YA
Zusak

Zusak, Markus

I am the messen-
ger

DUE DATE

2 1 MAY 2008		
2 1 MAY 2008		
2 5 JUN 2008		

i am the
messenger

markus
zusak

Alfred A. Knopf ✳ New York

THIS IS A BORZOI BOOK PUBLISHED BY ALFRED A. KNOPF

Text copyright © 2002 by Markus Zusak
Jacket illustration copyright © 2005 by David Goldin
All rights reserved under International and Pan-American Copyright
Conventions. Published in the United States by Alfred A. Knopf, an imprint
of Random House Children's Books, a division of Random House, Inc., New
York, and simultaneously in Canada by Random House of Canada Limited,
Toronto. Distributed by Random House, Inc., New York. Originally
published in Australia in 2002 as *The Messenger*
by Pan Macmillan Australia Pty Limited.
www.randomhouse.com/teens
KNOPF, BORZOI BOOKS, and the colophon are registered trademarks of
Random House, Inc.

Library of Congress Cataloging-in-Publication Data
Zusak, Markus.
[Messenger]
I am the messenger / by Markus Zusak.
p.   cm.
SUMMARY: After capturing a bank robber, nineteen-year-old cabdriver Ed
Kennedy begins receiving mysterious messages that direct him to addresses
where people need help, and he begins getting over his lifelong feeling of
worthlessness.
ISBN 0-375-83099-5 (trade) — ISBN 0-375-93099-X (lib. bdg.)
[1. Self-esteem—Fiction. 2. Heroes—Fiction. 3. Taxicab drivers—Fiction.]
I. Title.
PZ7.Z837Iae 2005
[Fic]—dc22
2003027388

Printed in the United States of America
February 2005
10 9 8 7 6 5 4 3 2 1
First American Edition

For Scout

Special thanks to Baycrew, the NSW Taxi Council, and Anna McFarlane for her expertise and commitment.

part one: **The First Message**

the holdup

The gunman is useless.

I know it.

He knows it.

The whole bank knows it.

Even my best mate, Marvin, knows it, and he's more useless than the gunman.

The worst part about the whole thing is that Marv's car is standing outside in a fifteen-minute parking zone. We're all facedown on the floor, and the car's only got a few minutes left on it.

"I wish this bloke'd hurry up," I mention.

"I know," Marv whispers back. "This is outrageous." His voice rises from the depths of the floor. "I'll be getting a fine because of this useless bastard. I can't afford another fine, Ed."

"The car's not even worth it."

"What?"

Marv looks over at me now. I can sense he's getting uptight. Offended. If there's one thing Marv doesn't tolerate, it's someone putting shit on his car. He repeats the question.

"What did you say, Ed?"

"I said," I whisper, "it isn't even worth the fine, Marv."

"Look," he says, "I'll take a lot of things, Ed, but . . ."

I tune out of what he's saying because, quite frankly, once Marv gets going about his car, it's downright pain-in-the-arse material. He goes on and on, like a kid, and he's just turned twenty, for Jesus' sake.

He goes on for another minute or so, until I have to cut him off.

"Marv," I point out, "the car's an embarrassment, okay? It doesn't even have a hand brake—it's sitting out there with two bricks behind the back wheels." I'm trying to keep my voice as quiet as possible. "Half the time you don't even bother locking it. You're probably hoping someone'll flog it so you can collect the insurance."

"It isn't insured."

"Exactly."

"NRMA said it wasn't worth it."

"It's understandable."

That's when the gunman turns around and shouts, "Who's talkin' back there?"

Marv doesn't care. He's worked up about the car.

"You don't complain when I give you a lift to work, Ed, you miserable upstart."

"Upstart? What the hell's an upstart?"

"I said shut up back there!" the gunman shouts again.

"Hurry up then!" Marv roars back at him. He's in no mood now. No mood at all.

4

He's facedown on the floor of the bank.

The bank's being robbed.

It's abnormally hot for spring.

The air-conditioning's broken down.

His car's just been insulted.

Old Marv's at the end of his tether, or his wit's end. Whatever you want to call it—he's got the shits something terrible.

We remain flattened on the worn-out, dusty blue carpet of the bank, and Marv and I are looking at each other with eyes that argue. Our mate Ritchie's over at the Lego table, half under it, lying among all the pieces that scattered when the gunman came in yelling, screaming, and shaking. Audrey's just behind me. Her foot's on my leg, making it go numb.

The gunman's gun is pointed at the nose of some poor girl behind the counter. Her name tag says Misha. Poor Misha. She's shivering nearly as bad as the gunman as she waits for some zitty twenty-nine-year-old fella with a tie and sweat patches under his arms to fill the bag with money.

"I wish this bloke'd hurry up," Marv speaks.

"I said that already," I tell him.

"So what? I can't make a comment of my own?"

"Get your foot off me," I tell Audrey.

"What?" she responds.

"I said get your foot off me—my leg's going numb."

She moves it. Reluctantly.

"Thanks."

The gunman turns around and shouts his question for the last time. "Who's the bastard talking?"

The thing to note with Marv is that he's problematic at the best of times. Argumentative. Less than amiable. He's the type of friend you find yourself constantly arguing with—especially when it comes to his shitbox Falcon. He's also a completely immature arsehole when he's in the mood.

He calls out in a jocular manner, "It's Ed Kennedy, sir. It's Ed who's talking!"

"Thanks a lot!" I say.

(My full name's Ed Kennedy. I'm nineteen. I'm an underage cabdriver. I'm typical of many of the young men you see in this suburban outpost of the city—not a whole lot of prospects or possibility. That aside, I read more books than I should, and I'm decidedly crap at sex and doing my taxes. Nice to meet you.)

"Well, shut up, Ed!" the gunman screams. Marv smirks. "Or I'll come over there and shoot the arse off you!"

It's like being in school again and your sadistic math teacher's barking orders at you from the front of the room, even though he couldn't care less and he's waiting for the bell so he can go home and drink beer and get fat in front of the telly.

I look at Marv. I want to kill him. "You're twenty years old, for Christ's sake. Are you trying to get us killed?"

"Shut up, Ed!" The gunman's voice is louder this time.

I whisper even quieter. "If I get shot, I'm blaming you. You know that, don't you?"

"I said shut *up,* Ed!"

"Everything's just a big joke, isn't it, Marv?"

"Right, that's it." The gunman forgets about the woman behind the counter and marches over to us, fed up as all buggery. When he arrives we all look up at him.

Marv.

Audrey.

Me.

And all the other hopeless articles like us sprawled out on the floor.

The end of the gun touches the bridge of my nose. It makes it itchy. I don't scratch it.

The gunman looks back and forth between Marv and me. Through the stocking on his face I can see his ginger whiskers and acne scars. His eyes are small and he has big ears. He's most likely robbing the bank as a payback on the world for winning the ugliness prize at his local fete three years running.

"So which one of you's Ed?"

"Him," I answer, pointing to Marv.

"Oh no you don't," Marv counters, and I can tell by the look on his face that he isn't as afraid as he should be. He knows we'd both be dead by now if this gunman was the real thing. He looks up at the stocking-faced man and says, "Hang on a sec. . . ." He scratches his jawline. "You look familiar."

"Okay," I admit, "*I'm* Ed." But the gunman's too busy listening to what Marv has to say for himself.

"Marv," I whisper loudly, "shut up."

"Shut up, Marv," says Audrey.

"Shut up, Marv!" calls Ritchie from across the room.

"Who the hell are *you?*" the gunman calls across to Ritchie. He turns to find out where the voice came from.

"I'm Ritchie."

"Well, shut yourself up, Ritchie! Don't *you* start!"

"No worries," returns the voice. "Thanks a lot." All my friends seem to be smart arses. Don't ask me why. Like many things, it is what it is.

In any case, the gunman starts to seethe. It seems to come pouring from his skin, right through the stocking on his face. "I'm completely bloody sick of this," he growls. His voice burns from his lips.

It doesn't shut Marv up, though.

7

"I think," he continues, "we might've gone to school together or something like that, you know?"

"You want to die," the gunman says nervously, still seething, "don't you?"

"Well, actually," Marv explains, "I just want you to pay the parking fine for my car. It's in a fifteen-minute zone outside. You're holding me up here."

"Damn right I am!" He points the gun.

"There's no need to be *that* hostile."

Oh God, I think. *Marv's gone now. He's about to get shot in the throat.*

The gunman looks out the glass doors of the bank, trying to figure out which car belongs to Marv. "Which one is it?" he inquires—politely enough, I must say.

"The light blue Falcon there."

"*That* piece of shit? I wouldn't piss on it, let alone pay a fine on it."

"Now hang on a second." Marv's getting all offended again. "Since you're holding up the bank, the least you can do is pay my parking fine, don't you think?"

Meanwhile.

The money's ready at the counter and Misha, the poor behind-the-counter girl, calls out. The gunman turns and heads back for it.

"Hurry up, bitch," he barks at her as she hands it over. I assume this is the mandatory tone for a holdup. He's seen the appropriate movies, all right. Soon he's on his way back to us, money in hand.

"You!" he screams at me. He's found new courage now that he's got the money. He's about to hit me with his gun when something catches his attention outside.

He looks closer.

Out the glass doors of the bank.

A slab of sweat falls from his throat.

He breathes hard.

His thoughts churn, and . . .

He goes off.

"No!"

The police are outside, but they have no idea what's happening in the bank. Word hasn't made it to the street yet. They're telling someone in a gold Torana to stop double-parking outside the bakery across the road. The car moves on and so do the cops, and the useless gunman is left holding the bag of money. His ride's gone.

An idea hits him.

He turns again.

Back to us.

"You," he orders Marv. "Give us your keys."

"What?"

"You heard me."

"It's an antique, that car!"

"It's a piece of shit, Marv," I abuse him. "Now give him the keys or I'll kill you myself!"

With a disgruntled look on his face, Marv reaches into his pocket and pulls out his car keys.

"Be gentle," he begs.

"Blow me," the gunman replies.

"There's no need for that!" Ritchie yells from under the Lego table.

"Shut up, you!" the gunman yells back, and he's off.

His only problem is the fact that Marv's car has about a 5 percent chance of starting first time round.

The gunman bursts through the doors of the bank and is on his way toward the road. He stumbles and drops the gun near the entrance but decides to keep going without it. All in a second, I can see the panic on his face as he decides whether to pick it up again or go on. There's no time, so he leaves it and continues running.

As we all get to our knees to watch him, we see him approaching the car.

"Watch this." Marv begins to laugh. Audrey, Marv, and I all watch, and Ritchie's on his way over to us.

Outside, the gunman stops and tries to work out which key opens the car. That's when we all crack up laughing at the incompetence of him.

He eventually gets in and tries to start the car countless times, but it never kicks over.

Then.

For some reason I'll never understand.

I run out, picking up the gun along the way. When I cross the road, I lock eyes with the gunman. He attempts to get out of the car, but it's too late now for that.

I'm standing at the Ford's window.

I have the gun pointed at his eyes.

He stops.

We both do.

He tries to get out and run, and I swear I have no idea I'm firing the gun until I've stepped toward him and hear the glass shatter.

"What are you doing?" Marv cries out in pain from the other side of the street. His world is crumbling. "That's my car you're shooting!"

Sirens arrive.

The gunman falls to his knees.

He says, "I'm such an *idiot*."

I can only agree.

For a moment, I look down and pity him because I realize that I'm quite possibly looking at the most hapless man on earth. First of all, he robs a bank with unutterably stupid people like Marv and me inside it. Then his getaway car vanishes. Then, when he's onto a good thing because he knows how to get his hands on a different car, it's the most pathetic car in the Southern Hemisphere. In a way, I feel sorry for him. Imagine it—the humiliation.

As the cops put the handcuffs on him and lead him away, I say to Marv, "Now do you see?" I continue on and become more forceful. Louder. "Do you see? This only goes to show the patheticness"—I point to it—"of this car." I pause a moment to let him think it over. "If it was even half decent, this bloke would've got away now, wouldn't he?"

Marv admits it. "I guess."

It's actually hard to tell if he would have preferred the gunman to get away simply to prove his car isn't so useless.

There's glass on the road and all over the seats of the car. I try to figure out which is more shattered—the window or Marv's face.

"Hey," I say, "sorry about the window, okay?"

"Forget it," Marv answers.

The gun feels warm and sticky, like melting chocolate in my hand.

Some more cops arrive to ask questions.

We go down to the police station and they ask us about the robbery, what happened, and how I managed to get my hands on the gun.

"He just dropped it?"

"That's what I told you, didn't I?"

"Look, son," the cop says. He looks up from his papers. "There's no need to get shirty with me." He's got a beer gut and a graying mustache. Why do so many cops feel the need to own a mustache?

"Shirty?" I ask.

"Yes, shirty."

Shirty.

I quite like that word.

"Sorry," I tell him. "He just dropped it on his way out, and I picked it up as I went to chase him. That's all. He was a complete shocker, all right?"

"Right."

We're in there for quite a while. The only time the beer-gutted cop becomes unsettled is when Marv keeps asking for compensation on his car.

"The blue Falcon?" the cop asks.

"That's the one."

"To be blunt, son—that car's an absolute outrage. It's disgraceful."

"I told you," I said.

"It doesn't even have a hand brake, for Christ's sake."

"So?"

"So you're lucky we're not fining you for it—it's unroadworthy."

"Thanks a lot."

The cop smiles. "My pleasure."

"And let me give you some advice."

We're almost out the door when we realize the cop still isn't finished. He calls us back, or at least he calls Marv.

"Yeah?" Marv replies.

"Why don't you get a new car, son?"

Marv looks seriously at the man. "I have my reasons."

"What—no money?"

"Oh, I've got money all right. I *do* work, you know." He even manages to sound sanctimonious. "I just have other priorities." He smiles now, as only someone who's proud of a car like that could possibly manage. "That—and I love my car."

"Fair enough," the cop concludes. "Goodbye."

"What priorities have *you,* of all people, got?" I ask Marv on the other side of the door.

Marv looks straight ahead blankly.

"Just shut up, Ed," he says. "You might be a hero to most people today, but to me you're just the dirty prick who put a bullet in my window."

"You want me to pay for it?"

Marv allows me another smile. "No."

To be quite honest, that's a relief. I'd rather die than put a solitary cent into that Falcon.

When we walk out of the police station, Audrey and Ritchie are waiting for us, but they're not alone. There are media people there as well, and a whole load of photos are taken.

"That's him!" someone calls, and before I can argue, the whole crowd is in my face, asking questions. I answer as fast as I can, explaining again what happened. The town I live in isn't small, and there are radio, TV, and newspaper people, all of whom will be presenting stories and writing articles for the next day.

I imagine the headlines.

Something like "Taxi Driver Turns to Hero" would be nice, but they'll probably print something like "Local Deadbeat Makes Good." Marv will get a good laugh out of that one.

After maybe ten minutes of questions, the crowd disperses and we walk back to our parking spot. The Falcon's got a nice big ticket slapped on the windscreen, under the wiper.

"Bastards," Audrey states as Marv rips it off and reads it. We were in the bank in the first place so Marv could deposit his paycheck. He can use it for the fine now.

We attempt to wipe the glass off the seats and get in. Marv turns the key about eight times. It won't start.

"Brilliant," he says.

"Typical," replies Ritchie.

Audrey and I say nothing.

Audrey steers and the rest of us push. We take it back to my place since it's closest to town.

A few days later I'll get the first message.

It changes everything.

2 sex should be like math: an introduction to my life

◆

I'll tell you a bit about my life.

I play cards at least a few nights a week.

It's what we do.

We play a game called Annoyance, which isn't particularly hard and is the only game we all enjoy without arguing too much.

There's Marv, who never shuts up, sitting there trying to smoke cigars and simultaneously enjoy it.

There's Ritchie, who's always quiet, sporting his laughable tattoo on his right arm. He sips on his longneck beer from start to finish and touches the whiskers that seem glued in patches on his man-boyish face.

There's Audrey. Audrey always sits opposite me, no matter where we play. She has yellow hair, wiry legs, the most beautiful crooked smile in the world, and lovely hips, and she watches a lot of movies. She also works as a cabdriver.

Then there's me.

Before I even mention me, I should tell you some other facts:

1. At nineteen, Bob Dylan was a seasoned performer in Greenwich Village, New York.
2. Salvador Dalí had already produced several outstanding artworks of paint and rebellion by the time he was nineteen.
3. Joan of Arc was the most wanted woman in the world at nineteen, having created a revolution.

Then there's Ed Kennedy, also nineteen. . . .

Just prior to the bank holdup, I'd been taking stock of my life.

Cabdriver—and I'd funked my age at that. (You need to be twenty.)

No real career.

No respect in the community.

Nothing.

I'd realized there were people everywhere achieving greatness while I was taking directions from balding businessmen called Derek and being wary of Friday-night drunks who might throw up in my cab or do a runner on me. It was actually Audrey's idea to give cab driving a shot. It didn't take much to convince me, mainly because I'd been in love with her for years. I never left this suburban town. I didn't go to university. I went to Audrey.

Constantly, I'm asking myself, *Well, Ed—what have you really achieved in your nineteen years?* The answer's simple.

Jack shit.

I mentioned it to a few different people, but all they did was tell me to pull my head in. Marv called me a first-class whinger. Audrey told me I was twenty years too early for a midlife crisis. Ritchie simply looked at me as if I was speaking in a foreign tongue. And when I mentioned it to my ma, she said, "Ohhh, why don't you have a bloody cry, Ed." You're going to love my ma. Trust me.

I live in a shack that I rent cheaply. Not long after moving in, I found out from the real estate agent that my boss is the owner. My boss is the proud founder and director of the cab company I drive for: Vacant Taxis. It's a dubious company, to say the least. Audrey and I had no trouble convincing them that we were old enough and licensed enough to drive for them. Mix a few numbers up on your birth certificate, show up with what appears to be the appropriate license, and you're set. We were driving within a week because they were short-staffed. No reference checks. No fuss. It's surprising what you can achieve with trickery and deceit. As Raskolnikov once said: "When reason fails, the devil helps!" If nothing else, I can lay claim to the title of Youngest Cabdriver in these parts—a taxi-driving prodigy. That's the kind of anti-achievement that gives structure to my life. Audrey's a few months older than me.

The shack I live in is pretty close to town, and since I'm not allowed to take the cab home, it's good walking distance to work. Unless Marv gives me a lift. The reason I don't have a car myself is that I drive people around all day or night. In my time off, the last thing I feel like doing is more driving.

The town we all live in is pretty run-of-the-mill. It's past the outskirts of the city and has good and bad parts. I'm sure it won't surprise you that I come from one of the bad parts. My whole family grew up at the far north of town, which is kind of like everyone's dirty secret. There are plenty of teenage pregnancies there, a plethora of shithead fathers who are unemployed, and mothers like mine who smoke, drink, and go out in public wearing Ugg boots. The home I grew up in was an absolute dump, but I stuck around until my brother, Tommy, finished school and got into university. At times I know I could have done the same, but I was too lazy at school. I was always reading books when I should have been doing math and the rest of it. Maybe I could have got a trade, but they don't give apprenticeships out down here, especially to the likes of me. Due to my aforementioned laziness I was no good at school, except at English, because of the reading. Since my father drank all our money away, I just went straight into work when school was done. I started out in a forgettable hamburger chain that I don't mention, due to shame. Next was sorting files in a dusty accountant's office that closed down within weeks of my arrival. And finally, the height, the pinnacle of my employment history so far.

Cab driving.

I have one housemate. He's called the Doorman, and he's seventeen years old. He sits at the flyscreen door, with sun painted onto his black fur. His old eyes glow. He smiles. He's called the Doorman because from a very early age he had a strong penchant for sitting by the front door. He did it back home, and he does it now at the shack. He likes to sit where it's nice and warm, and he doesn't let anyone in. This is because he finds it hard to move on account of the fact that he's so old. He's a cross between a Rottweiler and a German shepherd, and he stinks a kind of stink that's impossible to rid him of. In fact, I think that's why no one but my card-playing friends ever enters the shack. The initial stench of the dog slaps them in the face, and it's all over. No one's game enough to lengthen their stay and actually walk all the way in. I've even tried encouraging him to use some kind of deodorant. I've rubbed it under his arms in copious amounts. I've covered him all over with some of that Norsca spray, and all it did was make him smell worse. During that time, he smelled like a Scandinavian toilet.

He used to be my father's, but when the old man died about six months ago, my ma shifted him onto me. She got sick of him using the patch under her clothesline.

("Anywhere in the whole backyard he could use!" she'd say. "But where does he do it?" She'd answer the question. "Right under the bloody clothesline.")

So when I left, I took him with me.

To my shack.

To his door.

And he's happy.

And so am I.

He's happy when the sun throws warmth on him through the flyscreen door. He's happy to sleep there and move on a forward slant when I try to shut the wooden door at night. At times like that, I love the hell out of that dog. I love the hell out of him anyway. But Christ, he stinks.

I suppose he'll die soon. I'm expecting it, like you do for a dog that's seventeen. There's no way to know how I'll react. He'll have faced his own placid death and slipped without a sound inside himself. Mostly, I imagine I'll crouch there at the door, fall onto him, and cry hard into the stench of his fur. I'll wait for him to wake up, but he won't. I'll bury him. I'll carry him outside, feeling his warmth turn to cold as the horizon frays and falls down in my backyard. For now, though, he's okay. I can see him breathing. He just smells like he's dead.

I have a TV that needs time to warm up, a phone that almost never rings, and a fridge that buzzes like a radio.

There's a photo of my family on top of the TV from years ago.

Since I hardly ever watch the TV, I watch the photo once in a while. A pretty good show, really, although it gets dustier every day. It's a mother, a father, two sisters, me, and a younger brother. Half of us smile on the photo. Half don't. I like it.

In terms of my family, my ma's one of those tough women you couldn't kill with an ax. She's also developed a bit of a swearing habit, which I'll tell you more about later.

Like I said, my father died about six months ago. He was a lonely, kind, quiet, hard-drinking deadbeat. I could say that living with my ma wasn't easy and it drove him to drink, but there are no excuses. You can make them, but you don't believe them. He was a furniture deliverer. When he died they found him sitting on an old lounge chair still inside the truck. He was just sitting there, dead and relaxed. There was still so much to unpack, they said. They thought he was sitting in there bludging. His liver gave out.

My brother, Tommy, has done most things right. He's a year younger than me and goes to university in the city.

19

My sisters are Leigh and Katherine.

When Katherine got pregnant at seventeen, I cried. I was twelve then. She moved out of home soon after. She wasn't booted out or anything like that. She left and got married. It was a big event at the time.

A year later, when Leigh left, there were no problems.

She wasn't pregnant.

I'm the only one left in town these days. The others all left for the city and live there. Tommy's done especially well. He's on his way to becoming a lawyer. Good luck to him. I mean it.

Next to that picture on the TV, there's also a photo of Audrey, Marv, Ritchie, and me. We set the timer on Audrey's camera last Christmas, and there we are. Marv with cigar. Ritchie half smiling. Audrey laughing. And me holding my cards, still looking at the most shit hand in Christmas history.

I cook.

I eat.

I wash but I rarely iron.

I live in the past and believe that Cindy Crawford is by far the best supermodel.

That's my life.

I have dark hair, half-tanned skin, coffee brown eyes. My muscles are hugely normal. I should stand straighter, but I don't. I stand with my hands in my pockets. My boots are falling apart, but I still wear them because I love and cherish them.

Quite often, I pull my boots on and go out. Sometimes I go to the river that runs through town, or I go for a walk to the cemetery to see my father. The Doorman comes with me, of course, if he's awake.

What I like best is walking with my hands in my pockets, having the Doorman next to me, and imagining that Audrey's on my other side.

I always picture us from behind.

There's glow turning to darkness.

There's Audrey.

There's the Doorman.

There's me.

And I'm holding Audrey's fingers in mine.

I haven't written a song of Dylan proportions yet, or started painting my first attempt at surrealism, and I doubt I could start a revolution if I tried—because apart from everything else, I'm a bit of an unfit bastard, though I'm lanky and lean. Just weak, too.

Mainly, I think the best times I have are playing cards or when I've dropped someone off and I'm heading back to town, maybe from the city or even further north. The window's down, the wind runs its fingers through my hair, and I smile at the horizon.

Then I pull into town and the Vacant Taxis lot.

Sometimes I hate the sound of a car door slamming.

Like I've said, I love Audrey something terrible.

Audrey, who's had plenty of sex with plenty of people but never with me. She's always said she likes me too much to do it with me, and, personally, I've never tried to get her naked and new and all shivery in front of me. I'm too afraid. I've told you already that I'm quite pathetic when it comes to sex. I've had a girlfriend or two, and they didn't exactly rave about me in the sexual encounter department. One of them told me I was the clumsiest guy she'd ever met. The other one always laughed when I tried something on her. It didn't really work wonders on me, and she quit me soon after.

Personally, I think sex should be like math.

At school.

No one really cares if they're crap at math. They even proclaim it. They'll say to anyone, "Yeah, I don't mind science and English, but I'm absolutely *shithouse* at math." And other people will laugh and say, "Yeah, me, too. I wouldn't have a clue about all that logarithm shit."

You should be able to say that about sex, too.

You should be able to proudly say, "Yeah, I wouldn't have a clue about all that orgasm shit, ay. I'm okay at everything else, but when it comes to that part I wouldn't have a clue."

No one says that, though.

You can't.

Especially men.

We men think we *have* to be good at it, so I'm here to tell you I'm not. I should also explain that I honestly think my kissing leaves a lot to be desired as well. One of those girlfriends tried to teach me once, but I think she gave up in the end. My tongue work is particularly bad, I feel, but what can I do?

It's only sex.

That's what I tell myself, anyway.

I lie a lot.

Getting back to Audrey, though, I should really feel complimented that she won't even touch me because she likes me more than anyone else. It makes perfect sense, really, doesn't it?

If she ever gets down or depressed, I can make out the figure of her shadow through the front window of the shack. She comes in and we drink cheap beer or wine or watch a movie or all three. Something old and long like *Ben-Hur* that stretches into the night. She'll be next to me on the couch in her flannel shirt and jeans that have been cut into shorts, and eventually, when she's asleep, I'll bring a blanket out and cover her up.

I kiss her cheek.

I stroke her hair.

I think of how she lives alone, just like me, and how she never had any real family, and how she only has sex with people. She never lets any love get in the way. I think she had a family once, but it was one of those beat-the-crap-out-of-each-other situations. There's no shortage of them around here. I think she loved them, and all they ever did was hurt her.

That's why she refuses to love.

Anybody.

I guess she feels better off that way, and who can blame her?

When she sleeps on my couch, I think about all that. Every time. I cover her up, then go to bed and dream.

With my eyes open.

3 the ace of diamonds

There have been a few articles about the bank robbery in the local papers. They talk about how I wrestled the gun from the thief after chasing him down. Quite typical, really. I knew they'd make more out of it.

I go through some of them at my kitchen table, and the Doorman just looks at me like always. He couldn't give a shit if

I'm a hero. As long as he gets his dinner on time, he doesn't have a care in the world.

My ma comes over, and I give her a beer. She's proud, she tells me. According to her, all her kids have done quite well except me, but now she at least has a glimmer of pride in me to glimmer in her eye, if only for a day or two.

"That was my son," I can imagine her explaining to people she meets on the street. "I told you he'd amount to something *one* day."

Marv comes over, of course, and Ritchie.

Even Audrey pays me a visit with a newspaper tucked under her arm.

In each article, I'm known as twenty-year-old cabdriver Ed Kennedy, as I lied to every single reporter about my age. When you lie once, you have to make it uniform. We all know that.

My bewildered face is plastered all over the front pages, and even a guy from a radio show shows up and tapes a conversation with me in my lounge room. I have coffee with him, but we have to drink it without milk. He'd stopped me on my way out to get some.

It's a Tuesday evening when I get home from work and pull the mail out of the letter box. As well as my electricity and gas bills and some junk mail, there's a small envelope. I throw it down on the table with everything else and forget about it. My name's written in scrawl, and I wonder what it could possibly be. Even when I'm making my steak-and-salad sandwich, I tell myself to go into the lounge room soon to open it. Constantly, I forget.

It's fairly late when I finally get around to it.

I feel it.

Feel something.

There's something flowing between my fingers as I hold the envelope in my hands and begin tearing it open. The night's a cool one, typical of spring.

I shiver.

I see my reflection in the TV screen and in the photo of my family.

The Doorman snores.

The breeze outside steps closer.

The fridge buzzes.

For a moment, it feels like everything stops to watch as I reach in and pull out an old playing card.

It's the Ace of Diamonds.

In the echoes of light in my lounge room, I let my fingers hold the card gently, as if it might break or crease in my hands. Three addresses are written on it in the same writing as on the envelope. I read them slowly, watchfully. There's an eeriness slipping over my hands. It makes its way inside me and travels, quietly gnawing at my thoughts. I read:

45 Edgar Street, midnight
13 Harrison Avenue, 6 p.m.
6 Macedoni Street, 5:30 a.m.

I open the curtain to look outside.

Nothing.

I get past the Doorman and stand on the front porch.

"Hello?" I call out.

But again, there's nothing.

The breeze looks away—almost embarrassed at having watched—and I'm left there, standing. Alone. The card's still in my hand. I don't know the addresses I hold, or at least not exactly. I know the roads but not the actual houses.

It's without doubt the strangest thing that's ever happened to me.

Who would send me something like this? I ask myself. *What have I done to get an old playing card in my letter box with strange addresses scrawled on it?* I go back in and sit at the kitchen table. I try to work out what's happening and who has sent me what could be a piece of destiny in the mail. The visions of many faces reach me.

Could it be Audrey? I ask. *Marv? Ritchie? Ma?* I have no idea.

There's something in me that advises me to throw it out—to throw it in the bin and forget about it. Yet, I also feel pangs of guilt even for thinking of discarding it like that.

Maybe it's meant to be, I think.

The Doorman wanders over and sniffs the card.

Damn it, I can see him thinking. *I thought it might be something to eat.* After sniffing one last time, he pauses a moment and reflects on what he'd like to do next. As always, he shuffles back to the door, turns half a circle, and lies down. He gets comfortable in his suit of black and gold fur. His big eyes glow, but they also fall deep with darkness. His paws stretch out on the crusty old carpet.

He stares at me.

I stare back.

Well? I see him think. *What the hell do you want?*

Nothing.

Good.

Fine.

And we leave it at that.

It doesn't change the fact that I'm still holding the Ace of Diamonds in my hands, wondering.

Call someone, I tell myself.

The phone beats me to it. It rings. Maybe this is the answer I've been waiting for.

I pick it up and shove it to my ear. It hurts, but I listen hard. Unfortunately, it's my mother.

"Ed?"

I'd know that voice anywhere. That, and this woman shouts into the phone, every time, without fail.

"Yeah, hi, love."

"Don't 'Yeah, hi, love' me, you little bastard." Great. "Did you forget something today?"

I think about it, trying to remember. No thoughts or memories arrive. All I can see is the card as I turn it in my hands. "I can't think of anything."

"Typical!" She's getting a bit ropable now. Aggravated, to say the least. "You were s'posed to pick up that coffee table for me from KC Furniture, Ed." The words are spat through the phone line. They're loud and wet in my ear. "Y' big dickhead." She's lovely, isn't she?

As I've alluded to earlier, my mother really has quite a swearing habit on her. She swears all day every day, whether she's happy, sad, indifferent, everything. She blames it on my brother, Tommy, and me, of course. She says we used to swear our heads off when we were kids, playing soccer in the backyard.

"I gave up trying to stop you," she always tells me. "So I figured if you can't beat 'em, join 'em."

If I can go through a conversation with her without being called a wanker or dickhead at least once, I'm in front. The worst thing about it is the sheer *emphasis* she swears with. Whenever she calls me something like that, she spits it from her mouth, practically hurling it at me.

She's still going at me now, even though I'm not listening.

I tune back in.

". . . and what should I do tomorrow when Mrs. Faulkner turns up for morning tea, Ed? Should I just get her to put her mug on the floor?"

"Just blame me, Ma."

"Too bloody right I will," she snaps. "I'll just tell her that Dickhead Ed forgot to pick up my coffee table."

Dickhead Ed.

I hate it when she calls me that.

"No worries, Ma."

She goes on for quite a while longer, but again I focus on the Ace of Diamonds. It sparkles in my hand.

I touch it.

Hold it.

I smile.

Into it.

There's an aura to this card, and it's been given to *me*. Not to Dickhead Ed. To me—the real Ed Kennedy. The future Ed Kennedy. No longer simply a cab-driving hopeless case.

What will I do with it?

Who will I be?

"Ed?"

No answer.

I'm still thinking.

"Ed?" roars Ma.

I'm stunned back into the conversation.

"Are you listening to me?"

"Yeah . . . yeah, of course."

45 Edgar Street . . . 13 Harrison Avenue . . . 6 Macedoni Street . . .

"Ma, I'm sorry," I say again. "It just slipped my mind—I had a lot of pickups today. A lot of work in the city. I'll get it tomorrow, all right?"

"You sure about that?"

"I'm sure."

"You won't forget?"

"No."

"Good. Goodbye."

"Hey, wait!" I rush my voice through the phone.

She comes back. "What?"

I struggle to get the words out of my mouth, yet I have to ask her. About the card. I've decided I should really ask everyone I suspect of sending it to me. I may as well start with Ma.

"Yes, what?" she asks again, a bit louder this time.

I let the words out, each one tugging and pulling at my lips as they fight to stay in.

"Did you send me something in the mail today, Ma?"

"Like what?"

I pause a moment. "Like something small. . . ."

"Like *what*, Ed? I don't really have time for this."

All right. I have to say it. "It's a playing card—the Ace of Diamonds."

There's silence at the other end. She's thinking.

"Well?" I ask.

"Well what?"

"Was it you who sent it?"

She's had enough now, I can tell. The feeling reaches a hand through the phone line and shakes me.

29

"Of course it wasn't me!" It's like she's retaliating for something. "Why would I bother sending you a playing card in the mail? I should have sent you a reminder to pick up"—she raises her voice to a roar again—"*my goddamn coffee table!*"

"Okay, okay. . . ."

Why am I still so calm?

Is it the card?

I don't know.

But then, yes, I *do* know. It's because I'm always like this. Too pathetically calm for my own good. I should just tell the old cow to shut up, but I never have and never will. After all, she can't have a relationship like this with any of her other kids. Just me. She kisses their feet every time they come to visit (which isn't that much), and they just leave again. With me, at least she's got consistency.

I say, "All right, Ma, I was only checking to make sure it wasn't you. That's all. It just seemed like kind of a weird thing to get in the—"

"Ed?" she interrupts me, complete boredom attached to her voice.

"What?"

"Piss off, will you?"

"All right, I'll see you later."

"Yeah, yeah."

We hang up.

That bloody coffee table.

I knew I was forgetting something when I walked home from the Vacant Taxis lot. Tomorrow old Mrs. Faulkner will show up at Ma's place wanting to talk about my heroics in the bank a few days ago. All she'll hear is that I forgot to pick up the coffee table. I'm still not sure how I'm going to fit it in my cab, anyway.

I force myself to stop thinking about it. It's irrelevant. What I need to focus on is why this card's turned up and where it's come from.

It's someone I know.

That's certain.

It's someone who knows I play cards all the time. Which *should* make it either Marv, Audrey, or Ritchie.

Marv's out. For sure. It could never be him. He could never be that imaginative.

Then Ritchie. Highly unlikely. He just doesn't seem the type to do this.

Audrey.

I tell myself that it's most likely Audrey, but I don't know.

My gut feeling says it's none of them.

Sometimes we play cards on the front porch of my house or on the porch at someone else's place. Hundreds of people might have walked past and seen us. Once in a while, when there's an argument, people laugh and call out to us about who's cheating, who's winning, and who's whingeing.

So it could be anyone.

I don't sleep tonight.

Only think.

In the morning I get up earlier than normal and walk around town with the Doorman and a street directory, finding each house. The one on Edgar Street is a real wreck of a joint, right at the bottom of the street. The one on Harrison is kind of old, but it's neat. It has a rose bed in the front yard, though the grass is yellow and stale. The Macedoni place is up in the hilly part of town. The richer part. It's a two-story house with a steep drive-way.

I leave for work and think about it.

That evening, after delivering Ma's coffee table, I go to Ritchie's place and we play cards. I tell them. All at once.

"You got it here with you?" Audrey asks.

I shake my head.

Before I went to bed last night, I placed it in the top drawer of the cabinet in my bedroom. Nothing touches it. Nothing breathes on it. The drawer is empty but for that card.

"It wasn't any of you, was it?" I ask. I've decided I can't skirt around the question.

"Me?" asks Marv. "I think we all know I don't have the brains to come up with something like this." He shrugs. "That, and I wouldn't invest that much thought into the likes of you, Ed." Mr. Argumentative, as usual.

"Exactly," agrees Ritchie. "Marv's far too thick for something like this." Now that he's made his statement, he becomes silent.

We all look at him.

"What?" he asks.

"Is it you, Ritchie?" Audrey questions him.

He jerks a thumb over at Marv. "If he's too dumb, I'm too lazy." He holds his arms out. "Look at me — I'm a dole bludger. I spend half my days at the betting shop. I still live with my mum and dad. . . ."

To fill you in, Ritchie's name isn't even really Ritchie. It's Dave Sanchez. We call him Ritchie because he has a tattoo of Jimi Hendrix on his right arm but everyone reckons it looks more like Richard Pryor. Thus, Ritchie. Everyone laughs and says he should get Gene Wilder on the other arm and he'll have the perfect combination. They were a dynamic duo if ever there was one. How can you argue with movies like *Stir Crazy* and *See No Evil, Hear No Evil*?

Exactly.

You can't.

Just, if you ever meet him, don't mention the Gene Wilder thing. Trust me. It's the one thing that sends Ritchie into a bit of a frenzy. He can't stand it. Especially when he's drunk.

He's got dark skin and permanent whiskers on his face. His hair is curly and the color of mud, and his eyes are black but friendly. He doesn't tell people what to do and expects the same in return, and he wears the same faded jeans day in, day out— unless he's simply got several pairs of the same type. I've never thought to ask.

You can always hear him coming because he rides a bike. A Kawasaki something or other. It's black and red. Mostly he rides it without a jacket in summer because he's ridden since he was a kid. He wears plain T-shirts or unfashionable shirts that he shares with his old man.

We're all still staring at him.

It makes him nervous, and he turns his head now, with all of us, to Audrey.

"All right." She begins her defense. "I'd say out of all of us, I'm the most likely to think up something this ridiculous—"

"It isn't ridiculous," I say. I'm almost defending the card, as if it's part of me.

"Can I go on?" she says.

I nod.

"Good. Now, as I was saying—it definitely isn't me. I do, however, have a theory on how and why it ended up in your letter box."

We all wait as she gathers her thoughts.

She continues. "It all stems from the bank robbery. Someone

read about it in the paper and thought to themselves, *Now there's a likely-looking lad. Ed Kennedy. He's just the sort of person this town needs.*" She smiles but turns serious almost immediately. "Something's going to happen at each of the addresses on that card, Ed, and you'll have to react to it."

I think about it and decide.

I speak.

"Well, that's not real good, is it?"

"Why not?"

"Why *not*? What if there are people kicking the crap out of each other and I have to go in and stop it? It's not exactly uncommon around here, is it?"

"That's just luck of the draw, I guess."

I think of the first house.

45 Edgar Street.

In a shithole like that, I can't imagine anything too good happening.

For the rest of the night, I push thoughts of the card away, and Marv wins three games in a row. As usual, he lets us know it.

I'll be honest and say I hate it when Marv wins. He's a gloater. A real bastard of a gloater, puffing on his cigar.

Like Ritchie, he still lives at home. He works with his father as a carpenter. In truth, he works hard, though he doesn't spend a cent of what he earns. Even those cigars. He steals them from his old man. Marv's the maestro of meanness with money. The prince of penny-pinchers.

He has thick blond hair that stands up almost in knots, wears old suit pants for comfort, and jangles his keys in his pockets with his hands. He always looks like he's laughing with sarcasm at something, privately. We grew up together, which is the only reason we're friends. He's actually got a lot of other acquaintances, too, for a few reasons. The first is that he plays soccer in winter and has mates from there. The second and main reason is that he carries on like an idiot. Have you ever noticed that idiots have a lot of friends?

It's just an observation.

None of that helps me, though. Slagging off Marv doesn't solve the Ace of Diamonds problem.

There's no avoiding it, as much as I try.

It always sidles up to me and makes me recognize it.

I come to a conclusion.

I tell myself, *You have to start soon, Ed. 45 Edgar Street. Midnight.*

It's a Wednesday night. Late.

The moon leans down on me as I sit on my front porch with the Doorman.

Audrey comes over, and I tell her I'm starting tomorrow night. It's a lie. I look at her and wish we could go inside and make love on the couch.

Dive inside each other.

Take each other.

Make each other.

Nothing happens, though.

We sit there, drinking some suburban cheap-shit passion-pop alcohol she brought, and I rub my feet on the Doorman.

I love Audrey's wiry legs. I watch them a moment.

She looks at the moon as it holds itself up in the sky. It's higher now, no longer leaning. Risen.

As for me, I hold the card again in my hand. I read it and get ready.

35

You never know, I tell myself. *One day there might be a few select people who'll say, "Yes, Dylan was on the brink of stardom when he was nineteen. Dalí was well on his way to being a genius, and Joan of Arc was burned at the stake for being the most important woman in history. And at nineteen, Ed Kennedy found that first card in the mail."*

When the thought passes, I look at Audrey, the white-hot moon, and the Doorman, and I tell me to stop kidding myself.

4 ◆ the judge and the mirror

My next lovely surprise is a nice subpoena. I have to go to the local courthouse and tell my version of what happened in the bank. This has happened sooner than I thought.

It's set down for two-thirty in the afternoon. I'll get some time off during my shift and drive back into town to the court.

When the day arrives, I show up in my uniform and they make me wait outside the courtroom. When I go in to give the evidence, the chambers are spread out before me. The first person I see is the gunman. He's even uglier with the mask off. The only difference now is that he looks angrier. I guess a week or so in custody will do that to you. He's lost the pathetic, luckless expression on his face.

He wears a suit.

A cheap suit. It's all over him.

Once he sees me, I look immediately away because his eyes attempt to gun me down.

A bit late now, I think, but only because he's down there and I'm up here, in the safety of the witness-box.

The judge greets me.

"Well, I see you dressed up for the occasion, Mr. Kennedy."

I look down at myself. "Thank you."

"I was being sarcastic."

"I know."

"Well, don't get smart."

"No, sir."

I can see by now that the judge wishes he could put me on trial as well.

The lawyers ask me questions, and I answer them faithfully.

"So this is the man who held up the bank?" I'm asked.

"Yes."

"You're sure?"

"Absolutely."

"But tell me, Mr. Kennedy—how can you be so positive about that?"

"Because I'd know that ugly bastard anywhere. That, and he's exactly the same guy they put in handcuffs on the day."

The lawyer looks at me with disdain and explains himself. "Sorry, Mr. Kennedy, but we need to ask these questions in order to cover everything that needs to be covered, by the book."

I concede. "That's fair enough."

The judge chimes in now. "And as for ugly bastards—Mr. Kennedy, could you please refrain from casting such aspersions? You're not an oil painting yourself, you know."

"Thanks very much."

"You're welcome." He smiles. "Now answer the questions."

"Yes, Your Honor."

"Thank you."

When I'm finished, I walk past the gunman, who says, "Oi, Kennedy."

Ignore him, I tell myself, but I can't help it.

I pause and look at him. His lawyer tells him to keep his mouth shut, but he doesn't.

Quietly, he says, "You're a dead man. You just wait. . . ." His words attack me, faintly. "Remember what I'm telling you. Remember it every day when you look in the mirror." He almost smiles. "A dead man."

I fake it.

Composure.

I nod and say, "All right," and move on.

God, I pray, *give him life.*

The courtroom doors shut behind me, and I walk out into the foyer. It's caked in sunshine.

A policewoman calls me back and says, "I wouldn't worry about that, Ed." Easy for her to say.

"I feel like skipping town," I tell her.

"Now listen," she says. I like her. She's short and stocky and looks sweet. "By the time that chump's been through jail, the last thing he'll want is to go back." She considers it and seems confident in her appraisal. "Some people go hard in jail." She jerks her head back to the court. "*He* isn't one of them. He spent all morning crying. I doubt he'll be after you."

"Thanks," I reply. I allow some relief to filter through me, but I doubt it will last very long.

You're a dead man. I hear his voice again, and I see the words on my face when I get back in the cab and look in the rearview mirror.

It makes me think of my life, my nonexistent accomplishments and my overall abilities in incompetence.

A dead man, I think. *He's not far wrong.* And I pull out of the parking lot.

5 watching, waiting, raping

Six months.

He got six months. Typical of the leniency these days.

I've told no one about the threat, choosing instead to take the policewoman's advice and forget about him. In a way, I wish I didn't read about his jail term in the local paper. (The only good fortune is that early parole was denied.) I sit like normal in my kitchen with the Doorman and the Ace of Diamonds. The newspaper's on the table, folded over. There's a sweet picture of the gunman as a child. All I can see are his eyes.

Days pass, and gradually it works. I forget about him.

Really, I think, *what's a guy like* that *going to do?*

It makes more sense to look forward, and I slowly work my way toward the addresses on the card.

First up is 45 Edgar Street.

I try to go on a Monday but don't have the courage.

I make a second attempt on Tuesday but don't manage to leave the house, reading an awful book as an excuse.

On Wednesday, however, I actually make it out onto the street and head across town.

It's nearly midnight when I turn onto Edgar Street. It's dark, and the streetlights there have been rocked. Only one survives, and even that one winks at me. It's light that limps from the globe.

I know this neighborhood quite well because Marv used to come here a lot.

He had a girl here, on one of these slummy streets. Her name was Suzanne Boyd, and Marv was with her back in school. When the family picked up and left, almost without a word, he was devastated. Originally he bought that shitbox car to go and look for her, but he didn't even make it out of town. The world was too big, I think, and Marv gave up. That was when he became extra tight and argumentative. I think he decided he'd only care about himself from that moment on. Maybe. I don't know. I never give Marv too much thought. It's a policy I have.

As I walk, I remember all of that for a while, but it disappears as I edge forward.

I make it to the street's end, where number 45 is. I walk past it, on the other side of the road, and head for the trees that stand up and lean all over each other. I crouch there and wait. The lights are off in the house and the street is quiet. Paint flakes from the fibro and one of the gutters is rusting away. The flyscreen has holes bitten into it. The mosquitoes are feasting on me,

It better not be long, I think.

Half an hour passes and I nearly fall asleep, but when the time comes, my heartbeat devours the street.

A man comes stumbling over the road.

A big man.

Drunk.

He doesn't see me as he trips up the porch steps and struggles with the key before going in.

The hallway explodes with light.

The door slams.

"You up?" he slurs. "Get your lazy arse out here now!"

My heart begins to suffocate me. It keeps rising until I can taste it. I can almost feel it beating on my tongue. I tremble, pull myself together, then tremble again.

The moon escapes from the clouds, and I suddenly feel naked. Like the world can see me. The street is numb and silent but for the giant man who's stumbled home and talks forcefully to his wife.

Light materializes now in the bedroom as well.

Through the trees I can see the shadows.

The woman is standing up in her nightie, but the hands of the man take her and pull it from her, hard.

"I thought you were waiting up," he says. He has her by the arms. Fear has me by the throat. Next he throws her down to the bed and undoes his belt and pants.

He's on her.

He puts himself in.

He has sex with her and the bed cries out in pain. It creaks and wails and only I can hear it. Christ, it's deafening. *Why can't the world hear?* I ask myself. Within a few moments I ask it many times. *Because it doesn't care,* I finally answer, and I know I'm right. It's like I've been chosen. *But chosen for what?* I ask.

41

The answer's quite simple:
To care.

A little girl appears on the porch.
She cries.
I watch.
There's only the light now. No noise.
There's no noise for a few minutes, but it soon starts up again—and I don't know how many times this man can do it in one night, but it's certainly an achievement. It goes on and on as the girl sits there, crying.
She must be about eight.

When it finally ends, the girl gets up and goes inside. Surely this can't happen every night. I tell myself it isn't possible, and the woman replaces the girl on the porch.
She also sits down, like the girl. She's got her nightie on again, torn, and she has her head in her hands. One of her breasts is prominent in the moonlight. I can see the nipple facing down, dejected and hurt. At one point, she holds her hands out, form-ing a cup. It's like she's holding her heart there. It's bleeding down her arms.
I almost walk over, but instinct stops me.
You know what to do.
A voice inside me has whispered, and I hear it. It keeps me from going to her. This isn't what I have to do. I'm not here to comfort this woman. I can comfort her till the cows come home. That won't stop it happening tomorrow night and the night after.
It's him I have to take care of.
It's him I have to face.
All the same, she cries on the front porch, and I wish I could

42

go over there and hold her. I wish I could rescue her and hold her in my arms.

How do people live like this?

How do they survive?

And maybe *that's* why I'm here.

What if they can't anymore?

 pieces

I'm driving my cab, thinking, *It has to get better than this—my first message and it's a bloody rape case.* To top it all off, the bloke I have to take care of's built like a brick shithouse. He's a unit if ever I've seen one.

I tell no one. No friends. No authorities. Something beyond all that needs to be done. Unfortunately, it's me who's been chosen to do it.

Audrey asks about it when we're having lunch in the city, but I tell her she doesn't want to know.

She gives me that concerned look I love and says, "Just be careful, Ed, okay?"

I agree with her and we're back in our cabs.

All day, I can't help thinking about it. I also dread the other two addresses, although part of me explains that they can't be any worse than the first one.

I go there every night as, gradually, the moon goes through its cycle. Sometimes it doesn't happen. Sometimes he comes home and there's no violence. On those nights, the silence of the street is swollen. It's scared and slippery as I wait for something to happen.

A nervous moment arrives one afternoon when I go shopping. I'm walking along the dog food section when a woman walks past me with a little girl sitting in the trolley.

"Angelina," she says. "Don't touch that."

The voice is mild but unmistakable. It's the voice that calls to the night for help when she's slumped down on the bed, being raped by a drunk with a libido like Kilimanjaro. It's the voice of the woman who quietly sobs on her front porch in the silent, uncaring night.

For a split second, the girl and I lock eyes.

She's blond with green eyes and beautiful. The mother's the same, only tiredness has worn down her face.

I follow them awhile, and once, when the mother's crouched down looking at packet soups, I see her fall silently to pieces. She crouches there, dying to fall to her knees but not allowing herself.

When she stands back up, I'm there.

I'm there and we stare and I say, "You okay?"

She nods and lies.

"I'm okay."

I have to do something soon.

7 harrison avenue

At this point, you can probably tell what I've decided to do about the whole Edgar Street situation. Or at least you'll know if you're anything like me.

Cowardly.

Meek.

Positively weak.

Of course, in my infinite wisdom, I'm choosing to leave it for a while. *You never know, Ed. It might just work itself out.*

Now, I know that's pathetic in just about its purest form, but there's no way I can deal with this kind of thing so early. I need experience with this. I need a few wins under my belt before I can test myself against the rapist built like Tyson.

I pull out the card again one night as I drink coffee with the Doorman. I gave him some Blend 43 the previous night and he was quite taken by it.

At first, he wouldn't touch it.

He looked at me. He looked at his bowl.

Back and forth.

It took me nearly five minutes to realize that he saw me putting sugar in my mug that says Taxi Drivers Aren't the Biggest Shitheads on the Road. Once I gave him some sugar he became much more enthusiastic. He slurped and licked and carried on, demolishing the entire bowl and looking up for more.

So it's the Doorman and me in the lounge room. He's going at his coffee while I stare at the card, at the other addresses. Thirteen Harrison is next on the list, and I make my mind up to go there the next evening, six o'clock sharp.

"What do you say, Doorman?" I ask. "This one'll be better, you reckon?"

He gives me a grin because he's all hopped up on the Blend 43.

"I'm telling you." Marv points his finger at Ritchie. "I *did* knock. I don't care *what* you say."

"Did he knock?" Ritchie asks me.

"I can't remember."

"Audrey?"

She thinks a moment and shakes her head. Marv throws his hands in the air. He has to pick up four cards now. In Annoyance, that's the way it works. You get down to two cards and you knock. If you forget to knock before you put down that second-to-last card, you pick up four. Marv forgets to knock quite frequently.

He scowls as he picks up the cards, but secretly he's trying not to laugh. He knows he didn't knock, but he'll always try to get away with it. It's part of the game.

We're at Audrey's place, on her balcony. It's dark but the floodlights are on, and people look up as they walk past the lot of town houses. It's a street around the corner from mine. A bit of a dive, but nice enough.

In the first hour of play, I look at Audrey and know that I'm in nervous love with her. Nervous because I don't know what to do sometimes. I don't know what to say. What can I tell her when I feel the hunger rise in me? How would she react? I think she's frustrated with me because I could have gone to university and now I just drive a cab. I've read *Ulysses*, for God's sake, and half the works of Shakespeare. But I'm still hopeless, useless, and practically pointless. I can see she could never really see herself with me. Yet she's still done it with others who are pretty much the same. Sometimes I can't bring myself to think about it. Thinking about what they've done and how it feels and how she likes me too much to consider me.

Even though I know.

It isn't just sex I'd want from her.

I'd want to feel myself mold with her, just for a moment, if that's all I'm allowed.

She smiles at me when she wins a round, and I smile back.

Want me, I beg, but nothing comes.

"So whatever happened with that weird card thing?" Marv asks later.

"What?"

"You know very bloody well what." He points at me with his cigar. He could use a shave.

Everyone listens as I lie. "I threw it out."

Marv approves. "Good idea. Load of shit, that."

"Damn right," I agree. End of story. Supposedly.

Audrey looks at me, amused.

For the next few games I think of what happened earlier, when I went to 13 Harrison Avenue.

I was quite relieved, to tell you the truth, because nothing really happened at all. The only person there was an old woman who has no curtains on her windows. She was in there on her own, making her dinner and sitting there eating, and drinking tea. I think she ate a salad and some soup.

And loneliness.

She ate that, too.

I liked her.

I stayed in my cab the whole time, sitting there watching her. It was hot, and I drank some old water. Often, I hoped the woman was all right. She looked gentle and kind, and I recall the way her old-fashioned kettle whistled till she went over and soothed it. I'm quite sure she spoke to it, like she would to a child. Like a baby crying.

It kind of depressed me to think a human could be so lonely that she would comfort herself with the company of appliances that whistle, and sit alone to eat.

Not that I'm much better, mind you.

Let's face it—I eat my meals with a seventeen-year-old dog. We drink coffee together. You'd think we were husband and wife, the way we carry on. But still . . .

The old lady did something to my heart.

When her hands reached out and poured the tea, it was as if she also poured something into me while I sat there sweating in my cab. It was like she held a string and pulled on it just slightly to open me up. She got in, put a piece of herself inside me, and left again.

In there, somewhere, I still feel it.

I sit here playing cards, and the image of her is splayed across the table. Only I can see it. I see her hands shaking as she brought the spoon up to her mouth. I want to see her laugh or express some kind of happiness or contentment to let me know she's okay. I soon realize, though, that I have to find out for sure.

It's my go.

"Your go, Ed."

It's my go and I'm not going.

I'm down to two cards and I have to knock.

The Three of Clubs and the Nine of Spades.

The only trouble is, I want more cards tonight. I'm not interested in winning. I think I know what I have to do for the old woman, and I make a bet with myself.

If I pick up the Ace of Diamonds, I'm right.

If I don't, I'm wrong.

I forget to knock and everyone laughs at me as I go to pick up.

First card: Queen of Clubs.

Second card: Four of Hearts.

Third card: yes.

Everyone wonders why I could possibly be smiling, except Audrey. Audrey winks at me. She knows without asking that I did it on purpose. The Ace of Diamonds is in my hand.

This is much better than Edgar Street.

I'm feeling good.

It's Tuesday and I'm putting on my white jeans and my nice sandy-colored boots. I pull out a decent shirt. I've been to the Cheesecake Shop, having been ably assisted by a girl called Misha.

("Don't I know you?" she asked.

"Maybe. I can't quite—"

"Of course—you're the guy from the bank. The hero."

The fool, more like it, I thought, but I said, "Oh yeah—you're the girl behind the counter. You work here now?"

She nodded. "Yeah." She was a bit embarrassed. "I couldn't handle the stress in the bank."

"The robbery?"

"Nah, my boss was a total prick."

"The acne and the sweat patches?"

"Yeah, that's him. . . . Tried to stick his tongue in my mouth the other day."

"Ah well," I said. "That's men for you. We're all a bit that way."

"Ain't that the truth." But she was friendly from start to finish. When I was outside the shop, she called after me. "Enjoy the cake, Ed!"

"Thanks, Misha," I called back, but not loud enough, probably. I don't like making noise in public.

And I was gone.)

I think about it briefly as I open the box and look at half a mud cake. I feel for the girl because it can't have been too nice having that guy all over her like that, and it was *she* who quit. The bastard. I'm scared out of my mind before I try to put my tongue in a girl's mouth. And I don't have acne *or* sweat patches. Just shithouse confidence. That's all.

Anyway.

I give the cake a last examination. I smell good. I'm decked out in my nicest clothes, ready to go.

I step over the Doorman and close the door behind me. The day is silver gray and cool as I walk over to Harrison Avenue. I'm there by six o'clock, and the old lady is attending to the kettle again.

The grass on her front lawn is gold.

My feet crunch over it, like the sound of someone biting into toast. My boots seem to leave prints, and I truly feel like I'm walking over a giant piece of toasted bread. The roses are the only things alive, standing resolutely by the driveway.

Her front porch is cement. Old and cracked, like mine.

The flyscreen door is torn at the edges. Fraying. I open it and knock on the wood. The sound rhymes with my heartbeat.

Her footsteps climb to the door. Her feet sound like the tick-tock of a clock. Counting time to this moment.

She stands.

She looks up at me, and for a moment we both get lost in each other. She wonders who I am, but only for a split second. Then, with stunning realization clambering across her face, she smiles at me. She smiles with such incredible warmth and says, "I knew you'd come, Jimmy." She steps toward me and hugs me hard, her soft, wrinkled arms encasing me. "I knew you'd come."

50

When we move apart, she looks at me again, till a small tear lifts itself up in her eye. It trips out to find a wrinkle and follows it down.

"Ohh," and she shakes her head. "Thanks, Jimmy. I knew it, I *knew* it." She takes me by the hand and leads me into the house. "Come in," she tells me. I follow.

"Are you staying for dinner, Jimmy?"

"Only if you'll have me," I reply.

She chuckles. "'If you'll have me. . . .'" She waves me away dismissively. "You're such a card, Jimmy."

Damn right I'm a card.

"Of course I'll have you," she continues. "It'll be lovely to go over old times, won't it?"

"Of course." She takes the cake from me and puts it in the kitchen. I can hear her mucking around in there, and I call out to see if she needs any help. She tells me I should just relax and make myself comfortable.

The dining room and the kitchen both face the street, and as I sit at the dining room table, I see people walk past, rush past, and some wait for their dogs and move on. On the table is a pensioner's card. Her name's Milla. Milla Johnson. She's eighty-two.

When she comes back out, she brings a dinner identical to the one she had the previous day. Salad and soup and some tea.

We eat, and she tells me all about her day-to-day travels.

She talks for five minutes to Sid in the butcher's shop but doesn't buy any meat. Just chats and talks and laughs at his jokes, which aren't really funny.

She has lunch at five to twelve.

51

She sits in the park, watching the kids play and the skate-boarders do their tricks and swerves at the skate bowl.

She drinks coffee in the afternoon.

She watches *Wheel of Fortune* at five-thirty.

She has her dinner at six.

She's in bed by nine.

Later on, she gives me a question. We've cleaned up the dishes, and I'm sitting again at the table. Milla comes back in, nervously sitting in her chair.

Her shaking hands reach out.

To mine.

They hold them and her pleading eyes open me.

She says, "So tell me, Jimmy." The hands begin to shake a little harder. "Where have you been all this time?" Her voice is painful but soft. "Where have you been?"

Something's stuck in my throat—the words.

Finally, I recognize them and say, "I've been looking for you." I speak that sentence as if it's the one great truth I've ever known.

She returns my conviction, nodding. "I thought so." She pulls my hands over to her, leans over, and kisses my fingers. "You always did know what to say, didn't you, Jimmy?"

"Yes," I say. "I guess I did."

Soon, she tells me she has to go to bed. I'm pretty sure she's forgotten about the mud cake, and I'm dying to have some. It's close to nine o'clock, and I can sense I'm not getting a single crumb of that cake. I feel awful about it, of course. I ask myself what kind of person I am, worrying about missing out on a lousy piece of cake.

She comes to me at about five to nine and says, "I think I should probably go to bed, Jimmy. Do you think?"

I speak softly. "Yes, Milla, I think so."

We walk to the door and I kiss her on the cheek. "Thank you for dinner," I say, and walk out.

"My pleasure. Will I see you again?"

"Definitely." I turn and answer. "Soon."

The message this time is to soothe this old lady's loneliness. The feeling of it gathers in me as I walk home, and when I see the Doorman, I pick him up and hold all forty-five kilos of him in my arms. I kiss him, in all his filth and stench, and I feel like I could carry the world in my arms tonight. The Doorman looks at me with bemusement, then asks, *How about a coffee, old son?*

I put him down and laugh and make the old bludger a coffee, with plenty of sugar and milk.

"Would you like a coffee, too, Jimmy?" I ask myself.

"Don't mind if I do," I reply. "Don't mind at all," and I laugh again, feeling every bit like a true messenger.

8 being jimmy

It's been a while since I delivered the coffee table to Ma's place. I haven't dropped in on her for a good couple of weeks—to let her cool down a bit. She gave me a nice drubbing when I finally turned up with it.

I visit her on a Saturday morning.

"Well, look what the bloody cat dragged in," she says wryly when I walk through the door. "How's it going, Ed?"

"All right. You?"

"Workin' my freckle off. As usual."

Ma works in a gas station, behind the register. She does bugger all, but whenever you ask how she is, she claims to be "working her freckle off." She's making some sort of cake that she won't let me have a piece of because someone more important's coming over. Probably someone from the Lions Club or something.

I come closer to get a better look at what it is.

"Don't touch," she snaps. I'm not even within reaching distance.

"What is it?"

"Cheesecake."

"Who's coming over?"

"The old Marshalls."

Typical—rednecks from around the corner—but I say nothing. Better off that way.

"How's the coffee table going?" I ask.

She laughs almost deviously and says, "Pretty well—go have another look at it."

I do as she says, walk into the lounge room, and can't trust my eyes. She's done a bloody swap on me!

"Oi!" I shout to the kitchen. "This isn't the one I delivered!"

She comes in. "I know. I decided I didn't like that one."

I've got the shits now. Really. I knocked off work an hour early to pick up that other one, and now it's not good enough for her. "What the hell happened?"

"I was talking to Tommy on the phone and he said all that pine rubbish was pretty ordinary and wouldn't last." She props between sentences. "And your brother knows about that sort of thing, believe me. He bought himself an old cedar table in the city. Talked the guy down to three hundred and got the chairs half price."

"So what?"

"So he knows what he's doing. Unlike some people I know."

"You didn't get me to pick it up?"

"Now why in God's name would I do that?"

"You made me get the last one."

"Yeah, but let's face it, Ed," she says. "Your delivery service is a disgrace."

The irony of it isn't lost on me.

"Everything okay, Ma?" I ask later. "I'm going to the shops in a minute. Do you need anything?"

She thinks.

"Actually, Leigh's coming over next week and I want to make a chocolate-hazelnut cake for her and the family. You can get the crushed hazelnuts for me."

"No worries."

Now piss off, Ed, I think as I walk out. It's what she was thinking, I'm sure.

I like being Jimmy.

"Remember when you used to read to me, Jimmy?"

"I remember," I reply.

Needless to say, I'm at Milla's place again, in the evening.

She reaches out her hand and holds me by the arm. "Could you pick up a book and read me a few pages? I love the sound of your voice."

"Which book?" I ask when I reach the cabinet.

"My favorite," she answers.

Shit. . . . I rummage through the books that stand up in my eyes. *Which one's her favorite?*

But it doesn't matter.

Whichever book I pick will be her favorite.

"*Wuthering Heights?*" I suggest.

"How did you know?"

"Instinct," I say, and begin reading.

She falls asleep on the lounge after a few pages, and I wake her and help her to bed.

"Good night, Jimmy."

"Good night, Milla."

As I walk home, something writes itself to the edge of my mind. It's a piece of paper that was in the book, used as a bookmark. It was just a normal thin piece of pad paper, all yellow and old. The date said 1.5.41, and there was one small piece of typically scratchy male writing on it. A bit like my own writing.

It said:

Dearest Milla,
My soul needs yours.
Love,
Jimmy

During the next visit, she gets out her old photo albums and we look through them. She constantly points out a man who holds her or kisses her or just stands there on his own.

"You were always so handsome," she tells me. She even touches Jimmy's face on the photos, and I see what it is to love someone like Milla loved that man. Her fingertips are made of love. When she speaks, her voice is made of love. "You've changed quite a bit now, but you still look good. You always were the most handsome boy in town. All the girls said so. Even my mother told me how great you were, how loving and strong, and how I had to do good by you and treat you right." She looks at me now, almost panic-stricken. "I did right by you, Jimmy— didn't I? I treated you right, didn't I?"

I melt.

I melt and look her in her old but lovely eyes. "You did right by me, Milla. You treated me right. You were the best wife I could have ever—"

And that's when she breaks down and cries into my sleeve. She cries and cries and laughs. She shakes with such despair and joy, and her tears soak, nice and warm, through to my arm.

She offers me mud cake after a while. It's the one I brought her a few days ago.

"I can't remember who brought me this," she tells me, "but it's very nice. Would you like some, Jimmy?"

"That'd be great," I say.

It's older now and a bit stale, the mud cake.

But the taste is perfect.

A few nights later, we're all on the porch of the shack, playing cards. I'm going strongly until a sudden silence slits through the game. A sound follows it, from inside.

"It's the phone," Audrey says.

There's something about it that doesn't sit right. An uneasy feeling glides over me.

"Well, are you getting it?" Marv asks.

I get up and step over the Doorman with great trepidation.

The ring calls me toward it.

I pick it up.

Quiet. All quiet.

"Hello?"

Again.

"Hello?"

The voice attempts to find the very core of me. It finds it and says four words.

"How's it going, *Jimmy*?"

Something breaks in me.

"What?" I ask. "What did you say?"

"You heard me."

The phone dies, and I'm alone.

I stagger back out to the porch.

"You lost," Marv informs me, but I barely hear him. I couldn't care less about the card game.

"You look shockin'," Ritchie tells me. "Sit down, lad."

I heed his advice and take my place again in the game.

Audrey looks at me and asks whether I'm okay just by the expression on her face. I answer yes, and when she stays later, I nearly tell her about Milla and Jimmy. I come so close to asking what she thinks about it all, but I already know the answers. Her opinion can't change any of this, so I might as well face up to the fact that I have to go on. I've given Milla the companionship she's been needing, but it's time now to either move on to the next address or go back to Edgar Street. I can still visit her, of course, but it's time now.

It's time to move on.

That night, I go out walking with the Doorman, late. We go down to the cemetery and see my father and wander through the rest of the graves.

A flashlight hits us.

Security.

"You know what time it is?" the guy asks. He's big and mustached.

"No idea," I answer.

"Eleven past midnight. Cemetery's closed, mate."

I almost walk away, but tonight I can't. I open my mouth and say, "I'm wondering, sir . . . I'm looking for a grave."

He looks at me, deciding. Should he help me or not? He goes for yes.

"What name?"

"Johnson."

He shakes his head and laughs, a hint of criticism. "Do you have any idea how many Johnsons there are in this joint?"

"No."

"A *lot*." He sniffs at his mustache, as if to erase an itch. It's red. He's a redhead.

"Well, can we give it a go anyway?"

"What sort of dog is that?"

"Rotty-shepherd cross."

"He stinks a real bloody treat, mate. Don't you wash him?"

"Of course I do."

"Whoa." He turns away, screwing up his face. "That's diabolical."

"The grave?" I ask.

His memory is jogged. "Oh yeah. Well, we can give it a shot. Any idea when the poor old sap died?"

"There's no need to be disrespectful."

He stops. "Look." He's getting a bit shirty now. "Do you want my help or not?"

"All right, I'm sorry."

"This way."

We walk almost half the cemetery and find a few Johnsons, but not the one I'm after.

"You're a bit of a fussy bastard, aren't you?" the security guard says at one point. "Won't this one do?"

"This is Gertrude Johnson."

"Who you after again?"

"Jimmy." But this time I add something. "Wife's name's Milla."

He jolts to a stop, looks at me, and says, "Milla? Shit, I think I know that one. I remember the name because she's mentioned on the stone." He mutters now as we walk quickly to the other end of the graveyard. "Milla, Milla . . ."

His flashlight slaps a stone, and it's there.

JAMES JOHNSON
1917-1942
DIED SERVING HIS COUNTRY
BELOVED TO MILLA JOHNSON

For a good ten minutes or so we stand there with the flashlight burning the grave with light. The whole time, I'm trying to guess where and exactly how he died and, more to the point, realizing that poor old Milla's been without him for sixty years.

I can tell.

No other man has entered her life. Not the way her Jimmy did.

She's been waiting sixty years for Jimmy to come back.

And now he has.

9 the barefoot girl

Still, I have to move on.

Milla's story is beautiful and tragic, but there are other messages to deliver. The next one is 6 Macedoni Street, 5:30 a.m. For a moment I consider going back to Edgar Street, but I'm still too frightened by what I've heard and seen there. I go there once more, just to check that things are still the same. They are.

I arrive with the sun on Macedoni Street, mid-October. Overall, this spring has been unusually hot and it's already nice and warm as I hit the hilly street. I see the two-story house standing at the top.

Just after five-thirty, a lone figure comes from around the side of the house. I think it's a girl but can't be sure because the figure has a hood over its head. It wears red athletic shorts, a hooded gray sweatshirt, but no shoes. It's about five foot nine.

I sit down between two parked cars, waiting for the figure to come back.

When I give up waiting and begin to leave for work, I finally see her (it's definitely a her) come running around the corner. The sweatshirt's off now, tied around her waist, so I can see her face and her hair.

She takes me by surprise because we both hit the corner together, from opposite directions.

We both stop, momentarily.

Her eyes land on me, only for a second.

She looks at me, and she has sunshine-colored hair in a pony-tail and clear eyes, like water. The mildest blue I've ever seen. Soft lips that form a gentle shape of recognition.

And she keeps running.

I can only watch as she tilts her head and turns away.

Her legs are shaved, making me think I should have known earlier that it was a girl. They're long and lovely. She's one of those girls who are pretty much straight down. Skinny with a small but well-formed chest, long back, straight hips, and tall legs. Her bare feet are medium-sized, and they hit the ground lightly.

She's beautiful.

She's beautiful, and I'm ashamed.

She's fifteen if she's a day, and I'm being stepped on. I'm being crushed from the inside. Feelings of love and lust fight each other inside me, and I realize I'm drawn instantly to this girl who runs barefoot at five-thirty in the morning. I can't escape it.

I walk home and think about what she needs—what I need to deliver. In a way, it's a process of elimination. If she lives in the hills, she doesn't need money. I don't think she needs someone to befriend her, either, but who knows?

She runs.

It's something to do with that. It has to be.

Each morning I'm there, though I hide myself and don't think she sees me.

One day, I decide to progress the relationship and follow her. I'm in my jeans, my boots, and an old white T-shirt, and she's way out in front of me.

The girl strides.

I struggle.

When I started running, I felt like I was in the Olympic four-hundred-meter final. Now I feel like exactly what I am—a suburban taxi driver who doesn't exercise enough.

I feel pitiful.

Uncoordinated.

My legs labor to lift and drag me forward. My feet feel as though they're plowing the earth, sinking in. I breathe as deeply as I can but there's a wall in my throat. My lungs are starving. Inside me, I can feel the air climbing the wall to get down there but it's not enough. Still, I keep running. I have to.

She goes to the edge of town to the Grounds, where the athletic field is. It's at the bottom of a small valley, so I'm relieved it's a downhill run. It's the coming back that makes me nervous.

When we make it to the field, she jumps the fence, peeling off the sweatshirt to leave it hanging there. As for me, I stagger myself back to a walk and collapse under the shade of a tree.

The girl does laps.

The world does laps around me.

A dizziness circles me, and I need to throw up. I'm also dying for a drink, but I can't be bothered going over to the tap. So I'm just there, all sprawled out and sweating profusely.

Christ, Ed, I breathe. *You're an unfit bastard, aren't you? Even more than I thought.*

I know, I answer.

It's disgraceful.

I know.

I also know that I shouldn't just lie here all long and awkward under this tree, but I'm beyond hiding from the girl now. If she sees me, she sees me. I can barely move, let alone hide, and I know I'll be stiff as all hell tomorrow.

She stops for a while and stretches as the air finally breaks through to reach my lungs properly.

Her right leg is up on the fence. It's long and lovely.

Don't think about it. Don't think about it, I tell myself. Halfway through those thoughts, she notices me but looks immediately away. She tilts her head and sends her eyes to the ground. Exactly like the other morning. Just for that second. It makes me see that she'll never come to me. I understand this as she takes the leg off the fence and changes to the other. I'll have to go to her.

When she stops stretching and reaches for her sweatshirt, I climb from the ground and make my way toward her.

She begins to run but stops.

She knows.

I think she can feel that I'm here for her.

We're about six or seven meters apart now. I look at her, and she looks at the ground about a yard or so from my right ankle.

"Hello?" I say. The stupidity of my voice feels beyond repair.

There's a pause.

A breath.

"Hi," she says back. Her eyes are still focused on the ground beside me.

I take one step. No more. "I'm Ed."

"I know," she says. "Ed Kennedy." Her voice is high-pitched but soft, so soft you could fall down into it. It reminds me of Melanie Griffith. You know that soft-high voice she's got? That's what the girl has, too.

"How do you know who I am?" I ask.

"My dad reads the paper, and I saw your picture—after the bank robbery, you know?"

I walk forward. "I know."

Some time etches past, and she finally looks at me properly. "Why are you following me?"

I stand there, among my tiredness, and speak.

"I'm not sure yet."

"You're not a pervert or something, are you?"

"No!" I'm thinking, *Don't look at her legs. Don't look at her legs.*

64

She looks back to me now and gives me the same look of recognition as the other day. "Well, that's a relief. I saw you nearly every day." Her voice is so sweet it's almost ridiculous. It's like strawberry-flavored or something, that voice.

"I'm sorry if I scared you."

Warily, she dares to allow me a smile. "It's okay. It's just . . . I'm not too good at talking to people." She looks away again as her shyness smothers her. "So, do you think it'd be all right if we don't talk?" She hurries her words now to not hurt me. "I mean, I don't mind if you're out here in the morning with me, but I just can't talk, okay? I feel kind of uncomfortable."

I nod and hope she sees. "No worries."

"Thank you." She gives the ground a final look, takes her sweatshirt, and gives me one last question. "You're not much of a runner, are you?"

I savor that voice for a moment. It tastes like strawberry on my lips. Maybe this is the last time I'll ever hear it. Then, "No, I'm not," I say, and we exchange a final few seconds of acknowledgment before she runs away. I watch her and hear her bare feet lightly touching the earth. I like that sound. It reminds me of her voice.

I go out to the athletic field every morning before I head off for work, and she's there. Every day, without fail. One morning the rain pours down, and still she's there.

On a Wednesday, I take a day off work (telling myself it's the kind of sacrifice you're required to make when you've got a higher calling). With the Doorman in tow, I walk to the school at around three o'clock. She comes out with a few friends, which gladdens me because I hoped she wouldn't be alone. Her shyness made me worry about that.

It's funny how when you watch people from a long distance, it all seems voiceless. It's like watching a silent movie. You guess what people say. You watch their mouths move and imagine the sounds of their feet hitting the ground. You wonder what they're talking about and, even more so, what they might be thinking.

The strange thing I notice as I watch is that when a boy comes along and talks to the girls and walks with them, the running girl shifts back into the mode of looking to the ground. When he leaves she's all right again.

I stand and wonder for a while and conclude that she probably just lacks confidence, like me.

She probably feels too tall and gawky, not realizing how beautiful everyone knows she is. I think if it's only that, she'll be okay soon enough.

I shake my head.

At myself.

Listen to you, I tell me, s*aying she'll be okay. How the hell would you know? Is it because* you've *turned out okay, Ed? I very much doubt it.* I'm absolutely right. I have no business plotting or predicting anything for this girl. I only have to do what I'm *supposed* to do and hope it'll be enough.

A few times, I watch her house at night.

Nothing happens.

Ever.

As I stand there and contemplate the girl, and old Milla, and the dread of Edgar Street, I realize I don't even know this girl's name. For some reason I imagine it to be something like Alison, but mostly I just think of her as the running girl.

I go to the athletics meet that's on every weekend during summer. She's there and I find her sitting with the rest of her family. There's a younger girl and a small boy. They all wear black shorts and a light blue tank top with a rectangular patch sewn on the back. The girl's patch has number 176 on it, just under the slogan that says You've Gotta Be Made of Milo.

The under-fifteens' fifteen hundred meters is called, and she stands up, brushing dried grass from her shorts.

"Good luck," her mother says.

"Yeah, good luck, Sophie," the father echoes.

Sophie.

I like it.

I hear it in my mind and place the name carefully to her face. It fits nicely.

She's still brushing the grass from her shorts when I remember the other two kids even exist—once they were gone I was able to focus completely on Sophie. The girl's out doing shot put, and the boy's gone off somewhere to play army men with an ugly little bastard called Kieren.

"Can I go with Kieren, Mum? Please?"

"All right, but make sure you're listening out for your events—the seventy meters is coming up."

"Okay. Let's go, Kieren."

For a moment I feel glad to be called simple, no-problems Ed. Not Edward, Edmund, Edwin. Just Ed. Sheer mediocrity feels nice for a change.

Sophie sees me once she stands up, and a small piece of contentment finds itself on her face. She looks happy to see me, but she still turns from me almost straightaway. She walks to the marshaling area with a pair of crappy old spiked shoes in her hand (I assume the older kids are allowed to wear them in the longer races) when her father calls out again.

"Hey, Soph."

She turns to face him.

"I know you can win it—if you want it."

"Thanks, Dad."

She walks hurriedly away, turning once more to where I sit in the sun, shoving a Lamington into my mouth. There's a coconut sprinkle stuck to the side of my lips, but it's too late to remove it. She wouldn't see it, anyway. Not from that distance. She only gives me a quick glance and goes on. I know what I have to do now.

If I was a cocky sort of guy, I'd tell you this one's a piece of piss. A snack.

But I'm not.

I can't bring myself to say it because I still think of Edgar Street. I realize that for every good message, there will always be one that will agonize me. So I'm thankful for this. It's a nice day, and I like this girl. I like her even more when she runs alongside another tall and skinny girl who always looks like she's got the wood on her. They run together, but at the end, the other girl finishes more strongly. Her stride lengthens, and a man keeps yelling, "Go, Annie! Go, Annie! Dig 'em in, love! Dig 'em in! *Beat* her, darlin', you can do it!"

I'd rather come in second than have shit like that yelled at me.

Sophie's father is different.

For the race he goes down to the fence and watches intently. He yells nothing. Only watches. At times, I can sense some tension in him as he wills his daughter ahead of the other girl. When the other one nudges ahead, he looks briefly over to the other father, but that's all. When she wins, he applauds her, and he applauds Sophie, too. The other father only stands there with obscene pride, as if it was *he* who'd just run his stomach out and won the race.

When Sophie comes and stands next to her father, he puts his arm around her. Her disappointment is written heavily across her shoulders.

In a way, Sophie's dad reminds me of my own father, except my own father never put his arm around me. Not to mention he was an alcoholic. It's in his mannerisms and his quietness. My own father was a quiet man who never had a bad word for anyone. He'd go to the pub and stay there till closing. He'd walk the streets to sober up but it never quite worked. Still, I must say, he'd get up and make it to work the next day without fail. My ma would rant and rave and scream abuse at him for being out, but he never reacted. He never told her off in return.

Sophie's father looks the same, except for the alcoholic part. In short, he looks like a gentleman.

They walk back to the mother together and sit there on the hill. The father and mother hold hands as Sophie drinks one of those sports drinks. They look like the type of family who tell each other they love each other when they go to bed, and when they wake up, and before they go to work.

The spiked shoes come off Sophie's feet. She looks at them and sighs, "I thought these were meant to be good luck." I can only assume they've been handed down from her mother or perhaps another successful relative.

As they sit on the ground, I take a closer look at those shoes. They're a faded blue and yellow. They're old and worn through.

And they're wrong.

The girl deserves better.

10 the shoe box

"Haven't seen you for a while."

"I've been busy."

Audrey and I are on my front porch, drinking cheap alcohol, as usual. The Doorman comes out and asks for some, but I give him a big pat instead.

"You still getting those cards in the mail?" She knew all along of course that I was lying about throwing out the diamonds. No one in their right mind would throw diamonds out, would they? They're valuable. If anything, they need protecting.

Milla, I think. *Sophie. The woman on Edgar Street and her daughter, Angelina.*

"No, I'm still on the first one."

"Do you think there'll be more?"

I think about it and can't figure out if I want another one or not. "The first one's hard enough." We drink.

I drop in regularly at Milla's place, and she shows me her photos again and I continue reading from *Wuthering Heights*. I'm actually starting to like it. The cake got finished a few nights ago, thank God, but the old lady's as nice as ever. Shaky as hell but nice as ever.

Sophie loses again the next week at athletics, this time in the eight hundred. She doesn't run the same in those patchy old shoes. She needs something better to even come close to how she runs in the mornings. That's when she's true. She's apart. Almost out of herself.

Early next Saturday morning, I go to her house and knock on the door. Her father answers.

"Can I help you?"

I feel nervous, like I've come to convince him to let his daughter go out with me. I'm holding a shoe box in my right hand, and the man looks down at it. Quickly, I lift it and say, "I've got a delivery for your daughter Sophie. I hope they're the right size."

The shoe box passes between our hands, and the man looks confused.

"Just tell her a guy brought her some new shoes."

The man looks at me as if I'm heavily intoxicated. "Okay." He tries his hardest not to mock me. "I will."

"Thank you."

I turn around and start walking away, but he brings me back. "Wait," he calls out.

"Yes, sir?"

He holds the box out, puzzled, lifting it into the conversation.

"I know," I say.

The box is empty.

I haven't shaved, and I feel like death warmed up at the track. I didn't bring the cab in till six this morning and went straight over to Sophie's place and over to the track. I've got a sausage roll for breakfast and some coffee.

She gets called for the fifteen hundred, and she goes barefoot.

I smile at the thought of it.

Barefoot shoes . . .

"Just don't let her get stepped on," I say.

A few minutes later, her father approaches the fence. The race begins.

The other dickhead starts yelling out.

And Sophie gets tripped up on the back straight after a lap.

She falls among the lead group of five, and the rest of them stretch out, up to maybe twenty-five meters in front. When she gets back up, it reminds me of that bit in *Chariots of Fire* when Eric Liddell falls over and runs past everyone to win.

There are two laps to run, and she's still well behind.

She gets the first two runners easily, and she's running like she does in the morning. There's no strain. The only thing you can see on her is the feeling of freedom and the purest sense that she's alive. All she needs is the hood and the red pants. Her bare feet carry her past the third one, and soon she's up alongside her nemesis. She goes past her and holds her with two hundred to go.

Just like the mornings, I think, and people have stopped to watch. They saw her fall and stand and keep going. Now they watch her out in front, beyond everything that's ever been done on a normal weekend in this town. The discus has stopped, and the high jump. Everything has. All there is is the girl with the sunshine hair and the killer voice breathing and being in front.

The other girl comes at her.

She pushes for the lead.

There's blood on Sophie's knees, from the fall, and she also got spiked, I think, but this is how it has to be. The last hundred meters nearly kill her. I can see the pain tightening on her face. Her bare feet bleed on their way across the balding grass. She almost smiles from the pain—from the beauty of it. She's out of herself.

Barefoot.

More alive than anyone I've ever witnessed.

They run at the line.

And the other girl wins.

Like always.

*   *   *

As they go over the line, Sophie collapses, and down there, on the ground, she rolls onto her back and looks up at the sky. There's ache in her arms and ache in her legs and heart. But on her face is the beauty of the morning, and for the first time, I think, she recognizes it: 5:30 a.m.

Sophie's father claps, like always, only this time, he's not alone. The other girl's father claps now, too.

"That's a hell of a daughter you got there," he says.

Sophie's father only nods modestly and says, "Thank you. So have you."

J another stupid human

I throw my Styrofoam coffee cup in the bin with my sausage-roll wrapper and begin to walk away. As usual, I've got sauce all stuck on my fingers.

I can hear her feet behind me, but I don't turn around. I want to hear her voice.

"Ed?"

It's unmistakable.

I turn around and smile at a girl who's got blood on her knees and feet. From her left knee, it runs crookedly down her shin. I point to it and say, "You better get that looked after."

Calmly she answers. "I will."

Some discomfort stands between us now, and I know I don't

73

belong here anymore. Her hair's out and it's beautiful. Her eyes are worth drowning in, and her mouth speaks to me.

"I just," she says, "wanted to say thanks."

"For getting you spiked and hurt?"

"No." She refuses my lie. "Thanks, Ed."

I give in. "It's a pleasure." My voice sounds like gravel compared to hers.

When I step closer, I notice she doesn't look away from me now. She doesn't tilt her head or send her eyes to the ground. She lets herself look and be with me.

"You've got beauty," I tell her. "You know that, don't you?"

Her face goes a little red as she accepts it.

"Will I see you again?" she asks, and to be honest, I think I'll regret what I say next.

"Not at five-thirty in the bloody morning."

She twists on one of her feet, laughing, silently, to herself.

I'm about to leave when she asks, "Ed?"

"Sophie?"

It shocks her that I know her name, but she goes on. "Are you some kind of saint or something?"

Inside, I laugh. *Me? A saint?* I list what I am. *Taxi driver. Local deadbeat. Cornerstone of mediocrity. Sexual midget. Pathetic cardplayer.*

I say my final words to her.

"No, I'm not a saint, Sophie. I'm just another stupid human."

We smile a last smile, and I walk away. I feel her watching me, but I don't look back.

edgar street revisited

It feels like the mornings clap their hands.
To make me wake.

In the mornings of my eyes, I see three things each time.
Milla.
Sophie.
45 Edgar Street.
The first two hold me up with the rising of the sun. The third strips me and hands shivers to my skin and to my flesh and bones.

I spend the late of each night watching repeats of *Dukes of Hazzard*. The big fat guy always sits there eating marshmallows at his desk. *What's that bloke's name again?* I asked myself when I saw the first episode. Then Daisy came on-screen and said, "What's up, Boss Hogg?"
Boss Hogg.
Of course.
God, Daisy looks fantastic in her tight jeans. Each night when I see her my pulse quickens immeasurably, but she's always gone quicker than she arrives.
The Doorman shoots me a dirty look every time.
"I know," I say.
But then she comes on again and there's no point arguing. Beautiful women are the torment of my existence.

The nights and Dukes pass by.
I drive my cab with a headache that waits behind me. Every time I turn around, it's there.

"Thanks, mate," I say. "That'll be sixteen fifty."

"*Sixteen* fifty?" whinges the old guy in his suit. His words are like froth in my head, boiling, rising, and falling.

"Just pay up." I don't have the patience for this today. "You can walk next time if it costs too much." I'm sure he puts it on his company's account, anyway.

He gives me the money and I thank him. *Wasn't so difficult now, was it?* I think. He slams the door hard. My head may as well have been in it.

In a way, I'm waiting for another phone call to arrive at my place, telling me to get over to Edgar Street again, pronto. I wait a few nights, but there's nothing.

On Thursday night, I leave the card game at Audrey's early. A feeling clutters me. It makes me stand up and leave, almost without saying a word. The time has arrived, and I know I need to be standing outside that house at the end of Edgar Street—a house held up by the violence that occurs inside it almost every night.

As I walk there, I realize I'm hurrying. I've had the success I felt I needed.

Milla and Sophie.

Now I have to face this.

I turn onto Edgar Street, forming fists inside my jacket pockets. I check to see that no one's watching me. With Milla and Sophie, I always felt at ease. They were the nice ones. There was practically no risk involved, unlike here, where all the answers seem to be painful ones. For the wife and the girl and for the husband. And me.

Waiting, I pull a forgotten piece of chewing gum from my pocket and put it in my mouth. It tastes like sickness, like fear.

The feeling escalates when the man comes down the road and walks up the porch steps. Silence moves closer then. It clips me, pushing past.

It happens.

The violence interferes. It sticks its fingers into everything and tears it open. It all comes apart, and I loathe myself for waiting this long to end it. I despise myself for taking the easy options night after night. A hatred is wound up and let go in me. It hacks at my spirit and brings it to its knees, next to me. It coughs and suffocates as my own hatred for myself becomes overwhelming.

The door, I tell myself. *Go to the door—it's open.*

But I don't move.

I don't move because my cowardice tramples me, even as I try to lift my spirit from its knees. It only keels over. It sways off to the side and hits the earth with a silent, beaten thud. It looks up at the stars. They're stars that dribble across the sky.

Go, I tell myself again, and this time, I walk on.

Everything shakes as I walk up the porch steps and stand at the door. Distant clouds watch me, but they're backing away. The world wants nothing to do with this. I don't blame it.

Inside, I hear them.

He's waking her in every moment.

Disturbing her.

Reaching through her and abandoning her at the same time.

He throws her down and takes her and cuts her open. The bedsprings leak—a howling, desperate noise of falling down and springing up, even though they don't want to. Refusal is point-less. Complaint has no use. Some crying crawls to the doorway where I stand. It hobbles out from the gap in the door and lands at my feet.

How can you not go in? I ask myself, but still I wait.

The door opens a little more, and a presence stands there now, opposite me. It's the girl.

The girl is in front of me, planting her fist in her eye to wrestle out the sleep that has lodged there. She wears yellow pajamas with red boats on them, and her toes curl and rub together.

She looks at me, but without fear. Anything's better than where she's coming from.

In a whisper, she asks, "Who are you?"

"I'm Ed," I whisper back.

"I'm Angelina," she says. "Are you here to save us?" I can see a tiny spark of hope awaken in her eyes.

I crouch down to look at her properly. I want to tell her I am, but nothing comes out. I can see that the silence from my mouth has all but extinguished the hope she has conjured up. It's almost gone when I finally speak. I look at her truthfully and say, "You're right, Angelina—I'm here to save you."

She steps closer as it rekindles. "Can you?" she asks with surprise. "Really?" Even a girl of about eight years can see there's almost no rescue from her life. She has to double-check if she can believe me.

"I'll try," I say, and the girl smiles. She smiles and hugs me and says, "Thanks, Ed." She turns around now and points. Her voice whispers even quieter. "It's the first room on the right."

If only it was that easy.

"Well, come on, Ed," she says. "They're just in there. . . ."

But again, I don't move.

The fear has tied itself around my feet, and I know there's nothing I can do. Not tonight. Not ever, it seems. If I try to move, I'll trip over it.

I expect the girl to scream at me. Something like, "But you promised me, Ed! You *promised*!" She says nothing, though. I think she understands how physically powerful her father is and how scrawny *I* am. All she does is stumble over to me and hug me again.

The girl tries to crawl inside my jacket as the noise from the bedroom reaches us from inside. She hugs me so tight I wonder how her bones survive. When she lets go and leaves, she says, "Thanks for at least trying, Ed."

I answer nothing because the only thing I feel now is shame. I watch her feet as they turn and walk away beneath the yellow pajamas. She turns once more and says, "Goodbye, Ed."

"Goodbye," I say through my curtain of shame.

She closes the door completely, and I crouch there. I allow myself to fall forward and rest my head on the door frame. My breath bleeds. My heartbeat drowns my ears.

I'm in bed now, swallowed by the night. How can a person sleep when all he can feel are the arms of a tiny kid in yellow pajamas holding on to him in the dark? It's impossible.

I feel insanity will come after me soon. If I don't get back down to Edgar Street in the next few nights, I fear I might go crazy. If only the kid didn't come out—but I knew she would. Or at least I should have known. She'd always come out before and cried on the porch, followed later by her mother. I know as I lie here, flat on my back, that I'd meant to meet her. I wanted her to give me the courage. To force me inside. But it failed miserably. In fact, it couldn't have been more disastrous. Now a worse feeling empties itself into me.

At 2:27 a.m. the phone rings.

It shocks through the air, and I jump up, run to it, look at it. This can't be good.

"Hello?"

The voice at the other end waits.

"Hello?" I say again.

It finally speaks, and I can picture it now, mouthing the words. The voice is dry, permanently cracked. It's friendly enough, but it still means business. It says:

"Check your letter box, Ed."

A silence overhauls us, and the voice leaves me completely. There's no more breathing at the other end.

I hang up and walk slowly out my front door and over to the letter box. The stars are gone completely now and a haze of rain is falling as each of my footsteps step me closer. My hand shivers as I bend down and open the latch. I reach in.

I touch something cold and heavy.

My finger touches the trigger.

I shudder.

K♦ murder at the cathedral

There's only the one bullet in the gun. One bullet for one man, and this is where I feel like the unluckiest person on earth. I tell myself, *You're a cabdriver, Ed! How in the hell did you end up in all this mess? You should have just stayed on the floor in that bank.*

I'm sitting at my kitchen table with a gun warming up in my

hand. The Doorman's awake and demanding coffee, and all I can do is stare at the gun. It also doesn't help that whoever's setting all this up gives me just the one bullet. Don't they realize I'm most likely to shoot off one of my own feet before I even get started? I don't know. This has gone too far now. A gun, for God's sake. I can't kill anyone. For starters, I'm a coward. Second, I'm weak. Third, the day of the bank robbery was obviously a fluke—nobody's ever even showed me how to use a gun. . . .

I'm angry now.

Why have I been chosen for this? I beg, despite knowing without question what I have to do. *You were happy with the other two,* I castigate myself. *So now you have to do this one.*

What if I don't do it? Maybe the person on the phone will come after me. Maybe that's what it's all about. Maybe it's a case of either I do the job or the rest of the bullets wind up inside *me*.

Shit, I can't sleep now!

I'm about to have a hernia, for Jesus' sake.

I look through the old record collection my dad gave me. Stress relief. I shuffle through the albums feverishly and find what I'm looking for—the Proclaimers. I chuck it on and watch it spin. The ridiculous first notes of "Five Hundred Miles" come on, and I feel like going berserk. Even the Proclaimers are giving me the shits tonight. Their singing's an abomination.

I pace the room.

The Doorman looks at me as if I'm insane.

I *am* insane. It's official.

It's three in the morning, I'm playing the Proclaimers too loud for their own bloody good, and I'm pretty sure I have to go and kill someone. My life has really become worthwhile, hasn't it?

A gun.

81

A gun.

Those words shoot through me, and I constantly look at it to check this is real. White light from the kitchen stretches into the lounge room, and the Doorman's paws reach out and lightly scratch me, asking for a pat.

"Piss *off,* Doorman!" I spit, but his huge brown eyes plead for me to calm down.

I break and pat him on the stomach, apologize, and make us some coffee. There's no way I'm sleeping tonight. The Proclaimers are just warming up on that misery-to-happiness song—the follow-up to "Five Hundred Miles."

Insomnia must kill people, I think as I drive the cab back from the city. It's the next day. My eyes are itchy and burning as I drive with the window down. The warmth of the air feeds on my eyes, but I let it. The gun is under my mattress, where I left it last night. I've got the gun under the mattress and the card in my drawer. It's hard to tell which has cursed me more.

I tell myself to stop whingeing.

Back at the Vacant Taxis lot, I see Audrey kissing one of the new blokes who works there. He's about my height but obviously goes to the gym. Their tongues touch and massage each other. His hands are on her hips, and hers are in the back pockets of his jeans.

Lucky I don't have the gun now, I think, but I know I'm all talk.

"Hi, Audrey," I say as I walk by, but she doesn't hear me. I'm heading to the office to see my boss, Jerry Boston. Jerry's a particularly obese man with greasy hair combed over his bald spot.

I knock on his door.

"Come in!" he calls out. "It's about time you—" He stops midsentence. "Oh, I thought you were Marge. She was s'posed to bring me some coffee half an hour ago." I saw Marge smoking a cigarette in the car park but choose not to mention it. I like Marge, and it's not the sort of thing I like to get involved in.

The door closes behind me, and Jerry and I watch each other.

"Well?" he asks. "What?"

"Sir, I'm Ed Kennedy and I drive one of your—"

"Fascinating. What do you want?"

"My brother's moving house today," I lie, "and I was wondering if I could take my cab home to drive a few things over to his new place."

He looks at me generously and says, "Now why on earth would I let you do that?" He's smiling. "Do my taxis have Removalists painted on the doors? Do I look like a charity to you?" He's irritated now. "Buy your own car, for Christ's sake."

I remain calm but move closer. "Sir, I've driven night and day sometimes, and I've never taken a holiday." To be honest, due to my nine months of experience, my shifts fluctuate from night to day week after week. I'm not sure if that's legal. The new people get nights. The veterans get days. I get both. "I'm only asking for one night. I'll pay for it if you want."

Boston leans forward on the desk now. He reminds me of Boss Hogg.

His coffee comes in with Marge, who says, "Oh, hi there, Ed. How's it going?"

Ah, this tight arse won't let me have a cab for the night, I think, but all I say is, "Not bad, Marge, how are you?" She puts the coffee on the table and politely leaves.

Big Jerry takes a sip, says, "Ah, that's lovely," and has a change of heart. Thank God for Marge. Impeccable timing. He says, "Okay, Ed, since you work well enough, I'll let you have it. One night only, right?"

83

"Thank you."

"You working tomorrow?" He checks the roster and answers his own question. "Night shift." He ponders his coffee and resolves the issue. "Get it back to me by midday tomorrow. Not a minute later. I'll put a check on it in the afternoon. It needs a service."

"Yes, sir."

"Now let me drink my coffee in peace."

I leave.

I walk past Audrey, who's still going at it with the new bloke. I say goodbye, but again she doesn't hear. She won't be at cards tonight, and neither will I. This will annoy Marv no end, but I'm sure he'll survive. He'll get his sister to fill in for Audrey and his old man for me. His fifteen-year-old sister's a good kid but cops an awful lot for having a brother like Marv. He makes her life a living hell in many different ways. For example, all her teachers hate her because Marv was such a smart arse in school. They all think she's hopeless when she's actually quite intelligent.

Either which way, I've got more on tonight than cards. I attempt to eat but fail. I pull the Ace of Diamonds and the gun out and stare at them on the kitchen table.

The hours trickle past.

When the phone rings I feel afraid for a moment but then know it's Marv, without a doubt. I pick up.

"Hello?"

"Where the hell are you, Ed?"

"At home."

"Why? Ritchie and me are sitting here bored shitless. And where's Audrey? Is she with you?"

"No."

"Well, where is she?"

84

"With some guy from work."

"Why?" He's like a kid, I swear it. Always asking why for no reason. If she's not there, she's not there. Marv doesn't understand there's nothing that can be done about it.

"Marv," I say, "I've got a lot on tonight. I can't make it."

"What have you got on?"

Should I tell him or not? I wonder. I go for yes, saying, "All right, Marv, I'll tell you why I can't make it. . . ."

"Well, go on."

"Okay," I say. "I have to kill someone, all right? Is that all right with you?"

"Look"—he's getting frustrated now—"don't shit me, Ed. I'm in no mood for your litany of crap." *Litany?* Since when does Marv have a vocabulary? "Just get over here. Get over here or I won't let you in on the Annual Sledge Game this year. I was talking to some of the fellas about it today." The Annual Sledge Game is a preposterous game of soccer played at the Grounds before Christmas. It's played barefoot by idiots like Marv, who's conned me into playing the last few years. And every year I nearly break my neck.

"Well, count me out this year," I tell him. "I'm not coming over." I hang up. As expected, the phone rings again, but I lift it and put it straight back down. I almost laugh at the thought of Marv swearing at the other end in disgust. Right about now he's turning to yell, "Okay, Marissa! Get out here for a game of cards!"

It doesn't take me long to focus on the job at hand. This is the only night I can carry out my plan. One night with the cab. One night with my mark. One night with the gun.

Sooner than I hope, it's close to midnight.

85

I kiss the Doorman on the cheek and walk out. I don't look back because I'm determined to walk through the door again later tonight. The gun is in my right jacket pocket. The card is in my left, with a flask of doped vodka. I put a lot of sleeping tablets in it. It better work.

The difference tonight is that I don't go down to Edgar Street. Instead, I stay closer to Main Street and wait there. At closing time, one man isn't going home.

It's late when all the drunks drop out from the pubs. My bloke can't be missed because of the sheer size of him. He yells good-bye to his mates, not knowing it's for the last time. I turn my cab around so I'm facing the same way he's walking. He looms closer in my side mirror and goes past. When he's further down the road, I start up and drive toward him. The sweat I feel is normal now, and I know I'm going to do it. I'm inside the mo-ment. There's no getting out.

I pull up beside him and call out quietly.

"You need a lift, mate?"

He looks over and burps. "I'm not payin'."

"Come on, you look to be in a pretty bad way there—I'll give you a free one." At that, he smiles and spits, then comes around to the passenger side. When he gets in, he begins to explain his address. "Don't worry," I say. "I know where you live." There's something around me, numbing me. Without it, I could never go on. I remember Angelina and the way her mother fell to pieces in the supermarket. I have to do this. *You have to, Ed.* I nod in agreement.

I pull the vodka out of my pocket and offer it to him. He grabs it without a second thought.

I knew it, I congratulate myself. *A man like this takes everything he wants without even thinking about it.* A man like me thinks too much.

"Don't mind if I do," he says, and he takes a good hard swig.

"Keep it," I say. "It's yours."

He says nothing but keeps drinking as I drive past Edgar Street and head west, circling to the back end of town. There's a place out there on a dirt track called the Cathedral. It's the rocky summit of a mountain that looks over miles and miles of bushland. We're not even out of town when he falls asleep. The vodka flask drops and pours itself onto him as I drive on.

I drive for over half an hour, hit the dirt road, then go for another half hour. We get there just after one o'clock, and when I cut the engine, we're alone, in silence.

Time to get fierce, or at least as fierce as I get.

I get out of the car and go to the passenger side. I open the door. I beat him in the face with the gun.

Nothing.

I hit him again.

After five attempts, he's momentarily startled, tasting his own blood from his nose and mouth.

"Wake up," I order him.

He stutters a moment, not knowing where he is and what's happening.

"Get out."

I have the gun pointed exactly between his eyes.

"If you're wondering if this is loaded, it might be the last thought you ever have."

He's still groggy, but his eyes grow wide. He thinks about a sudden movement but understands very quickly that he can barely pull himself out of the car. Eventually he makes it out, and I walk him up the track with the gun grinding into his back.

"This'll go straight through your spine," I say, "and then I'll leave you here. I'll call your wife and kid and they can come out and look at you. They can dance around you. Would you like that? Or should I put this through your skull and let you die fast? Your choice." He falls down, but I follow him hard with my knees. I cripple him with my boyish boniness and have the gun pointed at the back of his neck. "You feel like dying?" My voice shivers but remains hard. "You deserve it, I can tell you that much." I jump off him and bark, "Now get up and keep walking or you die now."

There's a sound.

It rises from the ground.

I realize it's the sound of a man sobbing. Tonight, however, I don't care. I have to kill him because slowly, almost effortlessly and with complete contempt, this man kills his wife and child every night. And it's me alone, Ed Kennedy, a less than ordinary suburbanite, who has the chance to end it.

"Get up!" I get stuck into him again, and we press on to the top, to the Cathedral.

When we reach the summit, I make him stand there, about five meters from the edge. The gun's pointed at the back of his head. I'm about three meters behind him. Nothing can go wrong.

Except.

I begin to shiver.

I begin to shake.

I begin to lurch and quake at the thought of killing another human. The aura that surrounded me earlier is gone. The air of invincibility has deserted me, and I'm suddenly aware that I have to do this surrounded by nothing but my own human frailty. I breathe. I almost break.

I ask you:

What would you do if you were me? Tell me. Please tell me!

But you're far from this. Your fingers turn the strangeness of these pages that somehow connect my life to yours. Your eyes are safe. The story is just another few hundred pages of your mind. For me, it's here. It's now. I have to go through with this, considering the cost at every turn. Nothing will be the same. I'll kill this man and also die myself, inside. I want to scream. I want to scream out, asking why. The scattered stars shower down like icicles tonight, but nothing soothes me. Nothing allows me an escape. The figure in front of me collapses, and I stand above him, waiting.

Waiting.

Trying.

To reach a better answer than this.

God, the gun is so stiff in my hand. It's cold and warm and slippery and rigid, all at once. I tremble uncontrollably, knowing that if I do this, I will have to press the gun into the man's flesh or I'll miss. I'll have to bury it in him and watch as his human blood blankets him. I'll watch him die in a stream of unconscious violence, and even when I explain to myself that I'm doing the right thing, I still beg for an answer as to why it has to be me. Why not Marv, or Audrey, or Ritchie?

The Proclaimers thunder through my head.

Imagine it.

Imagine killing someone to the tune of two Scottish nerds wearing glasses and flattop haircuts. How will I ever listen to that song again? What will I do if it comes on the radio? I'll think of the night I murdered another man and stole his life with my own hands.

I shake and wait. Shake and wait.

He starts snoring. For hours.

* * *

First light seeps through the air, and when the sun comes up closer to the east, I decide it's time.

I wake him up with the gun. This time he responds immediately, and again I stand three meters behind him. He gets to his feet, attempts to turn around, but thinks again. I step closer and hold the gun behind his head, saying, "Now, I got chosen to do this to you. I've been watching what you do to your family, and now it's going to stop. Nod if you understand." He complies, slowly. "Do you realize you're going to die for what you've been doing?" No nod this time. I hit him again. "Well?" This time he nods.

The sun hits its head on the horizon, and I fasten my hand to the gun. My finger's on the trigger. Sweat slides down my face.

"Please," he pleads. He bends forward in a half breakdown. He feels like he'll die if he falls completely. A disturbing kind of sobbing takes hold of him. "I'm sorry, I'm so—I'll stop, I'll stop."

"Stop what?"

He hurries his words. "You know. . . ."

"I want to hear you say it."

"I'll stop forcing her when I get—"

"Forcing?"

"Okay—raping."

"Better. Continue."

"I'll stop doing it, I promise."

"How in God's name can I rely on your word?"

"You can."

"That isn't the answer I'm looking for. You'd get naught for that in an essay," and I dig the gun in a little harder. "Answer the question!"

"Because if I do, you'll kill me."

90

"I'm killing you now!" I'm feverish again, coated in sweat and what I'm doing, struggling to believe it. "Put your hands on your head." He does it. "Walk closer to the edge." He does it. "Now how do you feel? Think before you answer. A lot depends on whether you're right or wrong."

"I feel like my wife does every night when I come home."

"Scared out of your mind?"

"Yes."

"Exactly."

I follow him over to the edge, aim the gun, and make sure.

The trigger sweats across my finger.

My shoulders ache.

Breathe, I remind myself. *Breathe.*

A moment of peace shatters me and I pull the trigger. The noise of it burns through my ears, and just like the day of the bank robbery, the gun now feels warm and soft in my hand.

part two: **The Stones of Home**

Say a prayer
at the stones of home

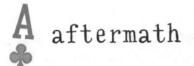 aftermath

Dryness.

I stagger out of the car and slip toward the flyscreen door. There's a feeling in me that resembles complete and utter desolation. It trips through me. No. It zigzags. I don't care that I'm a messenger anymore. The guilt of it handles me. I shrug it off, but always it climbs back on. No one said this was going to be easy.

The gun.

All I can feel in my hand is the gun. The warm, soft metal merging with my skin. It's in the trunk of the cab now, cold again and stony, feigning innocence.

As I walk toward the porch, I hear his body hit the earth again. I think it was a shock to him that he was still alive. Each breath he took was a gasp, sucking up life, collecting it, to keep. It was over. I'd shot at the sun, but of course it was too far. At the time, I wondered vaguely where the bullet landed.

Often on the way back, my tires retreading the path we'd driven, I looked over at the passenger seat. It was filled with emptiness. An aftermath of a dead man was probably still lying on the flat, flat earth, breathing up the dirt till it lined his lungs.

I find that all I want to do is make it inside and hug the Doorman. I hope he hugs me back.

We share a coffee.

"Good?" I ask him.

Brilliant, he answers.

Sometimes I wish I was a dog.

The sun's well and truly up and people are going to work. I sit at the kitchen table and feel quite sure that no one on my anonymous, dew-covered street has had a night like mine. I picture them all getting up in the night to have a leak or having orgasms together in their beds—while I was out channeling the end of a gun into the neck of another human. *Why me?* I think, but typically, no answer is forthcoming. I only know it would have been nice to be making love instead of attempting murder. I feel like I've lost something, and my coffee's getting cold. The stench of the Doorman reaches up and pats me. His sleeping comforts me, in spite of my thoughts.

The phone rings pretty soon.

Oh no, you can't handle this, Ed.

It's them, isn't it?

My heartbeat doubles. It tangles itself up.

An incompetent pulse.

I sit.

The phone rings.

Fifteen times.

96

I step over the Doorman, stare at the receiver, and finally decide to pick it up. My voice crumbles in my throat.

"Hello?"

The voice on the other end is irritated but, thankfully, belongs to Marv. In the background, I can hear men at work. Hammering. Swearing. Foundations for Marv's voice, on top.

"Well, thanks for picking up the bloody phone, Ed," he tells me. Personally, I'm in no mood for this right now. "I was beginning to think—"

"Shut up, Marv." I hang up.

Predictably, it rings again. I pick up.

"What the hell's wrong with you?"

"Nothing at all, Marv."

"Now, don't start this rubbish with me, Ed. I had a real rough night."

"Did you try to kill someone, too, did you, Marv?"

The Doorman looks at me as if to inquire whether the phone might be for him. Quickly, he gets back to his bowl and licks it, searching for a few stray coffee fumes.

"Again with this nonsense?" *Nonsense.* I love it when a guy like Marv uses a word like that. "I've heard some excuses in my time, Ed, but nothing like this."

I give up. "Forget it, Marv. It's nothing."

"Well, good." Marv's always happiest when I have nothing to say. He gets to the point he's been hoping to make all along. "So have you thought about it?"

"Thought about what?"

"You know."

My voice loudens. "No, Marv, at this point, I wouldn't have a single clue what you're talking about. It's early, I've been out all night, and for some reason I'm not really emotionally equipped for this little heart-to-heart of ours right now." I feel like hanging up again but resist. "Could you help me out and tell me exactly what we're talking about?"

"Okay, okay." He acts like I'm the biggest bastard on earth now and that he's doing *me* a favor by not hanging up on me. "It's just that some of the fellas are asking whether you're in or out."

"Of what?"

"You know."

"Fill me in, Marv."

"You know—the Annual Sledge Game."

Well, shit, I chastise myself, *that barefoot game of soccer. How in the hell can I have forgotten about that? What a selfish bastard I am.* "I really haven't given it much thought, Marv."

He's unhappy now, and not just an unhappy kind of unhappy. Marv's boiling. He delivers me an ultimatum. "Get keen then, Ed. Let me know within twenty-four hours if you can play. If not, we'll get someone else. There's a big waiting list, you know. These games are a highly sought-after tradition. We've got blokes like Jimmy Cantrell and Horse Hancock dying for a run. . . ." I tune out. Horse Hancock? I don't even want to think about just who in the hell that could be. Only when the phone starts beeping do I realize that Marv's hung up on me. I'd better ring him later and tell him I'll play. Hopefully someone will break my neck in the middle of a giant nettle patch. That'd be nice.

As soon as I get off the phone, I take a plastic bag out to the cab and unload the guilty party from the trunk. I put it back in the drawer and try to forget about it. I fail.

I sleep.

The hours go numb around me as I lie in bed.

I dream about last night, the crackling sun of morning, and the shivering giant of a man. Is he already back in town? Has he walked back in or even managed to hitch? I try not to think about it. Every time those thoughts climb into bed with me, I roll over, trying to squash them. They seep out.

It feels like midafternoon when I wake up for good, but it's barely eleven. The Doorman's wet nose kisses my face. I return the cab, come home, and take him for a walk.

"Keep your eyes peeled," I tell him when we make our way onto the road. Paranoia has broken into me. I think of the guy from Edgar Street, though I know he's most likely the least of my concerns. It's whoever sent me the Ace of Diamonds I need to worry about. I've got a bad feeling they'll know I've completed the card and will deliver the next one soon enough.

Spades. Hearts. Clubs.

I wonder which card will end up in my letter box next. It's the spades that worry me most, I think. The Ace of Spades scares me—always has. I try not to think about it. I feel watched.

Late in the afternoon, we walk a fair way and end up at Marv's place, where a lot of guys are hanging around out back.

Once in the backyard, I call out. Marv doesn't hear me at first, but when he comes over, I say, "I'm in, Marv."

He shakes my hand like I've just asked him to be best man at my wedding. It's important to Marv that I play because we've both been in it the last few years and he wants it to become a tradition. Marv believes in it, and I realize I shouldn't look down on that. It's what it is.

I look at Marv and the other people in his backyard.

They'll never leave this place. They'll never want to, and that's okay.

I talk with Marv awhile longer and attempt to leave, despite being offered beer by several cooler-toting suburban men. They're in board shorts, tank tops, and flip-flops. Marv comes with me through the gate to where the Doorman waits. When I'm nearly midway back up the street, he calls out.

"Hey, Ed!"

I turn. The Doorman doesn't. He doesn't care much for Marv.

"Thanks, okay?"

"No worries," and I keep walking. I take the Doorman home, make my way to the Vacant lot, and clock on. As I drive back through town, I think again of last night. Fragments of it stand by the road and run next to the car. When one image slows down and drops off, it's replaced by another. For a moment, when I glance in the rearview mirror, I don't seem to recognize who I am. I don't feel like me. I don't even seem to remember who Ed Kennedy's supposed to be.

I don't feel anything.

One piece of luck is that I have the next day off, completely. The Doorman and I sit in the park on the main street of town. It's afternoon, and I've bought us both ice creams. Single cone, two flavors. Mango and Jaffa orange for me. Bubble gum and cappuccino for the Doorman. It's nice, sitting in the shade. I watch intently as the Doorman gently lunges for the sweet taste and softens the cone with his slobber. He's a beautiful individual.

Footsteps crease the grass behind us.

My heart seizes up.

I see shadow. The Doorman keeps eating—a beautiful individual but a useless guard dog.

"Hi, Ed."

I know the voice.

I know it and shrink back down inside me. It's Sophie, and I see a glimpse of her athletic legs now as she asks if she can sit down.

"Of course," I say. "You want an ice cream?"

"No, thanks."

"You don't feel like sharing one with the Doorman here?"

She laughs. "No, thanks. . . . The Doorman?"

Our eyes come together. "Long story."

We're silent now, both waiting, till I remind myself that I'm the older one and should therefore initiate conversation.

But I don't.

I don't want to waste this girl with idle chitchat.

She's beautiful.

Her hand falls down to gently stroke the Doorman, and all we do is sit there for about half an hour. Eventually, I feel her looking at my face. Her voice enters me.

She says, "I miss you, Ed."

I look across and say, "I miss you, too."

The scary thing is, it's the truth. She's so young, and I miss her. Or do I cling to her because she was a good message? I think I miss her purity and truth.

She's curious.

I feel it.

"You still running?" I ask, denying it.

She nods politely and plays along.

"Barefoot?"

"Of course."

There's still a graze on her left knee, but as we both look at it, there's no regret inside the eyes of the girl. She's content, and if nothing else, I take comfort in her comfort with me.

You're so beautiful when you run barefoot, I think, but I don't bring myself to say it.

The Doorman finishes his ice cream and laps up the pats from Sophie's hand and fingers.

A car horn blows from behind us, and we both know it's for her. She gets up. "I have to go."

There's no goodbye.

Just footsteps and a question when she turns around. "Are you okay, Ed?"

I turn and see her and can't help but smile. "I'm waiting," I answer.

"For what?"

"The next ace."

She's smart and knows what to say. "Are you ready for it?"

"No," I say, and resign myself to one clear fact. "But I'll get it anyway."

She leaves properly then, and I see her father watching me from the car. I hope he doesn't think I'm a miscreant or something, sitting in parks and preying on innocent teenagers. Especially after the shoe box incident.

I feel the Doorman's snout on my leg now, and he stares up at me with his lovely geriatric eyes.

"Well?" I ask him. "What's it to be, my friend? Hearts, clubs, or spades?"

How about another ice cream? he suggests.

He's no help really, is he?

I crunch through my cone and we stand up. I realize how stiff and sore I still am from two nights ago at the Cathedral. Attempted murder will do that to you.

2 the visit

A third day passes, and still nothing.

I've been down to Edgar Street, and the house is dark. The woman and the girl are asleep, and there's still no sign of the husband. I've contemplated going back out to the Cathedral to see if he jumped or if something else happened to him.

Yet.

How ridiculous am I?

I was supposed to kill the man, and here I am worrying about his well-being. I feel guilty about everything I did to him, but on the other hand, I feel guilty about *not* killing him. After all, that was what I was sent there to do. I think the gun in my letter box made that perfectly clear.

Maybe he made it to the highway and kept walking.

Maybe he threw himself off the cliff.

I stop myself before I think of every possible scenario. Soon I won't have time to worry. A few more days.

I return one night from playing cards, and the house smells different. There's Doorman's smell, but something else as well. It smells like some kind of pastry. It hits me.

Pies.

I move with hesitance toward the kitchen and notice that the light's on. There's someone sitting in my kitchen eating pies, which they've taken out of my freezer and cooked up. I can smell the processed meat and the sauce. You can always smell the sauce.

With pointless optimism, I look for something to pick up to use as a weapon, but there's nothing in my path except the couch.

When I make it to the kitchen, I see a lone figure.

I'm shocked.

There's a man in a balaclava sitting at the table, eating a meat pie with sauce. Many questions rush through my mind, but none of them stick. It's not every day you come home to something like this.

As I contemplate what to do, I realize with considerable panic that there's another one behind me.

No.

A big slurp wakes me up.

The Doorman.

Thank God you're all right, I tell him. I say it by shutting my eyes with relief.

He slurps again, and his tongue is red from the blood that's cracked down my face. He smiles at me.

"I love you, too," I say, and my voice is like a rumor. I'm not quite sure if it came out or not or if it's true. It makes me realize that I hear nothing outside me. It's all inner and like static.

Move, I tell myself, but I can't. I feel cemented to the kitchen floor. I even make the mistake of trying to remember what happened. This only makes a noise blur across me and the Doorman's face disfigure above. It feels like a kind of precursor to death. A prologue, maybe.

My mind folds itself down.

To sleep.

I fall deep inside me and feel trapped. I fall through several layers of darkness, almost reaching the bottom, when a hand seems to pull me up by the throat and into the pain of reality. Someone is literally dragging me through the kitchen. The fluorescent light knifes me in the eyes, and the smell of pies and sauce makes me want to vomit.

I'm propped up to sit there now, on the floor, barely conscious, holding my head in my hands.

Soon the two figures merge with the haziness, and I can see them under the kitchen-light whiteness.

They're smiling.

They're throwing smiles at me from the insides of two very thick balaclavas. They're slightly bigger than average, and both muscular and strong, especially in comparison to me.

They say:

"Hi, Ed."

"How are you feeling, Ed?"

I'm treading water in my thoughts.

"My dog," I begin to moan. My head soaks through my hands now, and my words are quickly drowned. I've already forgotten that it was the Doorman who'd previously brought me back into consciousness.

"He needs a wash," one of them says.

"Is he okay?" Quiet words. Scared words that break and shiver and fight to keep themselves in the air.

"And a flea collar."

"Fleas?" I respond. My voice is scattered on the floor. "He hasn't got fleas. . . ."

"Well what are these?"

One of the men grabs me gently by the hair and lifts my head to see. He shows me a forearm full of insect bites.

"They're not from the Doorman," I say, wondering why in God's name I would choose to be obstinate in this situation.

"The Doorman?" Like Sophie, the intruders are curious about his name.

I confirm it with a nod of my head, which, surprisingly, wakes me up a little. "Look—fleas or no fleas—is he okay or not?"

The two of them look at each other now, and one takes another bite from his pie.

"Daryl," he says casually, "I'm not sure if I like Ed's tone just this minute. It's . . ." He struggles for the appropriate word. "It's . . ."

"Sour?"

"No."

"Unappreciative?"

"No." But he's got it now. "Worse—it's disrespectful." The last word is spoken with quiet, complete disdain. He looks directly at me as he speaks. His eyes warn me more than his mouth. It makes me suggest internally that I should break down and cry, begging them not to hurt my coffee-drinking dog.

"Please," I finally say, "you didn't hurt him, did you?"

The hard eyes flatten.

He shakes his head.

"No."

The best word I've ever heard.

"He's a useless guard dog, though," says the one still finishing his pie, dunking it in the sauce on his plate. "Do you know he slept through us breaking in?"

"I don't doubt it."

"Even when he woke up he only came in here wanting food."

"And?"

"We gave him a pie."

"Cooked or frozen?"

"Cooked, Ed!" He seems offended. "We're not savages, you know. In fact, we're quite civilized."

"Are there any left for me?"

"Sorry—the dog got the last one."

The big bloody greedy guts! I think, but I can't hold it against him. Dogs will eat anything. I can't argue with nature.

In any case, I try to catch them out.

I fire.

One quick question.

"Who sent you?"

Once in the air, my question loses its pace. The words float, and gingerly I stand and sit at one of the vacant kitchen chairs. I'm feeling a little more comfortable, knowing this is all part of what happens next.

"Who sent us?" The other one takes over now. "Nice try, Ed, but you know we can't tell you that. Nothing would give us greater pleasure, but we don't even know that ourselves. We just do the job and get paid."

I explode.

"What?" It's an accusation. Not a question. "No one pays *me*! No one gives me—"

I'm slapped.

Hard.

He then sits down again and resumes eating, dipping the last crust of pie in the big pool of sauce on his plate.

You overpoured, I think. *Thanks a lot.*

He calmly eats the crust, half swallows, and says, "Oh, do stop whining, Ed! We all have our duties here. We all suffer. We all endure our setbacks for the greater good of mankind."

He's impressed his mate and himself.

They're agreeing with each other, nodding.

"Nice," the other one tells him. "Try to remember all that."

"Yeah, what was it? The greater good of . . . ?" He thinks hard but can't come up with what he wants.

"Mankind," I answer, too quiet.

"What, Ed?"

"Man*kind*."

"Of course—you got a pen I can borrow, Ed?"

"No."

"Why not?"

"This isn't a newsagent's, you know."

"And there's that tone again!" He stands up and slaps me even harder, then sits back down, casual.

"That hurt," I tell him.

"Thanks." He looks at his hand—at the blood and the dirt and the smear. "You're in a pretty awful state there, Ed, aren't you?"

"I know."

"What's wrong with you?"

"I want a pie." I swear—and I'm sure you can back me up on this from previous actions—I'm definitely like a kid at times. A giant pain-in-the-neck kid. Marv's not the only one.

The one who slapped my face imitates me in a childlike voice. "'I want a pie. . . .'" He even sighs. "Would you listen to yourself? Grow up, for God's sake."

"I know."

"Well, that's the first step."

"Thanks."

"Now where were we, anyway?"

We all think.

Silently.

The Doorman walks in, looking guilty as all hell.

I s'pose a coffee's out of the question? he brings himself to ask me. The neck of him!

All I do is glare at him and he walks back out. He can tell he's in the bad books.

All three of us in the kitchen watch him make his exit.

"You can smell him coming, can't you?" one says.

"Damn right."

The slower eater of the two even stands up now and begins rinsing the plates in the sink.

"Forget it," I tell him.

"No, no—civilized, remember?"

"Oh yeah, that's right."

He claps his hands now and turns around. "Any sauce on my balaclava?"

"Not that I can see," replies the other. "What about me?"

He leans in and examines. "Nah, you're clean."

"Good." The slower eater wrestles with his own face a moment, saying, "Ah, this bloody shit thing. It's itchy as all get-out."

"Is that right, Keith?"

"Doesn't yours itch?"

"Of course it does!" Daryl can't believe he's having this discussion. "But you don't hear me complaining about it every five minutes, do you?"

"We've been here an hour."

"Even so, remember—these are the things we have to suffer for the greater good of . . ." He clicks his fingers over at me.

"Oh—mankind."

"That's right. Thanks, Ed. Lovely. Good work."

"No worries."

We're kind of friends now. I can feel it.

"Look, can we just get this over with so I can get this woolen mask off, Daryl?"

"Could you just show us a little discipline, Keith? All good hit men have impeccable discipline, all right!"

"Hit men?" I ask.

Daryl shrugs. "Well, you know, that's what we call ourselves."

"Sounds plausible," I concede.

"I suppose." And he thinks hard now.

He ponders. He speaks.

"Okay, Keith, you're right. We better head off soon. You got the pistol, didn't you?"

"I did, yes. It was in his drawer."

"Good." Daryl stands up and pulls an envelope from his jacket pocket. On it are the words *Ed Kennedy*. "Got a delivery for you, Ed. Please stand up, son."

I do it.

"I'm sorry," he now reasons, "but I'm under instructions. I have to tell you one thing—that so far you're doing well." He speaks more quietly. "And just between you and me—and I can get maimed for telling you this—we know you didn't kill that other man. . . ."

Again, he apologizes and delivers his fist beneath my ribs.

I'm bent over.

The kitchen floor is filthy.

There's Doorman hair everywhere.

The hammer of a fist lands on the back of my neck.

I taste the floor.

It joins my mouth.

Slowly, I feel the envelope land on my back.

Far, far away, I hear Daryl's voice one last time. He says, "Sorry, Ed. Good luck."

As their footsteps echo through the house, I hear Keith now as well.

"Can I take the mask off now?" he asks.

"Soon," Daryl answers.

The kitchen light fades, and again I'm sinking.

3 the envelope

I wish I could tell you that the Doorman's helping me up, but of course he isn't. He comes over and licks me a few times before I find enough strength to get to my feet.

The light dives at me.

Pain stands up.

As I try to keep balance, the Doorman sways, and I ask him desperately for help. All he can do, however, is sway and stare.

From the corner of my eye, I see something on the floor.

I remember.

The envelope.

It's fallen from my back, under the kitchen chairs, with all the Doorman hair.

I bend down and pick it up, holding it in my fingers like a kid holds something filthy, like a used hankie.

With the Doorman in tow, I retire to the lounge room and slump gracefully onto the couch. The envelope wavers, mocking its own danger, as if to say, *It's only paper. Only words.* It never mentions that the words might be of death or rape or awful, blood-filled duties again.

Or Sophies or Millas, I remind myself.

Either way, we're sitting on the couch.

The Doorman and me.

Well? he asks, chin on ground.

I know.

It has to be done.

I tear the envelope open and the Ace of Clubs falls out, with a letter.

Dear Ed,

All appears to be going well if you're reading this. I certainly hope your head isn't too sore. Undoubtedly, Keith and Daryl mentioned that we're all quite pleased with your progress. If my instincts serve me well, they probably also let it slip that we know you didn't kill the man from Edgar Street. Well done. You dealt with the situation in a neat, well-executed manner. Very impressive indeed. Congratulations.

Also, in case you're wondering, Mr. Edgar Street boarded a train to some old mining town not long ago. I'm sure you'll be glad to hear of it. . . .

Now some more challenges await.

Clubs are no snack, my son.

The question is, Are you up to it?

Or is that question irrelevant? Surely you weren't up to the Ace of Diamonds.

But you did it.

Good luck and keep delivering. I'm quite sure you realize your life depends on it.
Goodbye.

Perfect.

Just perfect.

I tremble at the thought of the Ace of Clubs disclosing its intentions. All reason tells me to keep from picking it up. Against all reality, I even envision the Doorman eating it.

The only problem is that I can feel it just beyond my big toe. The damn card is like gravity itself. Like a cross to strap across my back.

It's in my fingers now.

I hold it.

It's in my eyes.

I read it.

You know when you do something and realize only a few seconds afterward that you've actually done it? That's what I've done now, and as a result, I'm reading the Ace of Clubs, expecting another list of addresses.

I'm wrong.

Typically, it's not going to be that easy. There are no addresses this time. There's no uniform to this. There's nothing to make any part of it secure. Each part is a test, and part of that is in the unexpected.

This time, it's words.

Only words.

The card reads:

Say a prayer
at the stones of home

So could you tell me, please? Could you please tell me what that might mean? At least the addresses were cut-and-dried. The stones of home could be anything. Anywhere. Anybody. How do I find a place that has no face and nothing to point me in the right direction?

The words whisper to me.

The card softly speaks itself in my ear as if recollection should be immediate.

There's nothing, though.

Only the card, me, and a sleeping dog who gently snores.

Later on I wake up, crumpled on the couch, realizing that I've been bleeding again from the back of my head. There's blood on the couch and rust on my neck. The pain's back, but not sharp or gashing anymore. Just constant.

The card's on the coffee table, floating on the dust. Growing among it.

Outside is dark.

The kitchen light is loud.

It deafens me as I walk toward it.

The rusty blood scratches my neck and reaches down my back. I decide on the way that I need a drink, hit the light, and stumble through the dark toward the fridge. At the bottom I find a beer and go back to the lounge room, attempting to drink and be merry. In my case, merry means ignoring the card. I pat the Doorman with my feet, wondering what day and time it is and what might be on TV if I can be bothered getting up to turn it on. Some books sit on the floor. I won't be reading them.

Something leaks down my back.

My head's bleeding again.

4 ♣ just ed

"Another one?"

"Another one."

"What suit this time?"

"Clubs."

"And you still have no idea who's sending them?" Audrey's noticing the spilled beer on my jacket and now the crusty putrid blood on my neck. "God, what happened to you last night?"

"Don't worry."

I feel a bit pathetic, to tell you the truth. The first thing I've done when the sun's come up is gone over to Audrey's place for help. It's not till halfway through our front-door conversation that I realize how badly I'm shaking. The sun warms me, but my skin is trying to shake itself from me. It wrestles with my flesh.

Can I come in? I wonder, but my answer arrives within a few edgy moments when that guy from work enters the background, asking, "Who is it, darlin'?"

"Oh." Audrey shuffles.

Uncomfortable.

Then offhand.

"Oh, it's just Ed."

Just Ed.

"Anyway, I'll see you soon. . . ."

I begin walking backward, waiting.

For what?

For her.

But she doesn't come.

Finally, she takes a few steps out of the doorway and says, "Will you be home later, Ed?"

I continue backward. "I don't know." It's the truth. I *don't* know. My jeans feel a thousand years old as they wrap around my legs. Almost like a bluebottle. My shirt burns me cold. My jacket scrapes at my arms, my hair is frayed, and my eyes feel shot with blood. And still I don't know what day it is.

Just Ed.

I turn.

Just Ed walks on.

Just Ed walks fast.

He begins an attempt at a run.

But he trips.

He rips a foot into the earth and slips back to a walk, hearing her voice call out, coming closer.

"Ed?"

"Ed?!"

Just Ed turns back to listen to her.

"I'll come over later, right?"

He resigns, gives up.

"Okay," he admits. "See you then," and walks off. He has a vision of Audrey in the doorway:

A too-big T-shirt used as pajamas. Beautiful, great morning hair. Handled hips. The wiry, sun-showered legs. Dry, sleep-covered lips. Teeth marks on her neck.

God, I could smell the sex on her.

And I wished with silent anguish that it was also on me.

Yet I can only smell dried blood and a sticky spilled drink on my jacket.

It's a beautiful day.

Not a cloud in the sky.

*   *   *

For the record, Ed, I tell myself later, eating cornflakes, *it's Tuesday. You're working tonight.*

I dismiss the Ace of Clubs to the same top drawer as the Ace of Diamonds. For a moment, I imagine a full hand of aces in that drawer, fanned out as a player would hold them in a game. I never thought I wouldn't want four aces. In a card game, you pray for a hand like that. My life is not a card game.

I'm pretty sure Marv'll be at me again soon, wanting me to run with him in preparation for the Annual Sledge Game. For a while, I even manage a few laughs thinking of it—seeing us running barefoot through the dew and the frightening nettles of people's front lawns. There's no point running in shoes if the game's played barefoot.

Audrey arrives at about ten, all washed up and smelling like clean. Her hair is tied back except for a few gorgeous strands that fall over her eyes. She wears jeans, tan-colored boots, and a blue shirt with the Vacant Taxis badge embroidered on the pocket.

"Ed."

"Audrey."

We sit on the front porch with our legs dangling over the edge. A few clouds have formed now.

"So what does this one say?"

I clear my throat and speak quietly. "'Say a prayer at the stones of home.'"

Silence.

"Any idea?" she eventually asks. Her eyes have settled on me. I feel them. I feel their softness.

"None."

"And what about your head and"—she looks at me now with a

117

kind of concerned disgust—"the rest of you." She says it. "Ed, you're a complete mess."

"I know." My words land on my feet and slip off to the grass.

"What did you do at the addresses of the first card, anyway?"

"You really want to hear it?"

"I do."

I say it and see it.

"Well, I had to read to an old woman, let a sweet girl run barefoot till she was all trodden on and bloody and glorious, and"—I still speak calmly—"I had to kill a man who was pretty much raping his wife every night."

The sun emerges from a small cloud.

"Are you serious?"

"Would I say it otherwise?" I try to get some hostility in my voice, but none arrives. I don't have the energy.

Audrey doesn't dare to look at me now, scared she'll know the answer by the look on my face. "Did you do it?"

I feel guilty now, getting short with her like that and even telling her all this. There's nothing she can do to help. She can't even try to understand. She'll never know. Audrey will never feel the arms of that kid, Angelina, wrapped around her neck or see the pieces of the mother all over the supermarket floor. She'll never know how cold that gun was or how desperate Milla was to hear that she'd done right by Jimmy—that she'd never let him down. She'll never understand the shyness of Sophie's words or the silence of her beauty.

For a second or two I'm lost.

Inside those thoughts.

Inside those people.

When I climb back out and find myself still sitting next to Audrey, I answer her question.

"No, Audrey. I didn't kill him, but . . ."

"But what?"

I shake my head and feel some tears register in my eyes. I keep them in there.

"What, Ed? What did you do?"

Slowly. I talk the words. Slowly.

Slowly. . . .

"I took that man up to the Cathedral and had a gun jammed into his head. I pulled the trigger but didn't shoot him. I aimed for the sun." Treading over it like this doesn't help. "He's left town and hasn't come back. I'm not sure if he ever will."

"Does he deserve to?"

"What's *deserve* got to do with anything? Who the hell am I to decide, Audrey?"

"All right." Her hand touches me gently, in peace. "Calm down."

"Calm down?" I snap now. "Calm down? While you're screwin' that guy, while Marv plots his pointless soccer match, while Ritchie does whatever the hell he does when he's not playing cards, and while the rest of this town sleeps, I'm doing its dirty laundry."

"You're chosen."

"Well, that's comforting!"

"Then what about the old lady and that girl? Weren't they good things?"

I slow down. "Well, yeah, but—"

"Was the other one worth it for the sake of them?"

Damn.

I hate her.

I agree.

"It's just . . . I wish it was easier, for me, you know?" I make a special point not to look at her. "I wish it was someone else who

119

was chosen for this. Someone competent. If only I didn't stop that robbery. I wish I didn't have to go through with it all." It comes gushing out, with words like spilled milk. "And I wish it was me with you and not that other guy. I wish it was my own skin touching with yours. . . ."

And there you have it.

Stupidity in its purest form.

"Oh, Ed." Audrey looks away. "Oh, Ed."

Our feet dangle.

I watch them, and I watch the jeans on Audrey's legs.

We only sit there now.

Audrey and me.

And discomfort.

Squeezed in, between us.

She soon says, "You're my best friend, Ed."

"I know."

You can kill a man with those words.

No gun.

No bullets.

Just words and a girl.

We sit on the porch awhile longer, and I look down at Audrey's legs and her lap. If only I could curl up and sleep there. It's still just the beginning of all this, and already I'm exhausted.

It's decision time.

I have to pull myself together.

5 cabs, the hooker, and alice

It's evening now, and I'm driving into the city. The distant buildings shadow the sunset.

The night is quiet, for thinking.

The most interesting person I pick up is a prostitute-looking woman who sits in the front. Her body is hard. Physical. Her hair waves at me and her mouth is beautiful, though her teeth are ugly. Her words are blond and sweet. She ends all sentences with an endearment.

"Why the long face, honey?"

"I've never been this way before, sweetie."

Contrary to stereotypes, her makeup is very tasteful and light. She doesn't chew gum. She wears black knee-high boots, a white skivvy that gives her a lovely shape, and a dark jacket-vest.

Keep your eyes on the road, Ed.

"Honey?"

I turn to her.

"You remember where we're going, sweetie?"

I clear my throat. "The Quay Grand?"

"That's right—I gotta be there by ten, all right, sugar?"

"Sure." I give her a friendly look. I enjoy customers like this.

When we get there, the meter says eleven sixty-five but she gives me fifteen and tells me to keep the change. She leans in the window. "You look sweet."

I smile. "Thanks."

"For the cash or the compliment?"

"Both."

Now she even reaches a hand in and says, "My name's Alice."

121

I take it and hold it. "*They* get to call me Sheeba, but you can call me Alice, okay, honey?"

"Okay."

"And you are?"

"Oh." I let go of her hand reluctantly and reply. She mustn't have noticed my driver ID on the dash. "Ed. Ed Kennedy."

She gives me a last endearment. "Well, thanks for the lift, Ed. And don't worry so much. Enjoy yourself, all right, sweetie?"

"No worries."

When she walks away, I imagine her turning back around and saying, "Could you come and pick me up in the morning, Ed?"

But she doesn't.

She's gone.

Alice doesn't live here anymore.

Watching her all the way to the doors of the hotel, I'm sitting in the cab, alone.

Behind me, a car blows its horn in abuse, and a man roars out the window. "Get moving, cabbie!"

He's right. We're useless.

Driving through the night, I imagine Alice turning into Sheeba. I hear her voice and smell it in the dimly lit hotel room overlooking Sydney Harbor.

"That okay, sweetie?"

"Oh, honey. . . ."

"Yes, darlin', that's it, right there, sugar, keep going."

I see myself beneath her.

Being taken and made love to.

I feel her.

Know her.

Taste her champagne mouth.

Ignore the ugly teeth.

Just shut my eyes and taste her.

Touch her naked skin.

The skivvy on the floor.

The vest next to us.

The boots forgotten—triangled near the door.

Feel me in her.

"Oh," she says, breathless, "Ed, oh, Ed." I get lost in it. "Oh, Ed. . . ."

"Red!" the guy in the backseat screams at me.

I hit the brakes hard.

"Christ, mate!"

"Sorry."

I suck the air in deep.

It's been nice to forget about the Ace of Clubs and Audrey for a while, but now I'm back to the reality of it. The man's voice carried with it the memory of both.

"They're green now, buddy."

"Thanks."

Driving.

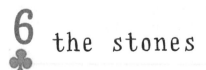

the stones

At home.

I drive into town as the sun edges up the sky. All roads are empty and I pull into the Vacant Taxis lot.

Like always, I walk back to the shack.

The Doorman's happy to see me.

We drink the obligatory coffee together, and I pull the card from the drawer. I watch it, trying to get new glimpses of it— trying to catch it off guard and have it reveal its secrets to me.

The night of driving could have gone either way, but I feel ready now. I want to throw my miserable, complaining, excuse-making mouth from my face and get on with it. I even corner myself in the widening light of the lounge room. I think, *Don't blame it anymore, Ed. Take it.* I even move out onto the front porch and see my own limited view of the world. I want to take that world, and for the first time ever, I feel like I can do it. I've survived everything I've had to so far. I'm still standing here. Okay, it's a crummy front porch I stand on, cracked to shithouse, and who am I to say that the world isn't the same? But God knows that the world takes enough of *us*. The Doorman sits at attention next to me, or at least as best he can. He even looks dependable and obedient. I look down at him and say, "It's time."

How many people get this chance?

And of those few, how many actually take it?

I crouch down and place my hand on the Doorman's shoulder (or the closest thing a dog has to one), and we go off to find the stones of home.

About halfway along the street, we stop.

We stop because we've got just the one problem.

We have no idea where to look.

The rest of the week trots by—a collection of card games, work, and hanging around with the Doorman. I kick a soccer ball around with Marv at the local grounds on Thursday night and watch him get drunk afterward at his place.

"Just over a month till the big game," he says. He sips his father's beer. He never buys his own. Never.

He still lives with his folks, Marv. The house is pretty nice inside, I must admit. Wooden floors. Clean windows. His ma and Marissa do all of it, of course. Marv, his lazy-arse brother, and their old man don't lift a finger. Marv pays a small boarding fee and throws the rest of his money into the bank. Sometimes I wonder what he's saving for. At last count, he said he was up to thirty grand.

"What position do you want, Ed? In the game."

"No idea."

"I want center," he confides in me, "though I'll probably get wing again. You'll get second row in spite of being lanky and weak."

"Thanks a lot."

"It's true, isn't it?"

He's got me there.

"But you can actually play when you pull your finger out," he continues.

This is where I should tell Marv that he's a good player, too, but I don't. I keep my mouth shut.

"Ed?"

Nothing.

I'm thinking about the Ace of Clubs again and where the stones of home might be.

"Ed?" He claps at me. "You there?"

For a brief moment, I consider asking Marv if he's heard of the stones of home, but something stops me. He won't understand, and I know without exception now that if I'm going to be this messenger, I have to do it alone.

"I'm fine, Marv," I tell him. "Just thinking of some things."

"That'll kill you," he warns. "You're better off not thinking at all."

In a way, I wish I could be like that. You'd never worry or care about anything that really mattered. You'd be happy, in the same pitiful way someone like our friend Ritchie is. Nothing affects you, and you affect nothing.

"Don't worry, Marv," I say. "I'll be all right."

Marv feels like talking tonight. He says, "Remember that girl I used to see?"

"Suzanne?"

He says her full name, drawing it out. "Suzanne Boyd." He shrugs now. "I remember when she left with her family and never even said a goddamn thing to me about it. That was three years ago now. . . . I thought about it till it drove me crazy." He echoes my previous thoughts now. "Someone like Ritchie, he wouldn't care less. He'd call her a slurry, drink a beer, and put a bet on at the betting shop." Marv smiles ruefully and looks down. "All over."

I want to talk to him.

I want to ask him about that girl and if he loved her and still misses her.

Nothing, however, exits my mouth. How well do we really let ourselves know each other?

There's a long quietness until I finally break it open. It reminds me of someone breaking bread and handing it out. In my case, I hand out a question to my friend.

"Marv?" I ask.

"What?" His eyes tear at me, suddenly.

"How would you feel if you had to be somewhere *right now* and didn't know how to get there?"

He examines the question. He seems to be over the girl for the moment. "Like missing the Annual Sledge Game?"

I allow him that much. "Okay."

"Well . . ." He thinks with all of him, rubbing his rough hand over the blond stubble on his face. That's how important the game is to him. "I'd always be imagining what's happening there, knowing I can't change it because I'm so far away."

"Frustrating?" I ask.

"Definitely."

I've looked up maps now. I've found some old books that belonged to my father and read local histories. Nothing, however, gives me any idea where I'll find the stones of home. The days and nights come apart. I feel them corroding at the seams. Every minute lets me know that something might be happening that I need to adjust or add to. Or stop.

We play cards.

I've been to Edgar Street a few times and nothing has changed. The man still hasn't returned. I don't think he's ever coming back.

The mother and the girl have looked happy when I've watched them. I leave it at that.

One night I go to Milla's place and read to her.

She's delighted to see me, and I must tell you it's nice to be Jimmy again. I drink tea and kiss Milla's wrinkled cheek on my way out.

On Saturday I go and watch Sophie run. She still comes in second, but, true to her word, runs barefoot. She sees me and nods. Nothing is said because it's while she's running. I'm standing behind the fence along the back straight. Just in that passing moment, we recognize each other, and it's enough.

I miss you, Ed, I hear her say from that afternoon in the park. Even today, in the look on her face as she runs past, I can tell she's saying, *I'm glad you came.*

I'm glad, too, but I leave as soon as the race is done.

At work that night, it happens.

I find the stones of home.

Or to be honest.

They find me.

Working in the city, I keep my eyes open for Alice, especially if I'm near the Quay or the Cross. She's nowhere, though, which is a bit disappointing. The only repeat pickups I get are old guys who always know a better way or yuppie businessmen who are always checking their watch or talking on the phone.

It's late now, about four in the morning, and I pick up a young man on my way home. As he waves me down I size him up. He looks stable enough and not in the least like a vomiter. The last thing I need is someone throwing up in my cab this close to the end of a shift. That can ruin your night within a few regrettable seconds.

I pull over and he gets in.

"Where to?" I ask.

"Just drive." His voice is threatening from the moment he speaks. "Drive me home."

I'm nervous, but I still talk. "Where's home?"

He turns and looks at me, ominous. "Where *you* live." His eyes are a strange yellow, like a cat's. Short black hair. Black clothes and two more words. "Drive, Ed."

Naturally, I do as he tells me.

He knows my name, and I know he's taking me where the Ace of Clubs wants me to go.

We sit in silence awhile, watching the lights lean past. He's sitting in front, and each time I attempt to look at him, I fail. I can always feel those eyes. They seem ready to claw me.

I try to initiate conversation.

"So," I say. Hopeless, I know.

"So what?"

So I try another angle. A gamble. "Do you know Daryl and Keith?" I ask.

"*Who?*"

His derision of me is horrifying, but still I battle on. "You know—Daryl and—"

"Look, mate, I heard you the first time." His voice hardens further. "Mention any more names like that and you won't even make it home, I swear it."

Why, I ask myself at this point, *are all the people who visit me either violent, argumentative, or both?* It seems that no matter what lengths I go to, I'm always winding up with people like *this* in my shack or in my cab.

For obvious reasons, I don't say another word as we near town. I only drive and try to steal a few more looks at him, unsuccessfully.

"Down the bottom end," he tells me when we reach Main Street.

"Near the river?"

"Don't get smart. Just drive."

Past my place.

Past Audrey's.

Down to the river.

"Here."

I pull over.

"Right, thanks."

"That'll be twenty-seven fifty."

"What?"

It takes courage to open my mouth. This guy looks like he wants to kill me. "I said, that's twenty-seven dollars fifty."

"I'm not paying."

I believe him.

I believe him because he simply sits there and lets his eyes grow round and black in the middle of all that yellow. This man is not paying. There's no discussion. There's no argument— although I try.

"Why not?" I say.

"I don't have it."

"I'll take your jacket, then."

He edges closer, bordering on friendly for the first time. "They were right—you are a stubborn son of a bitch, aren't you?"

"Who told you?"

But I don't get the answer.

His eyes go wild, and he opens the door and leaps from the cab.

Pause.

I feel trapped in the moment, then jump my own cab and go after him. Toward the river.

Wet grass and words.

"Get back here!"

Strange thoughts.

Thoughts of, *Get back here, Ed? "Get back here" is so common. It's what every cabdriver yells in this situation. You need to come up with some new material. It's a wonder you didn't add "punk" onto the end. . . .*

My legs tighten.

Air brushes past my mouth but doesn't seem to get in.

I run.

I run and realize that I've felt this feeling before—this sick feeling in my stomach.

It was when I was a kid, chasing my younger brother, Tommy. The one in the city with better prospects and better taste in coffee tables than me. He was faster, of course, even back then. Better. He always was, and it was embarrassing. It was shameful to have a younger brother who was faster, stronger, smarter, and better. At everything. But he was. It was that simple.

We used to fish at the river, upstream, and we'd race to see who could get there first. Not once did I win. Of course, I told myself, I could have if only I really tried.

So just once.

I did.

And I lost.

Tommy also found something extra that day and beat me by at least five yards.

I was eleven.

He was ten.

Nearly a decade later, here I am again, still chasing someone faster, stronger, and better.

After nearly a kilometer, my breathing collapses.

He looks back.

My legs buckle.

I stop.

It's over.

A laugh breaks from his lips, maybe twenty meters ahead.

"Bad luck, Ed," and he turns away again. He's gone.

Watching his legs disappear into the darkness, I stand there, climbing memory.

A dark wind makes its way through the trees.

The sky is nervous. Black and blue.

My heart applauds inside my ears, first like a roaring crowd, then slows and slows until it's a solitary person, clapping with unbridled sarcasm.

Clap. Clap.

Clap.

Well done, Ed.

Well given up.

I stand in long grass and hear the river now for the first time. It sounds like it's drinking. When I look toward it, I see the stars in it. They look like they're painted to the surface of the water.

The cab, I think. *It's open.* The keys are also still in it, which is the number one sin any cabdriver can make in pursuit of a runner. A cardinal sin, in fact. You always take the keys. You always lock up. Except me.

I see the cab in my mind.

On the road, alone.

Both doors are open.

"I have to go back," I whisper, but I don't.

I remain still until first light shows up, and I see my brother and me racing.

Myself, failing.

I see us fishing together, from the riverbank, and then going further upstream, past where you can see any houses. Up high, where you have to climb, where we fished from the rocks.

The rocks.

The smooth rocks.

More like—

I walk slowly at first, then hard. I walk hard upstream.

I follow my brother and me, and I climb.

The water crumbles on its way down as my hands and feet push me forward. The world is lightening, taking shape, and turning to color. It feels like it's being painted around me.

My feet are itchy.

Changing from cold to warm.

I see it.

I see us.

There, I point out. *There are the rocks. The giant stones.* God, I see us there, throwing down the lines, hoping, sometimes laughing. Vowing not to tell anyone about us coming here.

I'm nearly there.

Far away, the cab doors are still open.

The sun is up—an orange cutout in a cardboard sky.

I make it to the top and kneel down.

My hands touch the cool stone.

I breathe out.

Happy.

I hear the river and look up and realize that I'm kneeling down among the stones of home.

There are three names carved into the rock.

I see them a few moments later when I look back up, and I go over to them.

The names are these:

THOMAS O'REILLY
ANGIE CARUSSO
GAVIN ROSE

For a while the river rushes through my ears and sweat shoves itself under my arms. Down my left side, it runs past my rib cage to the top of my pants.

I search for pen and paper, knowing I don't have them, the same way you give a person the wrong answer in the unlikely hope that by some miracle it might suddenly be right.

It's confirmed. I have nothing, so I pencil the names into my mind and go over them in ink. Then I scratch them in.

Thomas O'Reilly.

Angie Carusso.

Gavin Rose.

None of the names is familiar, which is good, I decide. I think it would be even harder if I knew the people I'm sent to.

I take a last look and walk away, chanting the names so I don't forget.

It takes me nearly forty-five minutes to make it back to the cab.

When I get there, the doors are shut but unlocked, and the keys are no longer in the ignition. I sit behind the wheel, and when I pull down the sun visor, they fall into my lap.

7 ♣ the priest

"O'Reilly, O'Reilly . . ."

I'm going through the local phone book. It's midday. I've slept.

There are two T. O'Reillys. One in the better part of town. One in the slummy area.

That's the one, I think. *The slummy one.*

I know it.

To make sure, I go to the uptown address first. It's a nice cement-rendered house with a big driveway. I knock at the door.

"Yeah?"

A tall man opens up and stares at me through the flyscreen. He wears shorts, a shirt, and slippers.

"Sorry to bother you," I say, "but—"

"You selling something?"

"No."

"You a Jehovah?"

"No."

He's shocked. "Well, in that case, you can come in." His tone has changed immediately and his eyes are friendly for the first time. It makes me consider accepting his offer, but I decide against.

We remain on either side of the flyscreen door. I wonder how to do this properly and decide that straight out is probably best. "Sir, are you Thomas O'Reilly?"

He comes forward and waits a moment before answering. "No, mate, I'm Tony. Thomas is my brother. He lives down in some Henry Street shithole."

"Okay, sorry to keep you," and I start to leave. "Thanks."

"Hey." He opens the door and walks after me. "What is it you want with my brother?"

I pause. "I don't know yet."

"As long as you're going down there," he says, "could you do me a favor when you see him?"

I shrug. "No worries."

"Could you tell him greed hasn't swallowed me up yet?" The sentence lands between us like a ball with no air in it.

"Sure. No problem."

I'm nearly out the gate when Tony O'Reilly calls out one last time. I turn back to face him.

"I think I should warn you." He comes closer. "My brother's a priest."

We're both completely still for a few seconds as I consider it. "Thanks," I say, and move from the driveway.

I walk away, thinking, *It's still better than a wife-beating rapist.*

"How many times do you want me to tell you?"

"You're sure now?"

"It's not me, Ed. If it was me, I'd tell you."

I'm having this conversation with my brother, Tommy, on the phone. My thoughts have wandered toward him after being led to the river and the stones of home. To my knowledge, Tommy's the only other person who knows we went there since we never told anyone. We always thought we'd get a good hiding for going that far up the river alone. Then again, maybe someone knew but chose to ignore it. We could both swim.

Earlier, I told him about the cards, to which he said, "How does this sort of thing always seem to happen to you, Ed? If there's anything weird floating around, it always manages to land on *you*. You're like a weird-shit magnet."

We laughed.

I thought about it.

Taxi driver. Local loser. Cornerstone of mediocrity. Sexual midget. Pathetic cardplayer. And now weird-shit magnet on top of it.

Admit it.

It's not a bad list I'm building up.

"How are you, Tommy, anyway?"

"All right. You?"

"Not bad."

End of conversation.

It's not Tommy.

We've had a bit of a card-playing drought lately, so Marv organizes a big night. The decided venue is Ritchie's place. His folks have just gone on holiday.

Prior to going to Ritchie's, I head over to Henry Street and have a look for Thomas O'Reilly. As I walk there, my stomach fidgets inside me and my hands search for my pockets. The street's a complete shocker and has always been renowned for it. It's a place of broken roof tiles, broken windows, and broken people. Even the father's house is pretty objectionable. I can already tell from a distance.

The roof is corrugated, red, and rusty.

The walls are a dirty white fibro.

Blistered, sore-looking paint.

Crippled fence, struggling to remain standing.

And a gate that's in agony.

I'm nearly there when I realize there's no way I'm going to make it.

Three very big men step out of an alley and start asking me for things. They never threaten, but their presence alone makes me feel very awkward and alone.

"Hey, man, you got forty cents?" asks one of them.

"Or cigarettes?" says the next.

"Do you really need that jacket?"

"Come on, man—*one* cigarette. I know you smoke. It ain't gon' kill you to lend me just the one. . . ."

I freeze for a moment, turn, and walk away.

Very bloody quickly.

At Ritchie's, I keep reliving it while the others deal and talk.

"So where'd your folks go, Ritchie?" Audrey asks.

There's a lengthy gap as he considers the question. "I have no idea."

"You're joking, aren't you?"

"They told me, but I must have forgot."

Audrey shakes her head, and Marv laughs through his cigar smoke.

I think of Henry Street.

Tonight I win for a change.

A few rounds pass me by, but somehow I manage to win the most games out of all of us.

Marv still talks contentedly about the upcoming Sledge Game. "Did you hear?" he puffs at Ritchie and me. "The Falcons have got a new guy this year. People are saying he's something like one fifty."

Ritchie: "One fifty what? Kilos?"

Like Marv and me, Ritchie's played the last few years, on the wing, but he's even less interested than me. To give you an idea, he usually shares a beer or two with the crowd during the game's flat spots.

"That's right, Ritchie," Marv affirms. This is serious business. "One fifty big ones."

"You playing, Ed?"

That question comes from Audrey. She knows I am but asks only to comfort herself with me. Ever since the front-door just-Ed incident she hasn't really known what to say to me. I look up at her from the table and half smile. She knows it means we're okay.

"Yes," I tell her. "I'll be there."

Her smile back says, *That's good.* Good that we're okay, that is. Audrey couldn't care less about the Annual Sledge Game. She hates soccer.

Later, when the cards are over, she comes back to my place and we drink in the kitchen.

"New bloke still going well?" I ask. I'm emptying toast crumbs into the sink. When I turn around to meet her answer, I notice some dried blood on the floor. Blood from my head among all the dog hair. Reminders are everywhere.

"Not bad," she answers.

I want to tell her how sorry I am for showing up like I did the other morning, but I choose not to. We're okay now, and there's no point going over something I can't change. I come close a few times but let it go. It's better that way.

When I put the toaster back down in its familiar place, I catch my reflection in it—even if it is a touch filthy. My eyes are uncertain to the point of being injured. For just that instant I see the pitiful nature of my life. This girl I can't have. These messages I feel I can't deliver. . . . But then I see the eyes become determined. I see a future version of myself going down to Henry Street again to see Father Thomas O'Reilly. I'll be in my dirty old jacket, moneyless and cigaretteless, same as last time. Only next time I plan to make it to the front door.

I have to, I think, and I speak to Audrey.

"I know where I have to go," I tell her.

She sips on the grapefruit Sub I gave her and asks it. "Well, where?"

"Three more people."

The scratched names on the giant stone appear in my mind, but I don't speak them to her. Like I've said, there's no point.

She's dying to ask the names.

I can tell.

Not a solitary word makes it out of her mouth, though, and I must say this for Audrey—she never forces things. She knows I'll tell her nothing if she pushes too hard.

The one thing I do tell her is where I found the names.

"I had a runner, and that's where he went. . . ."

All Audrey can do now is shake her head. "Whoever this is sure is going to a lot of trouble."

"They also seem to know me unbelievably well—almost as well as I know myself."

"Yeah, but," Audrey begins, "who knows you real well, Ed?"

And that's just it.

"No one," I say.

Not even me? the Doorman walks in and asks.

I look back and reply.

Look, pal—a few cups of coffee don't mean you know me.

Sometimes I don't even think I know myself.

My reflection finds me in the eyes again.

But you know what to do, it says.

I agree with it.

I get to Henry Street the next night after work and make it to the front door, and I must say, Father O'Reilly's house gives new meaning to the word *atrocious.*

I introduce myself, and without much more, the father invites me in.

Without even thinking, I speak, in the hallway.

"Jesus, it wouldn't kill you to clean the place once in a while, would it?"

Did I just say that?

But I don't need to worry because the father responds immediately.

"Well, what about the state of *you?* When was the last time you washed that jacket?"

"Good point," I say, thankful for his quick reply.

He's balding, the father, and about forty-five. Not quite as tall as his brother, and he has bottle green eyes and fairly big ears. He's wearing a robe, and I wonder why he lives here and not at the church. I always thought priests lived at the churches so people could go there if they needed help or advice.

He leads me into the kitchen and we sit down at the table.

"Tea or coffee?" The way he says it, it's like I have no choice in the fact that I'm having *something*. It just depends which.

"Coffee," I reply.

"Milk and sugar?"

"Yes, please."

"How many sugars?"

I'm a bit embarrassed about this. "Four."

"*Four* sugars! What are you, David Helfgott?"

"Who the hell's that?"

"You know—piano player, half crazy." He's astounded I don't know. "He used to have about a dozen cups of coffee a day with ten spoons of sugar in each."

"Was he good?"

"Well, yes." He puts the kettle on. "Crazy but good." His glassy eyes are of kindness now. A giant kindness. "Are you crazy but good, too, Ed Kennedy?"

"I don't know," I say, and the priest laughs, more to himself than anyone else.

When the coffee's ready, the father brings it over and sits

down with me. Before he takes his first sip, he asks, "You get hassled for smokes and money out there?" He jerks his head back toward the street.

"Yeah, and one guy keeps asking me for my jacket."

"Really?" He shakes his head. "God knows why. No taste, I suppose." He drinks.

I look down at my arms. "Is it really that bad?"

"Nah." He speaks earnestly now. "I'm only messing with you, son."

I examine the sleeves again and the material next to the zipper. The black suede is almost worn through.

An uneasy quiet gets between us. It tells me it's time to get down to business. I think maybe the father can feel it, too, and the expression on his face is of curiosity, yet patience.

I'm about to speak when an argument breaks out in one of the neighboring houses.

A plate smashes.

Screams jump over the fence.

The fighting intensifies, voices slam, and doors shout shut.

The father notices my concern and says, "Just hang on a sec, Ed." He walks to the window and opens it wider. He yells. "Can you two do me a favor and calm down!" He persists. "Hey, Clem!"

A murmuring crawls to the window now, followed by a voice. "Yes, Father?"

"What's going on over there today?"

The voice answers. "She's getting on my nerves again, Father!"

"Well, that's obvious, Clem, but what about—"

Another voice arrives. A woman's. "He's been up at the pub again, Father. Drinking and doing all that gambling!"

The father's voice becomes reverend. Honorable and firm. "That true, Clem?"

"Well, yeah, but—"

"But nothing, Clem. Stay in tonight, okay? Hold hands and watch television."

Voice 1: "Okay, Father."

Voice 2: "Thanks, Father."

Father O'Reilly comes back to me then, shaking his head. "Meet the Parkinsons," he says. "They're bloody useless." His comment shocks me. I've never heard a priest talk like this before. In fact, I've never spoken to one at all, but surely they're not all like this.

"Does that happen often?" I ask.

"Couple of times a week. At least."

"How do you live with that?"

He simply holds out his arms, motioning to his robe. "That's what I'm here for."

We talk for a while, the father and me.

I tell him about cab driving.

He tells me about priesting.

His church is the old one at the edge of town, and I now realize why he's chosen to live here. The church is too far away for him to really help anyone, so this is the best place for him. It's everywhere, on all sides and angles. This is where the father needs to be. Not in some church, gathering dust.

Sometimes I wonder about the way he speaks, which is confirmed when he explains the church to me. He admits that if his church was any kind of shop or restaurant, it would have closed down years ago.

"Business no good lately?" I ask.

"The truth?" The glass in his eyes breaks and punctures me. "Shithouse."

That's when I have to ask him. "Can you really talk like that? Being holy and all?"

143

"What? Because I'm a priest?" He finishes the dregs of his coffee. "Sure. God knows what's important."

It's a relief at this point that he doesn't go on about God knowing all of us and the rest of that particular sermon. He doesn't preach, ever. Even when we both have nothing more to say, he looks at me with finality and says, "But let's not get caught up in religion today, Ed. Let's talk about something else." He turns slightly formal now. "Let's talk about why you're here."

We stare across the table.

Just briefly.

At each other.

After a long drawn-out silence, I confess to the father. I tell him I still don't know why I'm here. I don't tell him about the messages I've already done or the ones still left to do. I only tell him that I have a purpose here and that it will come to me.

He listens very intently, with his elbows on the table, his hands together, and his fingers entwined beneath his chin.

A while passes until he knows I have very little else to say. He then speaks very calmly and clearly. He says, "Don't worry, Ed. What you need to do will certainly arrive in you. I've got a feeling it has in the past."

"It has," I agree.

"Just do me a favor and remember one thing," he says, and I can see he's trying not to be too typically religious. "Have faith, Ed, all right?"

I search the coffee mug, but there's none in there.

He walks me out of his house and up the street. Along the way, we come across the cigarette, money, and jacket scabs, and the father rounds them all up and gets them together.

He says, "Now listen up, boys. I want you to meet Ed. Ed, this is Joe, Graeme, and Joshua." I shake all their hands. "Fellas, this is Ed Kennedy."

"Nice to meet you, Ed."

"Hi, Ed."

"How's it going, Ed?"

"Now you guys remember something." The father speaks sternly now. "Ed here is a personal friend of mine, and you're not to ask him for cigarettes or money. And especially not for his jacket." He flashes me a quick grin. "I mean, look at it, Joe. It's an outrage, isn't it? It's downright bloody awful."

Joe agrees with gusto. "It sure is, Father."

"Good. So we understand each other?"

They all understand.

"Good." The father and I progress to the corner.

We shake hands and say our goodbyes, and the father's nearly out of sight when I turn around upon remembering his brother. I run back, calling out, "Hey, Father!"

He hears me and swivels.

"I nearly forgot." I stop running and stand about fifteen meters in front of him. "Your brother." The father's eyes reach a little closer. "He said to tell you that greed hasn't swallowed him yet."

The priest's eyes lighten then, with a touch of regret poured gently into them. "My brother, Tony . . ." His words are soft, and they hobble toward me. "I haven't seen my brother in a long time—how is he?"

"Not bad." I say it with a confidence I don't understand. Only gut feeling tells me it's the right answer, and we stand there now, among awkwardness and the rubbish.

"You all right, Father?" I ask.

"I am, Ed," replies Father O'Reilly. "Thanks for the concern."

145

He turns and walks away, and for the first time, I see him not as a priest.

I don't even see him as a man.

At this moment, he's just a human walking home on Henry Street.

Complete contrast now.

I'm at Marv's place, watching *Baywatch* with the sound down. We don't care about the plot or the dialogue.

We're listening to his favorite group, the Ramones.

"Can I put something else on?" Ritchie asks.

"Yeah, put Pryor on," Marv says. We even call Jimi Hendrix Richard Pryor these days. "Purple Haze" starts up, and he says, "Where's Audrey?"

"I'm here." She walks in.

"What's that *smell*?" Ritchie asks. He cringes. "It's familiar."

Marv knows, without doubt, and he points a finger at me. Accusingly. "You brought the Doorman, didn't you?"

"I had to—he was looking lonely when I left."

"You know he isn't welcome here."

The Doorman's at the open back door, looking in.

He barks at Marv.

The only person he barks at.

"He doesn't like me," Marv points out.

Another bark.

"It's because you give him dirty looks and put shit on him all the time. He understands, you know."

We argue awhile longer, but Audrey breaks it up by dealing out the cards.

"Gentlemen?" She clears her throat.

We sit down, and I pick up.

In the third game, I pick up the Ace of Clubs.

Father O'Reilly, I think.

"What are you doing this Sunday, Marv?"

"What do you mean, what am I doing on Sunday?"

"What do you think I mean?"

Ritchie says, "I swear you're a goose, Marv. I believe Ed is simply asking if you're busy this Sunday."

Marv points at Ritchie now. He's all hostile today because I brought the Doorman along. "Don't you start on me, either, Pryor." Now he looks at Audrey. "And you can keep quiet, too."

Audrey's astonished. "What the hell did *I* do?"

I interrupt. "Anyway, not only you, Marv—all three of you." I place my cards on the table, facedown. "I need a favor."

"Like what?" says Marv.

They're all listening now.

Waiting.

"Well, I was wondering if we could all go"—I let the words hurry from my mouth—"to church."

"What?"

"What's wrong with that?" I argue.

Marv tries to recover from the shock. "What the hell do you want us to go to church for?"

"Well, there's this priest, and—"

"He isn't one of those Chesters, is he?"

"No, he isn't."

"What's a Chester?" Ritchie asks, but he gets no answer. In the end, he doesn't really care and forgets about it.

The next person to speak is Audrey, finally bringing some reason to all of this. She says, "So why, Ed?" I think she's figured out that this smells a lot like the Ace of Clubs.

"The priest's a nice guy, and I think it might be good, even just for a laugh."

"Is *he* going?"

Marv motions to the Doorman.

"Of course not."

And Ritchie's my savior. He might be a dole bludger and a gambler and have the shonkiest tattoo in the world on his arm, but he'll agree to almost anything. In his typically affable way, he says, "Why not, Ed. I'll go to church with you." He then adds, "For a laugh, right?"

"Sure," I say.

Then Audrey. "Okay, Ed."

Now to Marv, who knows he's in a delicate situation. He doesn't want to go, but he knows that if he refuses he'll look like a proper bastard. He finally lets the air out of his lungs and says, "God, I can't believe it. I'll come, Ed." He laughs, unhappily. "Church on Sunday." Shaking his head. "Christ."

I pick up my cards. "Exactly."

Later that night, the phone's ringing again. I don't let it intimidate me.

"Hello?"

"Hi, Ed."

It's Ma. I breathe a sigh of relief and get prepared for the barrage. I haven't heard from her for a while, so she must have at least a fortnight to a month's worth of abuse to level at me.

"How you going, Ma?"

"You rung Kath yet? It's her birthday."

Kath, my sister.

"Oh shit."

"Oh shit's right, Ed. Now get your arse into gear and ring her."

"Right, I'll—"

The phone line's dead.

No one can murder a phone call like my mother.

The only mistake I made was not thinking quickly enough to ask Kath's phone number, just in case I can't find it. I've got a bad feeling I've lost it, which proves to be true once I've scoured every drawer and every crack in the kitchen. It's nowhere, and she isn't in the book.

Oh no.

You've guessed right.

The dreaded return phone call to Ma.

I dial.

"Hello?"

"Ma, it's me."

"What is it now, Ed?" Her sigh tells me how fed up she is.

"What's her number?"

I'm sure you can imagine.

Sunday shows up, quicker than I thought.

We sit near the back of the church.

Ritchie's happy enough, and Audrey's content. Marv's hungover—drinking his father's beer again—and I'm nervous for some reason I can't pinpoint.

The church really only has about a dozen people in it besides us. The emptiness of it is kind of depressing. The carpet is eaten with holes, the pews look morose. Only the leaded windows look sacred and holy. The other people are old and sit hunched like martyrs.

When Father O'Reilly comes out, he says, "Thank you all for coming." For just a moment, he looks a beaten man. He then notices the four people up the back. "A special welcome to the cabdrivers of this world."

His bald patch glistens from a glint of leaded-window light.

He looks up to acknowledge me.

I laugh, the only one.

Ritchie, Marv, and Audrey all turn their heads to stare at me. Marv's eyes are bloodshot something terrible.

"Rough night?" I ask him.

"Shocker."

The father gathers his thoughts and scans the audience. I can see him mustering the strength to carry this out with vigor. Father O'Reilly reaches deep. He begins his sermon.

Afterward, we're all sitting outside, the ceremony gone and done.

"What was the point of all that shepherd shit?" asks Marv. He lies down in the grass. Even his voice sounds like a hangover.

We sit here under a huge willow tree that weeps down around us. Earlier, back inside the church, they handed the plate around for people to put money in just before we left. I put five dollars in, Ritchie had no money, Audrey handed over a few dollars, and Marv went through his pockets and put in a twenty-cent coin and a pen lid.

I looked at him.

"What?"

"Nothing, Marv."

"Damn right."

As we sit under the tree Audrey sings to herself and Ritchie lies back, leaning on the step. Marv falls asleep, and I wait.

Soon, a presence rears up behind me. I know it's Father O'Reilly even before he speaks. It's the impression of the man. The quiet, laughing down-to-earthness of him.

He's behind me and he says, "Thanks for coming, Ed." He looks now at Marv. "That lad looks to be in an even more shit state than you." Some wickedness crosses his face. "For Christ's sake," and we all laugh, except Marv. Marv wakes up.

"Oh." He scratches his arm. "Hi, Father. Nice sermon."

"Thanks." He looks at all of us again. "Thank you all for coming. I'll see you next week?"

"Maybe," I say, but Marv chooses to speak for himself.

"Not a chance," he says.

The father takes it well.

I don't think I know *exactly* what the father needs, but I know now what I plan to do. Back home, I sit with the Doorman, occasionally reading and watching the picture frames above the television. I make up my mind.

I'm going to fill his church up.

It's just a question of how.

151

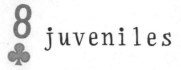

8 juveniles

A few days pass and I'm going over ideas on how to get people into that church. I think of asking Audrey, Marv, and Ritchie to bring all their family and friends, but first, none of them is really that reliable, and second, I'll have enough trouble just getting *them* there a second time.

I do a lot of driving early in the week, turning it over in my mind.

Only when I'm taking a man to the airport do I get the idea. We're nearly there when he says, "Hey, mate, I've actually got a bit of time up my sleeve—could you just drop us off at this pub up here?"

I look in the rearview and realize.

"That's it!" I tell him.

"Just one beer in a real pub," he says. "I can't stand those air-port lounges."

I pull over and let him out.

"Fancy one yourself?" he asks. "On me."

"No," I say. "I've got another quick pickup—but I can come and get you in about half an hour if you like."

"Certainly." He's quite happy with himself.

Quite frankly, so am I, because what I'm about to tell you is a fact.

In this country, there is only one thing that can draw a crowd without any shadow of a doubt. The answer?

Beer.

Free beer.

I go to the father, almost bursting through his front door, telling him we can organize something big for the upcoming Sunday. I tell him all about the idea. "Free beer, things for the kids, food. Did I mention the free beer?"

"Yes, Ed, I believe you did."

"Well? What do you think?"

He sits down calmly and considers it. "It sounds great, Ed, but you're forgetting one thing."

I can't be dampened today. "What?"

"We'll need money for all of that."

"I thought the Catholic Church was loaded—all that gold and shit in those big cathedrals. . . ."

He laughs a moment. "Did you see any gold in *my* church, Edward?"

Edward?

I think the father's the only person I'd ever allow to call me that. I'm even simply Ed on my birth certificate.

I continue. "You sure you haven't got any money lying around?"

"Well, not really, Ed. I've put it all into single teenage mothers' funds, alcoholics, the homeless, addicts, and my holiday to Fiji."

I assume he's joking about the Fijian holiday.

"Well, okay then," I say, "I'll raise the money myself. I've got a little stacked away. I'll put five hundred up."

"Five *hundred*? That's a lot, Ed. You don't seem the type to have a lot of money."

I walk fast and backward out his front door. "Don't worry about a thing, Father." I even laugh now myself. "Just have a little faith."

Now, I must say.

It really helps to have immature friends at a time like this. You get ideas on how to spread the word very quickly about something you want done. You don't bother with posters. You don't bother with an ad in the local paper. You realize there's only one real answer. Something to burn into every mind in town. . . .

Spray paint.

Marv is suddenly interested in going to church on Sunday. I tell him the plan and know without doubt that I can count on him. This is one area Marv excels and delights in. Juvenile behavior can be his specialty at times.

We steal both my ma's and Ritchie's barbecues, I ring up and book a jumping castle, and we borrow one of those karaoke machines from one of Marv's mates who works at the pub. We also get a few kegs, a half-decent deal from the butcher on sausages, and we're set.

Time for the paint.

We buy it from the local hardware on Thursday afternoon and descend on the town at three that morning. Marv's car staggers to a halt at my place, and we decide to walk into town from there. At each end of Main Street, we write the same thing in giant letters on the road:

MEET A PRIEST DAY
THIS SUNDAY 10 A.M.
ST. MICHAEL'S

FOOD, SINGING, DANCING, AND

FREE BEER

BE THERE OR MISS OUT
ON ONE **HELL** OF A PARTY

I don't know about Marv, but I feel a camaraderie as we kneel down and do the paint job. It feels like youth as we write the words. At one stage, I look across at my friend. Marv the argumentative. Marv the tight arse with his money. Marv with the girl who vanished.

When the job's done, he smacks me on the shoulder and we run off like handsome thieves. We both laugh and run, and the moment is so thick around me that I feel like dropping into it to let it carry me.

I love the laughter of this night.

Our footsteps run, and I don't want them to end. I want to run and laugh and feel like this forever. I want to avoid any awkward moment when the realness of reality sticks its fork into our flesh, leaving us standing there, together. I want to stay here, in this moment, and never go to other places, where we don't know what to say or what to do.

For now, just let us run.

We run straight through the laughter of the night.

With the arrival of tomorrow, everyone's talking about it. Absolutely everyone.

The cops have been around to the father's, asking him whether he knows anything about all this. He admits to knowing about the day, but nothing about the advertising techniques undertaken by some of his flock.

Over at his place on Friday afternoon, he tells me all about it.

"As you can imagine," he told the cops, "I have some rather dubious clientele. What church for the poor doesn't?"

They believed him, of course. Who wouldn't believe this man? "Okay, Father, but let us know if you find out anything, will you?"

"Of course, of course," and even when the cops began to leave, the father added one last question. "Will I be seeing you guys on Sunday?"

Apparently the cops are only human, too.

"Free beer?" they answered. "Can't say no to that."

Brilliant.

So it's all set up. Everyone's going. Families. Drunks. Complete bastards. Atheists. Satanists. Local gothics. Everyone. Free beer will do that. You can count on it. It's safe as houses.

I still work on Friday night, but I've got Saturday off.

That day, two things happen.

The first is that the father comes over to my place. I offer him some soup for lunch. Halfway through it, he stops and I see some emotion expand on his face.

He drops his spoon and says, "I have to tell you something, Ed."

I also stop. "Yes, Father?"

"You know, they say that there are countless saints who have nothing to do with church and almost no knowledge of God. But they say God walks with those people without them ever knowing it." His eyes are inside me now, followed by the words. "You're one of those people, Ed. It's an honor to know you."

I'm stunned.

I've been called a lot of things many times—but nobody has ever told me it's an honor to know me.

I suddenly remember Sophie asking if I was a saint and me replying that I'm just another stupid human.

This time, I allow myself to hear it.

"Thanks, Father," I say.

"The pleasure's mine."

The second thing that happens is that I make a few visits around town. First up, I see Sophie, very briefly. I ask if she can make it on Sunday, to which she says, "Sure, Ed."

"Bring the family," I suggest.

"I will."

Then I go to Milla's and ask if she'd allow me to escort her to church on Sunday.

"I'd be absolutely delighted, Jimmy." In short, she's thrilled.

Then.

The last visit.

As I find myself knocking on Tony O'Reilly's front door, I don't feel too optimistic.

"Oh," he says, "you." But he appears happy enough to see me. "You give that brother of mine my message?"

"I did," I say. "My name's Ed, by the way."

I'm a touch embarrassed now. I hate telling people what to do, or even asking. Still, I look now at Tony O'Reilly and talk. "I was kind of . . ." The rest of the sentence breaks off.

"What?"

I pick it back up but keep it. I use something else instead.

"I think you know what, Tony."

"Yes," he agrees. "I do. I've seen the spray paint."

I look down and back up. "So how about it?"

He opens the flyscreen, and I'm worried he might be coming out to abuse me, but he asks me to come in and we sit down in his lounge room. He wears a similar outfit to last time. Shorts, a tank top, and slippers. He doesn't look too mean, but I'm a firm believer in men in that sort of gear. All the best criminals wear stubbies, tank tops, and flip-flops.

Without asking, he brings out a cool drink. "Orange cordial okay?"

157

"Of course." It even has crushed ice in it. He must have one of those brilliant fridges that do everything.

I hear some kids running around in the backyard, and soon I see their faces appearing now and then, rising and falling from a trampoline.

"Little bastards," Tony sniggers. He has the same humor as his brother.

For a few minutes we watch a very interesting special on tug-of-war on some kind of *Wide World of Sports* show, but when a commercial comes onto his big-screen TV, Tony turns his attention back toward me.

"So tell me something, Ed—I guess you're wondering why my brother and I have a rift between us."

I can't hide it. "Well, yes."

"You feel like hearing what happened?"

I look at him.

Honestly.

And I shake my head. "No, that's none of my business."

Tony breathes out heavily and takes a sip of his drink. I hear him crush the ice even more inside his mouth. I don't realize it, but I've given him the right answer.

One of the kids comes in the room, crying.

"Dad, Ryan keeps—"

"Ah, stop whingein' and piss off!" Tony shouts.

The kid contemplates crying a bit harder but straightens up almost immediately. He pulls himself together. "Is that cordial, Dad?"

"Yes."

For a moment, I think the kid's asking if his dad's being friendly and approachable. Then I remember the drink.

"Can I have some?"

"What's the magic word?"

"Please?"

"Right. In a sentence."

"Can I have some cordial, please?"

"Yes. That's better, George. Now piss off to the kitchen and make some, will you?"

The kid beams. "Thanks, Dad!"

"Bloody kids," Tony laughs. "No manners these days. . . ."

"I know," I say, and we laugh.

We laugh and Tony says, "You know, Ed, if you look hard enough, you just might see me there tomorrow."

Inside, I rejoice, but I don't show it.

This is good.

"Thanks, Tony."

"Oh, Da-ad!" yells George from the kitchen. "I spilled it!"

"I bloody knew it!"

Tony gets up, shaking his head. "Can you see yourself out while I sort this shit out?"

"No worries."

I leave the big-screen TV and the big house, relieved. A pleasing result.

I sleep harder than I imagine possible and wake up early. I'd been reading a beautiful, strange book called *Table of Everything* last night. I search for it but realize it's fallen between my bed and the wall. Halfway through looking for it, I remember that today's the day. Meet a Priest Day. I abandon the search and get up.

Audrey, Marv, and Ritchie arrive at my place at eight o'clock and we head over to the church. The father's already there, pacing up and down, going over his sermon.

Other people show up.

Marv's mate with the kegs and the karaoke.

The jumping-castle people.

We've got the barbecues, and we arrange for Ritchie and a few of his friends to guard the beer while the sermon's on.

By quarter to ten, people start showing up in earnest, and I realize I have to pick up Milla.

"Hey, Marv"—I can't believe I'm doing this—"could I borrow your car for ten minutes?"

"*What?*" I can tell he's going to make the most of this. "*You* want to borrow *my* shitbox car?"

I don't have the time. "Yes, Marv. I take back everything I've ever said about it."

"And?"

And?

I realize. "I'll never say anything bad about it again."

He smirks in victory and throws me the keys. "Look after it, Ed."

Now, that wasn't called for. Marv knows I'll have to restrain myself from saying something. He even waits, the bastard, but I say nothing.

"Good boy," he says, and I leave.

Milla's waiting anxiously and has the door open before I even walk up the porch steps.

"Hello, Jimmy," she says.

"Hi, Milla."

At the car, I open the door for her and we drive back to the church. A nice breeze comes through the broken window.

When we arrive, it's five to ten and I'm amazed. The church is packed. I even spot Ma walking inside in a green dress. I don't think she gives a toss about the beer. She just doesn't want to miss out on what's happening.

I find one of the few vacant seats and ask Milla to sit there.

"What about you, Jimmy?" she asks nervously. "Where are *you* going to sit?"

"Don't worry," I tell her. "I'll find somewhere," but I don't. I join the people who stand at the back of the church, waiting for Father O'Reilly to come out.

When ten o'clock strikes, the bells of the church take possession of the congregation, and now everyone—the kids, the powdered ladies with handbags, the drunks, the teenagers, and the same people who are there week in, week out—falls down to silence.

The father.

Walks out.

He walks out, and everyone waits for the words.

For a while, he simply looks out into the crowd. Then his down-to-earth smile appears on his face and he says, "Hello out there," and everyone goes berserk. They clap and cheer, and the father looks more alive than I've ever seen him. What I don't know is that he also has a few tricks of his own.

There are no other words yet.

No prayers.

He waits again for silence, pulls a harmonica from his robe, and begins playing a soulful tune. Halfway through, three derelict men in suits also come out, one banging on top of a bin, the other playing violin, and the last also playing harmonica. A big one.

They play, and the music drums through the church, and an atmosphere I've never felt before spills through the entire crowd.

When they stop, the crowd roars again, and the father waits. Finally, he says, "That song was for God. It came from Him and is dedicated to Him. Amen."

"Amen," repeats the crowd.

The father speaks for a while then, and I love what he says and the way he says it. He doesn't speak like all those preachers in those fire-and-brimstone churches, where there's more bull- shit than anything else. The father speaks with a sincerity that's hypnotizing. Not about God, but about the people of this town getting together. Doing things together. Helping each other. And just getting together in general. He invites them to do that in his church every Sunday.

He gets those guys, Joe, Graeme, and Joshua, to do some read- ings. They're pretty hopeless and slow, but they're applauded like heroes when they finish, and you can see the pride ruffled on their faces. A far cry from scabbing money, cigarettes, and jackets.

For quite a while, I wonder where Tony might be. As I look over the crowd, Sophie catches my eye and we both raise a hand, and she resumes listening. I don't find Tony anywhere.

At the end, the father leads a rendition of the old favorite from school—"He's Got the Whole World in His Hands." Everyone sings and claps in time, and at the end of it, I finally see Tony.

He pushes through the crowd and stands next to me.

"Hi, Ed," he greets me. He's got a kid attached to each hand. "Any cordial?" he asks. "For the kids."

"No worries."

Maybe five minutes later, the father sees me with Tony, stand- ing up the back.

He's ending now, and there still hasn't been a prayer. Thomas O'Reilly finally gets around to it.

He says:

"People, I'm going to pray now, out loud, and then silently. Feel free then to say any prayers of your own." He bows his head and says, "Lord, I thank you. I thank you for this glorious moment and for all of these magnificent people. I thank you for free beer"—the crowd laughs—"and I thank you for the music and words you've given us today. Most of all, though, Lord, I thank you that my brother could be here today, and I thank you for certain people in the world who have awful taste in jackets. . . . Amen."

"Amen," the people repeat again.

"Amen," I say, delayed, and now, like many of these people, I pray for the first time in years.

I pray, *Let Audrey be okay, Lord, and Marv and Ma and Ritchie and all my family. Please take my dad in your arms, and please, please help me with the messages I have to deliver. Help me do them right. . . .*

The father's last words arrive about a minute later.

"Thank you, everyone. And let the party begin."

The crowd roars.

One last time.

Ritchie and Marv do the barbecue. Audrey and I do the beer. Father O'Reilly looks after the kids' food and drinks, and no one misses out on anything.

When the food and drink are all gone, we bring out the karaoke, and there are many people singing all kinds of things. I stay a long time with Milla, who also finds some girls, as she put it, that she went to school with. They all sit on a bench, and one of them doesn't have legs long enough to touch the ground.

With her legs crossed at the ankles, she swings them back and forth, and it's the most beautiful thing I see all day.

I even get Audrey to sing with me. "Eight Days a Week" by the Beatles. Of course, Ritchie and Marv bring the house down when they do a rendition of "You Give Love a Bad Name" by Bon Jovi. I swear, this whole town lives in the past.

I dance.

I dance with Audrey, Milla, and Sophie. I especially love twirling them and hearing laughter in their voices.

When it's over, and I've taken Milla home and returned again, we clean up.

The last thing I see that day is Thomas and Tony O'Reilly sitting on the steps of the church, smoking together. The odds are that they won't see each other for another few years, but I can ask for nothing more than this.

I didn't know the father smoked.

9 ♣ the cops show up

That night I get some visitors—first Father O'Reilly and later the police.

The father knocks on my door and stands there, saying nothing.

"What?" I ask him.

But the father doesn't speak. He merely stands there and watches me. He searches me for an answer for what happened today. In the end, I think he gives up on words. He only steps forward, places his hands on my shoulders, and looks very seriously into my eyes. I can see the feeling shifting the skin on his face. He contorts in a very peaceful, very holy way.

I think it's the first chance in a long time the father's had to say thank you. Usually it's people thanking *him*. I think that's why his expression is so stranded and why the recognition on his face stumbles in its attempt to reach me.

"No worries," I say. A quiet happiness stretches out between us. We hold it awhile.

When he turns and leaves, I watch him walk up the road till he disappears.

The police show up at about ten-thirty. In their hands, they hold scrubbing brushes and some kind of liquid solution.

"For washing that paint off the road," they say.

"Thanks a lot," I answer.

"The least we could do."

Again at 3 a.m. I'm on the main street of town, this time scrubbing the paint off the road.

"Why me?" I ask God.

God says nothing.

I laugh and the stars watch.

It's good to be alive.

10 the easy one and ice cream

My arms and shoulders are sore as all hell the next few days, but I still think it was worth it.

In that time, I find Angie Carusso. There are only a few Carussos in the phone book, and I eliminate them one by one till I find her.

She has three kids and looks to have been one of those typical teenage mothers in this town. It's two boys and a girl, and she works in the chemist part-time. Her hair is short and dark brown and she looks nice in her work dress. It's one of those white, knee-length clinical sort of garments that all chemist assistants seem to wear. I like them.

Every morning, she gets her kids ready for school and walks there with them. Three days a week she goes to work. The other two she walks back home.

I watch her from afar and notice she gets paid on the Thursday. On those afternoons, she picks up her kids and takes them to the same park I sat in with the Doorman when Sophie came and talked to me.

She buys each of her kids an ice cream, and they gulp them down quicker than I can believe. As soon as they're done, they want another.

"No, you know the rule," Angie tells them. "You'll get another one next week."

"Please?"

"Please?"

One of them starts having a tantrum, and I wish for a second that I have to straighten the kid out. Thankfully, he stops pretty fast because he wants a go on the slippery dip.

Angie watches them awhile until she gets too bored and drags them away with her.

I know.

I know already.

This one's easy, I think.

Easy as ice cream.

Watching her walk away, it's her legs that sadden me. I don't know why. I think it's because they move slower than what's natural for her. She loves those kids but they slow her down. She walks a little lopsided so she can hold her daughter's hand.

"What's for dinner, Mum?" asks one of the boys.

"I don't know yet."

She gently throws a wisp of dark hair from her eyes and moves on, listening to the words spoken by her daughter. She's telling Angie about a boy at school who keeps teasing her.

As for me, I continue watching the small steps of Angie's wandering legs.

They still make me sad.

I get a big share of day shifts after that and do a lot of walking in the evenings. My first stop is Edgar Street, where the lights are on and I can see the mother and her daughter eating. It strikes me that without the man there, they might not have enough money coming in to pay the bills. On the other hand, he probably drank a lot of the money away, and I'm fairly certain she'd prefer being a little poorer in return for his absence.

I also walk by Milla's place, and later on I call in on Father O'Reilly, who is still on a high after the Meet a Priest Day congregation. There were considerably fewer people at the following week's ceremony, but the church was still a lot fuller than it had been.

Last, I go to each address that houses someone by the name of Rose. There are about eight of them, and I find the one I'm looking for on my fifth attempt.

Gavin Rose.

He's about fourteen and wears old clothes and a permanent sneer. His hair is reasonably long and his flannel shirts all resemble rags. They stream down his back.

He goes to school.

He's teenage-smoker tough.

He has blue eyes the color of fresh toilet water and a dozen or so freckles flung across his face.

Oh, and one other thing.

He's a complete bastard.

For example, he goes into corner shops and shows disrespect to the owners who can't speak much English. He steals from those shops—anything that fits under his arms or in his pants. He shoves weaker kids and spits on them if he gets the opportunity.

While getting a look at him before school, I'm careful not to be spotted by Sophie. Some previous fears surface, and I cringe at the idea of her noticing me and thinking that I like to hang around school yards. Watching.

Mostly, I see Gavin Rose at home.

He lives with his mother and older brother.

His mother's a chain-smoking Ugg boot wearer who loves a drink, and his brother's just as bad as Gavin. It's actually quite a dilemma trying to decide which one's worse.

They live at the very bottom of town, not far from a dirty, frothy creek that stems from the river. The defining feature of the place is that the only thing the Rose brothers do is fight. If I go there in the morning, they're arguing. If I go in the evening, they're fistfighting. At all times, they're hurling abuse at each other.

Their ma can't control them.

To cope, she drinks.

She falls asleep on the couch as the latest soap washes over the screen.

Within a week, I've watched those boys fight at least a dozen times, until one night, the Tuesday, they have the worst one yet. It erupts out the front door and to the side of the house, and the older brother, Daniel, beats the absolute Christ out of Gavin. Gavin's buckled over, and Daniel lifts him up by the collar.

He lectures his brother and shakes his head back and forth at the same time.

"I told you not to touch *my* stuff, all right?"

He bangs him to the ground before walking purposefully back inside.

Gavin is left there, and after a few minutes he rises to his hands and knees as I watch from over the street.

Eventually, after checking his face for blood, he swears and begins half walking, half running down the street. All the way he's talking of hatred and killing his brother, until he finally stops and sits in the gutter at the very end of the slope, where bush lingers around the road.

This is my moment.

I walk over and stand in front of him, and I have to tell you, a nervousness manages to sidle up next to me. The kid's tough and won't give me anything for free.

There's a streetlight standing over us, watching.

There's a breeze, cooling the sweat on my face, and slowly I see my shadow step on Gavin Rose.

He looks up.

"What the hell do *you* want?"

There are hot tears cooking on his face, and his eyes bite.

I shake my head. "Nothing."

"Well get away from me then, you first-prize wanker, or I'll beat the living shit out of you."

He's fourteen, I think. *Remember Edgar Street?* This is a piece of cake.

I tell him, "Well, do it then, because I'm not moving." My shadow has covered him completely now, and he doesn't move. Like I thought, he's all talk. He pulls grass out of the ground and throws it to the road. He tears at it like it's hair. His hands are ferocious.

After a while, I sit down in the gutter a few meters away and get my mouth to wreck the nothingness that has followed his threat.

"What happened?" I ask, but I don't look at him. It'll work if I don't look.

His answer is succinct.

He says, "My brother's a complete arsehole and I want to kill him."

"Well, good for you."

He flares. "Are you taking the piss out of me?"

I shake my head, still refusing to look at him. "No, I'm not." *You little bastard,* I think.

He starts repeating it now. "I want to kill him. I want to kill him. I want. To kill. *Him.*" His angry hair shrouds his face. His freckles light up under the streetlight.

I look at the boy and think about what I have to do.

I wonder if these Rose boys have ever been tested in the world.

They're about to be.

J♣ the color of her lips

Thursday afternoon appears to be traveling well.

Angie Carusso goes through her usual routine at work and picks up her kids from school. She walks with them to the park, and they discuss which ice creams they're going to buy. One of them makes a cunning decision to get a cheaper one so he can have two. He suggests it to Angie and she tells him he's still only allowed one. He then switches back to a more expensive choice.

They go into the shop and I wait in the park. I sit on one of the far benches and wait for them to come out. Once they do, I go into the shop myself and try to figure out what kind of ice cream Angie Carusso would like.

Hurry up, I think, *or they'll be gone by the time you come back out.* In the end, I decide on two flavors. Peppermint choc chip and passion fruit, in a waffle cone.

When I walk out, the kids are still scoffing down their own ice creams. They're all on the bench.

I go over.

I topple over my words, surprised that they come out properly.

"Excuse me, I—" Angie and the kids all turn and face me. Up

close, Angie Carusso is beautiful and awkward. "I've seen you here a few times and noticed that you never get an ice cream yourself." She looks at me as if I'm a lunatic. "I thought you deserved one, too."

Clumsily, I hold it out to her. It already streams green and yellow down the side of the cone.

She eases her hand out gingerly and takes it, her expression startled and half broken. For quite a few seconds, she looks at it. Then her tongue rescues the streams on the side of the cone.

When she's cleaned it up enough, she attempts a bite as if it's the original sin. *Should I or shouldn't I?* She looks at me warily again before sinking her teeth into the peppermint choc. Her lips go light green right about the time her boys go charging down to the slippery dip. Only the girl stays and points out, "Looks like you got an ice cream as well today, Mum."

Angie strokes the fringe from her daughter's eyes. "Yes, Casey, looks like it, doesn't it? Go on," she tells her. "Go play with your brothers."

Casey goes, and now it's only she and me at the bench.

It's a warm day and humid.

Angie Carusso eats her ice cream, and I wonder what to do with my hands. She works her mouth around the peppermint and onto the passion fruit now, nice and slow. She uses her tongue to push it down so the cone won't be empty. She looks like she couldn't stand it if the cone was empty.

As she eats, she watches her kids. They've barely noticed that I'm there, more intent on calling out to their mother and arguing about who's going higher on the swings.

"They're beautiful," Angie says to the cone, "most of the time." She shakes her head and talks on. "I was the easy one when I was younger. Now I've got three kids and I'm alone." She looks at the swings, and I can see she's imagining what they'd look like if the kids weren't there. The guilt of this holds her down momentarily. It appears to be there constantly. Never far away, despite her love for them.

I realize that nothing belongs to her anymore and she belongs to everything.

She cries, momentarily, as she watches. She allows herself at least that. There are tears on her face and ice cream on her lips.

It doesn't taste like it used to.

Still, when she stands up, Angie Carusso thanks me. She asks my name, but I tell her it isn't important.

"No," she protests, "it is."

I relent. "It's Ed."

"Well, thanks, Ed," she says. "Thank you."

She thanks me a few times more, but the best words I hear all day come to me right when I think it's over. It's the girl, Casey. She twists herself onto Angie's hand and says, "Next week I'll give you a bite of mine, Mum."

In a way, I feel sad and empty, but I also feel that I've done what was intended. Just once, an ice cream for Angie Carusso.

I'll always remember the color of it on her lips.

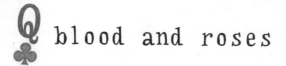 blood and roses

Now I have to deal with the Roses, and like I've said, I don't think they've been tested in the world. It seems they've never been asked how they would react if someone from outside came in and interrupted their fighting with foreign fists.

I have their address.

I have their phone number, and I'm ready.

Early next week I get a lot of day shifts, and I go over there every night I have free. Each time, they only argue. There's no actual fight, so I go home, disappointed. On the way back, I look for the closest phone booth to their house and find one a few streets away.

The next two nights I have to work, which I decide is a good thing. They had a big fight only recently, and they might need a few more days to build up properly to another one. All I need is Gavin to leave the house again. My job isn't a pleasant one.

On Sunday night, it happens.

I'm there for nearly two hours when the house shakes and Gavin storms out again.

He goes back to the same place and sits again in the gutter.

And again, I go down there.

My shadow only edges onto him when he says, "*You* again," but he doesn't even get a glimpse of me.

My hands reach down and grab him by the collar.

I feel like I'm outside myself.

I watch myself drag Gavin Rose into the bush and beat him down to the grass, the dirt, and the fallen tree branches.

My fists clutter on his face and I put a hole in his stomach.
The boy cries and begs. His voice twitches.

"Don't kill me, don't kill me. . . ."

I see his eyes and make sure not to meet them, and I put my fist onto his nose to eliminate any vision he might have had. He's hurt, but I keep going. I need to make sure he can't move by the time I'm done with him.

I can smell how scared he is.

It pours out of him.

It reaches up and stuffs itself into my nose.

I realize this could all backfire terribly, but it feels like my only option.

It's time to explain that before I had to sort out Edgar Street, I'd never even laid a finger on a person in this way. It doesn't feel good, especially when it's a young kid who doesn't have a chance. However, I can't let that stop me. I'm possessed as I continue beating Gavin Rose on his body and face. It's dark, and a gathering wind stalks through the bush.

No one can help him.

Except me.

And how do I do it?

I give him one last kick and make sure he won't be able to move for at least another five or ten minutes.

I get off him, breathing heavily.

Gavin Rose isn't going anywhere.

There's blood on my hands as I walk quickly from the bush and up the street. I can hear the television in the Rose house as I hurry past.

When I turn the corner and see the phone booth, I discover a big problem—there's someone in it.

"Well, I don't care what *she* says," a very large teenage girl with a navel ring booms inside the box. "It has nothing to do with me. . . ."

I can't help it.

I think, *Get out of there, you silly bitch.*

But she only gets more articulate.

One minute, I decide. *I'll give her one minute and then I'm going in.*

She sees me but clearly couldn't care less. She turns around and continues talking.

Right. I'm going in, and I knock on the glass.

She responds by turning around and asking, *"What?"* The word is spoken like gunshot.

I try manners. "Sorry to bother you, but I really need to make an urgent call."

"Piss off, mate!" She's not happy, to say the least.

"Look!" I hold up my hands and show her the blood on my palms. "A friend of mine just had an accident and I have to call an ambulance. . . ."

She talks into the phone again. "Kel? Yeah, I'm back. Listen, I'll call you back in a *minute*." She stares at me obscenely when she says that. "Okay?"

When she hangs up, she saunters out and I can smell a mixture of her sweat and deodorant inside the booth. It isn't too charming, but it isn't a smell of Doorman proportions, either.

I shut the door and dial.

Three rings and Daniel Rose picks up the phone.

"Yeah, hello."

I whisper, nice and hard. "Now you listen to me—if you go down to the bush at the end of your street, you'll find your brother in a pretty bad way. I strongly suggest you get down there."

"Who is this?"

I hang up.

"Thank you," I say to the girl on my way out.

"There better not be any blood on the phone."

Nice girl.

Back on the Roses' street, I make it just in time to see.

Daniel Rose is helping his brother walk back to their house. I'm far away, but I can see him supporting him, with his arm around his shoulder. For the first time, they look like brothers.

I even let myself imagine some words for them.

Come on, Gav, you can make it. We'll get you home and fix you up.

There is blood on my hands and blood at the bottom of the street. I hope for a moment that they both understand what they're doing and what they're proving.

I want to tell them, but I realize that all I do is deliver the message. I don't decipher it or make sense of it for them. They need to do that themselves.

I can only hope they're capable as I make my way home to some running water and the Doorman.

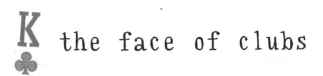

K the face of clubs

Well, I must say, I'm very pleased with myself. There were three names carved into that great rock at the stones of home, and I'm quite sure I've fulfilled everything I had to do.

I walk down to the river with the Doorman and head upstream to where the names are in the rock. It gets a little rough for the Doorman on the way up, and I look at him, disappointed. "You had to come, didn't you? I told you it was going to be a hard one for you, but did you listen?"

I'll just wait here, he replies.

I give him a pat as he lies down and I keep going up the river.

As I climb the large stones, I feel a pride swelling in me. It's a great feeling to be going there again in victory after the uncertainty of my first visit.

It's late afternoon but not hot, so I'm barely sweating when my eyes hit the names.

Immediately, I notice there's something different. They're the same names, but next to them, there's also a tick scratched in, obviously for each time I completed what I had to do.

I'm very happy to see the first name.

Thomas O'Reilly. Big tick.

Then Angie Carusso. Another one.

Then . . .

What?

I look at the stone in disbelief, as the name Gavin Rose is still naked and alone in the tick department.

I stand there with my arm bent around my body, scratching my spine.

"What do I still need to do?" I ask. "Gavin Rose was as complete as they come."

The answer can't be far away.

A few days pass, and the end of November is near. It's getting close to the Annual Sledge Game. Marv's been calling me up, still agitated about my apparent lack of interest.

December hits, and two nights before the game, I'm still nervous about Gavin Rose and that invisible tick on the stone. I've been back there and there's still nothing. I hoped whoever was doing that part was just running late, but there's no way three or four days could pass. Whoever's running this would never allow that to happen.

I'm having trouble sleeping.

I'm irritable with the Doorman.

When I haven't slept again after Thursday, I go to the all-night chemist at the top of Main Street to get something, anything, to help me sleep. I should have saved some of the sleeping pills I slipped the man from Edgar Street.

As I walk out, I notice a group of boys hanging around across the road.

Nearing home, it becomes obvious that they're following me, and when we're all standing at an intersection, waiting for the legs to go green, I notice the voice of Daniel Rose.

"This him, Gav?"

I try to fight them off, but there are too many. At least six. They drag me into an alley and handle me in much the same way I took care of Gavin. They club me with their hands and hold me down and all take turns. I can feel blood crawling across my face and bruises showing up along my ribs, my legs, and my stomach.

They enjoy themselves.

"Teach you to mess with my brother." This is Daniel Rose making conversation. He kicks me hard in the ribs. The loyalty hurts. "Come on, Gav—take the last shot."

Gav does as he's told.

He reefs a boot to my stomach and forces his fist into my face.

They run off into the night.

As for me, I try to get up but fall.

I drag myself home and feel like I've come full circle from when I had the Ace of Clubs first delivered.

When I stagger through the front door, the Doorman looks shocked. Almost concerned. All I can do is shake my head and assure him I'm okay with a small, painful smile. I imagine that while all this is going on, a large tick is being scratched into the stone next to the name of Gavin Rose. It's over.

Later that night I look in the bathroom mirror.

Two black eyes.

Swollen jaw.

A blood stream flowing to my throat.

I look at myself and try my hardest to attempt a smile.

Well done, Ed, I tell myself, and I stare for a final few seconds at my broken and bloodied face.

I stare strangely into the face of clubs.

part three: **Trying Times for Ed Kennedy**

A
♠
Graham Greene
Morris West
Sylvia Plath

A
♠

A
♠

A
♠

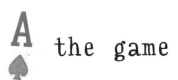

A the game

A mosquito sings in my ear, and I almost feel grateful for the company. I'm even tempted to sing along.

It's dark, there's blood on my face, and the mosquito could easily sit and drink without injecting. It could kneel down and sip the blood from my right cheek and my lips.

When I get out of bed and stand up, the floor is cool and my feet enjoy the relief. My sheets felt woven together with sweat, and now I lean on the wall in the hallway. Some sweat reaches my ankle and rolls under the arch of my foot.

I don't feel bad.

Laughter escapes my mouth as I check the clock, go to the bathroom, and have a cold shower. The icy water sets fire to my cuts and bruises, but everything feels good. It's close to four in the morning now, and I'm no longer afraid. After putting on a pair of old jeans and nothing else, I walk back to bed in search of the two aces. I open the drawer and lift the cards in my fingers. The yellow light of the room stands next to me as I happily look down at the stories of those cards. I'm gripped by feeling when I think of Milla and Edgar Street, and I hope for a brilliant life for Sophie. I laugh about Father O'Reilly, Henry Street, and Meet a Priest Day. Then Angie Carusso, whom I wish I could have done more for. And those bastard Rose boys.

What will the next card be? I wonder.

I expect it to be hearts.

I wait.

For daylight and the next ace.

This time I want it to be fast.

I want the card right now. No obscurity. No riddles. Just give me the addresses. Give me the names and send me there. That's what I want.

My only worry is that every time I've wanted something to go a certain way in all of this, it's gone the other, designed perfectly to challenge me with the unknown. I *want* Keith and Daryl to come walking through the door again. I want them to deliver the next card and criticize the Doorman for his smell and for having fleas. I've even left the door unlocked so they can enter my house in a civilized manner.

But I know they're not coming.

I find my book and head to the lounge room. I take the aces with me and hold them as I read.

When I wake up again, I'm on the floor with the two cards next to my left hand. It's about ten already and it's hot, and someone's banging at the door.

It's them, I think.

"Keith?" I call out, getting to my knees. "Daryl? That you?"

"Who the hell's Keith?"

I look up and see Marv standing over me. I rub my eyes.

"What are you doing here?" I ask him.

"Is that any way to speak to friends?" He sees my face properly now and the black and yellow rods that are my ribs. *God,* I see him think, but he doesn't say it. He answers my question with an answer to a *different* question. This is typically frustrating of Marv. Instead of saying what he's doing here, he tells me how he got in. "The door was unlocked, and the Doorman let me past for a change."

"See? I told you he's okay."

I walk through to the kitchen with Marv behind me. He asks about the state of me.

"How'd you end up like that, Ed?"

I switch the kettle on. "Coffee?"

Yes, please.

Of course, the Doorman's just walked in.

"Thanks," Marv answers.

As we drink, I tell Marv what happened. "Just some young fellas. They had a look at me and took me from behind."

"You get any shots in of your own?"

"No."

"Why not?"

"There were six of them, Marv."

He shakes his head. "Christ, the world's going crazy." He decides to get back to something sane. "Do you think you'll be right to play this afternoon?"

Of course.

The Sledge Game.

Today's the day.

"Yes, Marv." I make the answer very clear. "I'm playing." I'm suddenly very in the mood for this year's game. Despite being a physical disaster, I feel stronger than ever, and I'm actually relishing the idea of being hurt some more. Don't ask me why. I don't understand it myself.

"Come on." Marv stands up and begins for the door. "I'll buy you some breakfast."

"Really?" This isn't like Marv at all.

As we leave I ask him for the truth.

"Would you be doing this if I pulled out of the game?"

Marv opens his car and gets in. "No way."

At least he's honest.

His car doesn't start.

"Not one word." He eyes me.

We both snigger slightly.

This is a good day. I can feel it.

We walk to a crappy café at the bottom of Main Street. They serve eggs and salami and some sort of flat-looking bread. The waitress is a big woman with a wide mouth and a hankie in her hand. For some reason, to me, she looks like a Margaret.

"Whata you two bores want?"

We're shocked.

"Bores?" asks Marv.

She gives us an I-don't-have-time-for-this kind of look. She's bored shitless. "Of course. You both bores, ain't you?" It's then I realize she's saying *boys*.

"Hey," I say to Marv. "Boys."

"What?"

"*Boys.*"

Marv peruses the menu.

186

Margaret clears her throat.

Not wanting to annoy her further, I order fast. "I'll have a banana milk shake if that's okay."

She frowns. "We're out of milk."

"Out of milk? How in the hell can a café run out of milk?"

"Look, I don't buy the milk. I don't have anything to do with the milk. I only know we don't have any. Why don't you order something to eat?" She loves her job, this lady. I can sense it.

"Have you got bread?" I ask.

"Now don't get smart, bore."

I scout the rest of the café, checking out what everyone else is eating. "I'll have what that bloke over there's having." All three of us look over.

"You sure?" Marv warns. "That looks pretty borderline, Ed."

"Well they've at least *got it*, haven't they?"

And now Margaret's really unhappy. She says, "Now listen." She scratches her scalp with her pen. I'm almost waiting for her to clean her ears out with it. "If this place isn't good enough for you bores, you can bloody well piss off and find somewhere else to eat." She's very testy, to say the least.

"All right." I hold my hand up, almost backing away. "Give me what that guy's got and just a banana, okay?"

"Good thinking," Marv approves. "Potassium for the game."

Potassium?

I don't think that's really going to help.

"And you?" Margaret's transferred her attention now to Marv.

He shifts in his seat. "How about that flat bread you've got with your finest selection of cheeses?" He had to do it. Marv can't resist being a smart arse to a person like this. It's in his nature.

But Margaret's good. She puts up with complete shitheads

187

like us all the time. "The only cheese around here is you," she responds, and I must say, we both laugh and give her some encouragement. She chooses not to notice. "Anything else for you bores?"

"No, thanks."

"Right. That's twenty-two fifty."

"*Twenty-two fifty?*" We can't hide our exasperation.

"Well, yeah—this is a classy joint, you know."

"That's obvious—the service is incredible."

And now we sit in the boiling-hot outdoor section of the café, sweating and waiting for this breakfast. Margaret takes great pleasure in passing us while she delivers other people's food. We're close to asking her a few times just where ours has vanished to, but we know that will only serve to make us wait longer. People are actually eating lunch before we eat our breakfast, and when it finally comes, Margaret slops it down on our table like she's serving us compost.

"Cheers, love," Marv says. "You've outdone yourself."

Margaret blows her nose and walks off. Savage indifference.

"How's yours?" inquires Marv soon after. "Or more to the point, *what* is it?"

"Eggs and cheese and something."

"Do you even *like* eggs?"

"No."

"Then why'd you get it?"

"Well, it didn't look like eggs when it was on that other guy's plate."

"Fair enough. You want some of mine?"

I take up the offer and eat some of his flat bread. Not bad, really, and I finally ask Marv exactly why he's chosen today of all days to take me out to breakfast. It's never happened before.

I've never gone out for breakfast in my life. That, and Marv would never even consider paying for me. That simply wouldn't be on. Under normal circumstances, he'd rather die.

"Marv," I say, looking straight at him, "why are we here?"

He shakes his head. "I—"

"You're making sure I turn up to the game this afternoon, aren't you? You're sweetening me up."

Marv can't lie to me on this, and he knows it. "That would about cover it."

"I'll be there," I tell him. "Four o'clock sharp."

"Good."

The rest of the day glides by. Thankfully, Marv gives me the next few hours off, so I go home and sleep some more.

When the time comes around, I walk to the Grounds with the Doorman, who has picked up on my recent happiness, despite the mess I appear to be.

We stop off at Audrey's.

No one home.

Maybe she's already at the Grounds. She does hate the soccer, but she's always there, every year.

It's nearly quarter to four when we walk into the valley where the Grounds are, and I remember Sophie and me here, over at the athletic track. It makes this game look pitiful—which it is. A crowd is already gathering at the soccer field, while the athletic track is empty but for barefoot images of the girl.

I watch the beauty for as long as I can, then turn and face the rest of it.

The closer I get, the stronger the smell of beer. It's hot. About thirty-two.

189

The two teams are in different corners of the field, and a crowd of a few hundred is slowly growing bigger. It's always a bit of an event, the Sledge Game. It's held the first Saturday of December every year, and I think this is the fifth time it's been put on. As for me, this is my third year.

I leave the Doorman in the shade of a tree, and when I approach the team, the ones who notice me take a second look at my face. Their interest, however, leaves them pretty fast. They're the type of people who see bruises and blood quite a lot.

Within five minutes, I'm thrown a blue jersey with red and yellow stripes on it. Number 12. I change from my jeans into a pair of black shorts. There are no socks and no boots—they're the rules of the Sledge Game. No boots and no protective gear. Just a jersey, shorts, and a foul mouth. That's all you need.

Our team is known as the Colts. The opposition is the Falcons. They wear a green and white jersey with the same color shorts, though no one cares about that. We're lucky to have the jerseys at all, considering each side just flogged them one year from one of the real local clubs or took the discarded ones.

There are forty-year-old men in the Sledge Game. Big, ugly firemen or coal miners. Then there are some midrange players; some young ones, like Marv, Ritchie, and me; and some that can actually play well.

Ritchie's our last guy to show up.

"Well, look what the bloody dog brought along," says one of our fat guys. One of his mates tells him it's supposed to be *what the cat dragged in,* but, frankly, big fatso's too thick to understand. He's got what we'd call a Merv Hughes mustache. If you don't understand that, all you really need to know is that it's big, it's bushy, and it's downright reprehensible. The saddest comment on all of this is that he also happens to be our captain. I think his real name's Henry Dickens. No relation to Charles.

Ritchie throws down his bag and answers, "Hey, lads, how are we?" but he looks at the ground, and no one really gives a shit about how anyone is. It's five minutes to four and most of the team is drinking beer. One gets thrown to me, but I keep it for later.

I stand around a bit as the crowd continues piling toward the soccer field and Ritchie comes over.

He studies me, up and down, and speaks.

"Christ, Ed—you look bloody desperate. All bloodied and messed up and shit."

"Thanks."

He looks closer. "What happened?"

"Ah, just some young fellas having a bit of harmless fun."

He pats me on the back, hard enough to hurt. "That'll teach you, won't it?"

"For what?"

Ritchie winks at me and finishes his beer. "No idea."

You have to love Ritchie when he's like this. He doesn't care much for how things happen or bother asking why. He can tell I don't particularly feel like discussing the incident, so he makes a crack and we leave it behind us.

Ritchie's a good mate.

I find it curious that no one's even *suggested* that I should have called the police about what happened. You don't do that sort of thing around here. People get mugged or beaten up all the time, and in most cases you either get back straightaway or take it.

In my case, I'm taking it.

Doing a few lazy stretches, I look over at the opposition. They're bigger than us, and I set my eyes on the massive one Marv had been talking about a while back. He's gigantic, and to be honest, I can't tell if it's a man or a woman. In fact, from a distance, he looks like Mimi from *The Drew Carey Show*.

Then.

Worst of all.

I look at his number.

It's number 12, like me.

"That's who you're marking," says a voice behind me. I know it's Marv, and Ritchie comes over as well.

"Good luck, Ed," he says, suppressing his amusement. It makes a burst of laughter shoot from my mouth.

"Bloody hell, I'll get flattened by him. Literally."

"You sure that's a man?" Marv inquires.

I bend down and hold up my toes, stretching the backs of my legs. "I'll ask when he's on top of me."

Strangely, though, I'm not overly concerned.

The crowd's getting restless.

"Right, get in here," says Merv.

That's right, I said Merv, not Marv—I've named the fat guy with the mustache Merv because I have no confidence at all that his name is in fact Henry. I think his mates call him Merv, anyway, on account of the mustache.

Everyone gathers in nice and close, and here's where we all get pumped up for the game. It's a collection of nasty underarm sweat, beer breath, missing teeth, and three-day growth.

"Right," says Merv, "when we get out there, what are we going to do?"

192

No one says anything.

"Well?"

"I don't know," someone finally says.

"We're going to *smash* these pricks!" shouts Merv, and now there's a rumble of agreement, except for Ritchie, who yawns. A few of the others shout as well now, but it's hardly a wall of sound. They swear and snort and talk of everything short of disemboweling the Falcons.

These are grown men, I think. *We never grow up.*

The ref blows his whistle. As always, it's Reggie La Motta, who is very popular in town for being a complete drunk. The only reason he refs the game is that he gets two free bottles of spirits we all chip in for. One from each side.

"All right, let's kill these blokes" is the general consensus, and the side runs on.

Quickly, I head back to the tree where I left the Doorman. He's asleep and a small boy's patting him.

"You want to look after my dog?" I ask.

"Sounds good," he replies. "My name's Jay."

"He's the Doorman," and I run onto the field and join the lineup.

"Now listen up, fellas," begins Reggie. His voice is slurred. The game hasn't even begun and the ref's already pissed. It's quite funny, actually. "If there's any of that same shit as last year, I'm walking away and you can ref yourselves."

"You won't get your two bottles then, Reg," someone says.

"Bullshit I won't." Reggie sharpens. "Now, no rubbish, you hear?"

Everyone goes along with it.

"Thanks, Reggie."

"Right, Reg."

Everyone moves forward and we shake hands. I shake with my opposite number, who towers over me and puts me in the shade. I was right. He's a man all right, but a dead ringer for Mimi from *Drew Carey*.

"Good luck," I say.

"Give me a few minutes," Mimi answers throatily. Some heavy eye makeup would really do the trick. "I'm going to tear you to pieces."

Let the games begin.

The Falcons kick off, and soon enough I get my first run.

I get killed.

Then I have another run.

I get killed again, and I also receive the trash talk in my ear as big Mimi squashes my head into the ground. This is what the Sledge Game is all about. The crowd is constantly oohing and aahing, screaming obscenities, and cracking up—all between drinking beer and wine and eating pies and hot dogs from the same guy who shows up every year to sell them. He sets up shop on the sideline, even catering for the kids with soft drinks and lollies.

The Falcons go in to score a few times and spring to a good lead.

"What the hell's going on?" someone asks as we stand next to the posts. It's big Merv. As captain, he feels he should at least say something. "Jesus, there's only one of us having a chop and that's . . . Hey, what's your name again?"

I'm startled because he's pointing at me.

Taken aback, I answer. "Ed," I say, "Kennedy."

"Well, Ed here's the only one running hard and tackling. Now come on!"

I keep running.

Mimi keeps monstering and abusing me, and I'm wondering if he'll ever run out of breath. Surely someone that big in *this* heat can't go much longer.

I'm on the ground when Reggie calls halftime and everyone goes off for a beer. Each player will then convince himself, with difficulty, to go back on.

During the interval, I lie down in the shade near the Doorman and the boy. That's when Audrey turns up. She asks nothing about the state of me because she knows it's just more messenger work. It's becoming normal now, so I don't go into it.

"You all right?" she asks.

I sigh happily and say, "Sure, I'm loving life."

In the second half there's a turnaround and we fight back. Ritchie scores in the corner and then another guy goes in under the posts. It's even.

Marv's playing well now, too, and it's tight for a long time.

Mimi's finally getting tired, and during an injury break Marv comes over and stirs me up. "Oi," he digs into me, "you still haven't hurt that big bloody sheila yet." He's all blond sticky hair and determined eyes.

I object. "Well, look at the size of him, Marv. He's bigger than Mama Grape, for Christ's sake!"

"Who's Mama Grape?"

"You know—from that book." I give in. "And they made a movie out of it. Don't you remember? Johnny Depp?"

"Either way, Ed—get up there and give him some!"

So I do.

There's a guy being assisted from the field, and I go over to Mimi.

We look at each other.

I say, "Run at me next time you get the ball."

And I walk away, positively shitting myself.

Play resumes then, and Mimi does it.

He winds up and runs at me, and for some reason I know that I'm going to do it. He charges onto the ball, I line him up, go forward, and all I hear is the sound. There's a big collision and everything shakes. As the crowd goes insane I realize I'm still standing—and Mimi's lying in a crumpled heap on the ground.

Soon everyone's around me, saying great work and such, but a sudden sickness falls to my stomach. I feel awful for what I've done and the big number 12 on Mimi's back stares forlornly back at me, motionless.

"Is he alive?" someone asks.

"Who gives a shit?" comes the answer.

I vomit.

Slowly, I walk from the field as everyone argues about how to get rid of Mimi so they can resume play.

"Just get the stretcher," I hear.

"We haven't got any, and besides—look at the *size* of this guy. He's too big, anyway. We'll need a bloody crane."

"Or a Bobcat."

The suggestions are limitless. People like this couldn't care less about digging into someone. You name it. Size, weight, stench. If you've got it, they'll tell you, even if you're stomped all over the ground.

The last voice I hear is big Merv's. He says, "That's the best don't-argue I've seen in a long time." He expressed a great deal of joy in that sentence, and the other players agree with him.

I keep walking. I still feel terrible. Guilty.
For me, the game's over.
The game's over, but something else begins.

I make it back to the tree, and the Doorman's gone.
A familiar fear quickens in me.

2 ♠ twenty dollars for the dog and the card

I stand and turn frantically in a circle, trying to find my dog and that kid.

Past the field there's a small creek, and I elect to start there. I run as fast as I can in this state, the game forgotten, and from the corner of my eye, I see a girl with yellow hair coming toward me.

"The Doorman," I call to Audrey. "He's gone," and I realize how much I love that dog.

She joins me for a while, then moves off in a different direction.

At the creek, there's nothing.

I return to the expansive grass of the field. The game's moving along and I can still hear the crowd somewhere in the miles of the back of my mind.

"Anything?" Audrey asks. She'd been further down the creek.

"No."

We stop.

Calmness.

That's the best way, and now, as I turn back to the tree where the Doorman sat originally, I see him and the kid going back there. The kid holds a can of drink and a long stick of licorice, and now I see there's someone else with them.

She sees me.

It's a youngish sort of woman, and when she finds my glare, she quickly kneels down and grabs hold of the kid. She gives him something, speaks, and heads off immediately in the opposite direction.

"It's the next card," I say to Audrey, and I take off. I run harder than I ever have before.

When I reach the boy and the dog I stop and see that I was right. The kid holds a playing card, but for now I don't see what suit it is. I resume my pursuit of the young woman. She's disappeared in the crowd but I run anyway because I'm sure. I feel *absolutely* certain that I'm chasing a person who at least knows who's behind all this.

But she's gone.

She's disappeared, and I only stand on the sideline, without breath.

I could keep chasing, but there's no point. She's gone and I need to get back to the card. That boy could be ripping it to pieces for all I know.

Thankfully, when I make it back, he still holds it. Tightly. He looks like he's not going to let it go without a fight.

As it turns out, I'm absolutely correct.

*   *   *

"No," he says.

"Look." The last thing I want is to muck around with this kid. "Just give me the card."

"No!" The kid's attempting to cry.

"Well, what did that lady say to you?"

"She said"—he wipes his eyes—"that the card belongs to the owner of this dog."

"Well, that's *me*," I say.

"No—he's mine. The dog's mine!"

Give me Daryl, Keith, and another trouncing any day, I think. *Anything'd be better than this kid.*

"All right." I adjust the game plan. "I'll give you ten bucks for the dog and the card."

The kid isn't stupid. "Twenty."

I'm displeased, to say the least, but I ask Audrey for a twenty and she gives it to me. "I'll pay you later," I tell her.

"No worries."

I hand over the twenty and receive the Doorman and the card.

"Nice doing business with you." The kid revels in his victory.

I feel like strangling him.

It's not what I expect.

"Spades," I say to Audrey.

She's close enough for her hair to touch my shoulder. The Doorman stands on my foot.

"And you," I accuse him. "*You* stay put next time."

Okay, okay, he responds, and soon he goes into a coughing fit.

Sure enough, a piece of licorice jumps from his mouth, and guilt crawls into his eyes.

"That'll teach you." I point at him viciously. He tries to ignore me.

"Is he all right?" Audrey asks as we walk away.

"Of course," I answer. "He'll outlive me, the gluttonous bastard." But secretly I smile.

3♠ dig

Apparently, we won the game, and there's a victory party at big Merv's place. Marv rings me in the evening and orders me to go since everyone voted me best player for ironing out old Mimi.

"You have to, Ed."

So I go.

Again, I stop by at Audrey's on the way but she's not there. I assume she's out with the boyfriend. It almost turns me off going to Merv's, but I find my way there and go in.

No one recognizes me.

No one speaks to me.

At first, I can't even find Marv, but he locates me later on the front porch.

"You made it. How you feeling?"

I look at my friend and say, "Better than ever." Behind us, we can hear the drunk people yelling and yahooing, and there are people in the front bedroom doing what people do there.

We sit awhile, and Marv describes the later events of the game to me. He wonders where I disappeared to, but I only tell him that I felt sick and couldn't go on. We talk at length about the hit I put on Mimi.

"It was glorious," Marv confides.

"Why, thank you." I try to push the edges of guilt back to my stomach. I still feel for him, or her, or whatever.

After another ten minutes or so, I detect that Marv might want to head back inside.

In my pocket, I have the new card.

Ace of Spades.

It makes me look deeper into the street, trying to find the future events in store. I'm happy.

"What?" Marv asks. "What are you grinning at, bore?" *Bore*, I think, and we both laugh and connect for a moment. "Come on," Marv goes on. "What is it, Ed?"

"Time for digging," I say, and walk off the porch. "I have to go, Marv. Sorry. I'll see you later."

I feel bad because all I ever seem to do is walk away from Marv these days. Tonight, he allows me some room. I think he finally understands that what's important to him doesn't have to be to me.

"Bye, Ed," he says, and I can tell by his voice. He's happy enough.

The night's dark but lovely, and I walk home. At one point I stop under a blinking streetlight and examine the Ace of Spades again. I'd already looked at it several times, at home and on Merv's front porch. I'm most confused about the choice of suit because I'd expected hearts. Hearts would have followed a red-black pattern, and I thought spades, being the most dangerous-looking suit, would be last.

The card has three names on it:

Graham Greene
Morris West
Sylvia Plath

The names are familiar, although I'm not too sure why. They're nobody I know, but I've heard of them. Definitely. When I arrive home I look them up in the local phone book and there's a Greene and a few Wests but none with a *G* or an *M* before it. Still, there might be other people at those addresses with those names. I make up my mind that I have to travel the town tomorrow.

I relax in the lounge room with the Doorman. I've made chips in the oven, and we share them. I can feel my body developing some extra soreness from the Sledge Game, and by midnight I can barely move. The Doorman's at my feet and I sit there, waiting for sleep.

My head rolls back.

The Ace of Spades slips from my hand to a crack in the couch.

I dream.

It's a long night, where I'm trapped inside a dreamworld and can't decipher whether I'm awake or asleep. When I wake up near morning, I'm still in the Sledge Game, and I'm chasing the woman who brought the card and arguing with the kid. Bargaining.

Later, I dream that I'm in school again, but no one else is there. It's only me, and the air in the classroom is dusty yellow. I'm sitting there with books strewn on the desk and words on the board. The words are in running writing, and I can't decipher them.

A woman walks in.

A teacher with long skinny legs, black skirt, white blouse, and purple cardigan. She's nearly fifty but sexy in some way. She ignores me for the most part, until a bell rings, loudly, as if it's right outside the room. That's the first time she even acknowledges my existence.

She looks up.

"Time to start, Ed."

I'm ready. "Yes?"

"Could you read the words behind me please?"

"I can't."

"Why in God's name not?"

I focus harder on the words but still can't make them out.

She's shaking her head at me now. I don't see it but feel the disappointment as I glue my eyes to the desk. I stare for a long time and actually feel upset that I've let this woman down.

A few minutes later.

I hear it.

A whipping noise followed by some creaking reaches into my ears.

I look up, and what greets my sight is a shock. It boots the breath from my lungs—the teacher is hanging from a rope in front of the blackboard.

She's dead.

She swings.

The ceiling's gone and the rope is tied tightly around one of the rafters.

Horrified, I sit there, suffocating on air that seems to have no oxygen as I breathe it frantically in. My hands stick to the table, so much that I need to pry them off when I stand up and

203

attempt to run out for help. My right hand hits the door handle when, slowly, I stop and turn again to the woman hanging from the rope.

Slow.

Almost creeping.

I walk over to face her.

Just when I think she looks even vaguely peaceful, her eyes shock open and she speaks.

It's strangled and coarse, her voice.

"Recognize the words now, Ed?" she says, and I'm left standing there, looking beyond her at the board. Now I see the title at the top and understand what it says:

"Barren Woman."

That's when the body tumbles to the floor at my feet, and I wake.

Now it's the Doorman at my feet, and the dusty yellow air is in the lounge room from the rising sun outside.

The dream lunges at me a few seconds after I open my eyes and I see the woman, the words, and the title again. I feel her falling at my feet and hear what she said. *Recognize the words now, Ed?*

"'Barren Woman,'" I whisper.

I know I've heard it before. In fact, I know I've read a poem called "Barren Woman." I read it in school because I had a depressed English teacher. She loved that poem, and I recall some of the lines even today. Words like "the least footfall" and "museum without statues" and comparing her life to a fountain that rises and falls back into itself.

"Barren Woman."

"Barren Woman."

I rise fast when it comes to me. I nearly trip over the Doorman, who, by the way, is not impressed. He gives me a look of *You just woke me, pal.*

"'Barren Woman,'" I tell him.

So what?

I repeat the title, and this time I grab him joyously by the snout because now I know the answer to the Ace of Spades. Or at least I'm on the way.

The poem "Barren Woman" was written by a woman who committed suicide, and I'm pretty sure of it—her name was Sylvia Plath.

I search the couch for the card and see her name again, third on the list. *They're writers,* I think. *They're all writers.* Graham Greene, Morris West, and Sylvia Plath. It surprises me that I've never heard of the first two, but then you can't know of everyone who ever wrote a book. But I know for sure about Sylvia. We're even on a first-name basis now. That's how proud of myself I am.

I rejoice in the moment for quite a while, feeling like I've unlocked some great mystery by accident. I'm incredibly stiff now and my ribs are killing me, but I'm still able to eat cereal with milk that's dubious, to say the least, and loads of sugar.

It's around seven-thirty when I discover that I've only solved part of the problem. I still have no idea where I have to go or what messages I need to deliver.

I'll start at the library, I think. It's a shame it's Sunday. It won't open till later.

Audrey comes over.

We watch a movie she highly recommends.

It's good.

I refrain from asking where she was last night.

I tell her about the spades, the names, and that I'm heading over to the library in the afternoon. I'm pretty sure it's open on Sunday between twelve and four.

When she drinks the coffee I made, I look at the redness of her lips and wish I could just stand up, walk over, and kiss them. I want to feel the flesh of them and the softness against my own. I want to breathe in her and *with* her. I want to be able to put my teeth to her neck and have my fingers touch her back and run them through the lovely, mild yellow color of her hair.

Honestly.

I don't know what it is this morning.

But soon I understand why I feel like this — I *deserve* something. I'm going around fixing people's lives, even just for a moment or two. I'm hurting people that need hurting, when inflicting pain goes against everything that comes naturally to me.

I at least deserve something, I reason. *Audrey could love me just for a second, surely.* But I know. Without doubt, I know nothing will happen. She won't kiss me. She'll barely touch me. I'm running all over town, getting trodden on, beaten up, abused, and for what? What do I get out of it? What's in it for Ed Kennedy?

I'll tell you what.

Nothing.

But I'm lying.

I'm lying, and I vow, right this instant, to stop. I've been through all this and thought I'd really turned a corner after the Ace of Clubs.

I stop.

Stop everything.

And I do something stupid.

I stand up completely on impulse and walk over to Audrey and kiss her on the mouth. I feel the red lips and the flesh and the air inside her, and with my eyes closed I feel her for just a second. I feel all of her and it rushes past me. Through me and past me and over me and I'm hot and cold and shivering and shot down.

I'm shot down by the sound of my mouth slipping away from hers till silence staggers between us.

I taste blood.

Then I see blood on Audrey's lips that are on Audrey's surprised face.

God, I couldn't even kiss her properly. I couldn't do it without opening up and bleeding on her.

I close my eyes.

I clench them shut.

Soon I stop everything and say, "I'm sorry, Audrey." I turn away. "I didn't know what I was doing. I'm . . ." And the words stop now, too. They cut themselves down before it's too late, and the two of us stand in the kitchen.

We both have blood on our lips.

She doesn't want to feel that way about me, and I can accept that, but I wonder if she'll ever know that no one will love her as hard as I do. She wipes the blood from her mouth, and I say again how sorry I am. Audrey is as gracious as ever and takes the apology, explaining that she just can't do that sort of thing with me. I think she'd rather do it without any meaning or truth. Just what it is, without the risk of any of that. If she doesn't *want* love from anyone, I have to respect that.

"Don't worry, Ed," she says, and she means it.

One great thing is that Audrey and I are always okay. Somehow, we manage it. It doesn't seem to matter what happens. I consider this fact for a moment, and to be perfectly honest, I wonder how long it can possibly last. Surely not forever.

"Give us a smile, Ed," she says later, when she's leaving.

I can't help it.

I give her one.

"Good luck with the spades," she says.

"Thanks."

The door closes.

It's nearly twelve now, and I put on my shoes and head for the library. I still feel stupid.

Now it's true that I've read a lot of books, but I bought them all, mainly from secondhand bookshops. The last time I actually used a library, they still had big long catalog drawers. Even at school, when the computers came in as stock standard, I still used the drawers. I liked pulling out the card of an author and seeing the books listed.

When I walk into the library, I'm expecting an old lady behind the counter, but it's a young guy, about my age, with long, curly hair. He's a bit of a smart mouth, but I like him.

"You got any of those cards?" I ask him.

"What kind of cards? Playing cards? Library cards? Credit cards?" He's enjoying himself. "What exactly do you mean?"

I can tell he's trying to make me look uneducated and useless, though I don't really need his help. "You know," I explain to him, "the cards with all the writers and authors and that."

"Ohh," and he laughs fully now. "You haven't been in a library for a long time, have you?"

208

"No," I say. Now I *really* feel uneducated and useless. I might as well wear a sign that says Total Dropkick on it. I act on it. "But I've read Joyce and Dickens and Conrad."

"Who are they?"

Now I have the upper hand. "What? You haven't read those guys? You call yourself a librarian?"

He acknowledges me now with a devious smile. "Touché."

Touché.

I can't stand that expression.

Nonetheless, the guy becomes a lot more helpful now. He says, "We don't use those cards anymore—it's all on the computer. Come on."

We go over to the computers and he says, "Right, give me an author."

I stutter because I don't want to tell him one of the people on the Ace of Spades. They're mine. I give him Shakespeare.

He types it in and all the titles come up on the screen. Then he types in the number next to *Macbeth* and says, "There it is. You got it?"

I read the screen and understand. "Thanks."

"Just yell out if you need me."

"No worries."

He goes off, and I'm alone with the keys, the writers, and the screen.

First up, I go for Graham Greene. I'll go in the same order as they're listed on the card. I search my pocket for some paper but all I've got is a decrepit napkin. There's a pen tied to the table, and when I punch the name in and hit return, all the titles of Graham Greene come up on-screen.

Some of the titles are brilliant.

The Human Factor.

Brighton Rock.
The Heart of the Matter.
The Power and the Glory.
Our Man in Havana.

I write them all on the napkin, as well as the call number for the first one.

Next, I type *West, Morris.* Some of his titles are just as good, if not better.

Gallows on the Sand.
The Shoes of the Fisherman.
Children of the Sun.
The Ringmaster.
The Clowns of God.

Now, Sylvia.

I must admit, I have a soft spot for her because I've read her once and it was her writing that came to me in the dream. If it wasn't for her, I wouldn't be sitting here, closer to knowing where I have to go. I want her titles to be the best, and whether it's biased or not, to me, they are.

The Winter Ship.
The Colossus.
Ariel.
Crossing the Water.
The Bell Jar.

I take the napkin to the shelves and look them all up again, in order. They're all beautiful. All old and hard-covered in plain red or blue or black. I take all of them. Every one, and I go and sit down with them. What now?

How the hell am I going to read all of these in a week or two? The poems of Sylvia, maybe, but the other two have written some pretty long books, to say the least. I hope they're good.

"Listen," says the library man. I'm at the counter with all the books. "You can't borrow this many. There's a limit, you know. Do you even have a card?"

"What kind of card?" I can't help it. "A playing card? A credit card? What kind of card do you mean?"

"Okay, smart arse."

We both enjoy the moment, and he reaches under his counter and gives me a sheet of paper.

"Fill this out, please."

Once I receive the card, I try buttering him up a little to get my hands on all the books.

"Thanks, mate. You're doing a hell of a job."

He looks up. "You still want all those books, don't you?"

"That's right." I pile them up onto the counter from the floor. "Basically, I really need them, and one way or the other, I'm going to get them. Only in today's sick society can a man be persecuted for reading too many books." I look back into the emptiness of the library. "They're hardly jumping off the shelves, now, are they? I don't think anyone else wants them just now."

He allows me to talk, going through the motions. "Look, to be honest," he says, "I personally couldn't give a pinch of shit how many you borrow. It's regulations. If my boss catches me, I'm in it."

"In what?"

"I don't bloody *know*, but I'll be in it deep."

Still, I look at him, not giving an inch.

He caves in.

"All right, give 'em here. Let's see what I can rig up for you." He starts scanning them. "My boss is a total knob anyway."

When he's done, there are exactly eighteen books on the other side of the counter.

"Thanks," I tell him. "Much appreciated."

How am I going to get them all home? I ask myself.

I consider ringing Marv for a lift, but I manage on my own. I drop some along the way, rest a few times, but in the end, each book makes it home.

My arms are killing me.

I didn't know words could be so heavy.

All afternoon, I read.

I fall asleep once as well, no disrespect to the writers. I'm still worn out from the Rose beating and the Sledge Game.

As I read, I enjoy the work of Graham Greene. I don't pick up any clues as to where I have to go, but I think it must be simpler than this. I look over at the small book mountains I've built. It's demoralizing, to say the least. How am I ever going to find what I need among those thousands of pages?

When I wake up, a southerly's blowing outside and it's actually pretty cool for this time of year. It being early December, I feel a little strange going to put a sweatshirt on. I walk past the front door and see a piece of paper lying there.

No, it's a napkin.

Anxious, my eyes close for a second, and I bend down to pick it up. It really brings home the fact that I've been followed all this time. They watched me go to the library. They watched me *in* the library and on the way home. They knew I wrote the titles on the napkin.

My eyes read it.

Just a few words, in red.

Dear Ed,

Good work—but don't worry, it's simpler than you think.

I go back and sit with the books. I read "Barren Woman" until I know it word for word.

The Doorman wants a walk later, so we go. We meander through the streets of town, and I try to guess where the next addresses will be. "Any clues, Doorman?" I ask.

There's no reply. He's far too busy carrying out his casual, investigative style of sniffing.

What I haven't recognized till now is that the answers are signposted. They're everywhere, at the top of every street and at every intersection. *What if the messages are hidden in the titles?* I wonder. *The book titles.* All I'd have to do is match the street to one of each writer's books.

Simpler than you think, I tell myself. The napkin's still in my pocket, along with the Ace of Spades. I pull both out and look at them. The names watch me, and I swear they see it when I understand. I lean down a moment and speak excitedly to the Doorman.

"Come on," I say. "We have to get moving."

We run home, or at least we go as fast as the Doorman will allow. I need the books, the street directory, and, hopefully, a few minutes.

Yes, we run.

Each book waits and I sit there with my old *Gregory's,* trying to find a match with any of the titles. I go through Graham first again. There's no Human Street, no Factor Street, no Heart Street.

After a minute or so, I find it.

I hold the book in my hand.

It's black, and the title's written in gold on the spine. *The Power and the Glory.* There's no Power Street, but my eyes grow large with realization when I go back a few pages. The name greets my eyes like a fist. Glory Road.

I grin and ruffle up the Doorman's fur. Glory Road. That's bloody brilliant. I'd love to live on Glory Road.

On the map, it's way up on the edge of town.

Now I go through the Morris West titles. It's faster this time. *The Clowns of God.*

I find a Clown Street in the upper part of town.

Last of all, Sylvia's one is Bell Street, from *The Bell Jar.* According to the directory, Bell Street is one of the small side streets off the main street of town.

Now I check that none of the other titles also match, but I'm safe. They're the ones.

Just one question for each street.

What number?

Now I have to dig.

This is spades, so I have to dig.

The clues must be in the books, so now I shove the other ones to the side and focus on the three finalists. I feel kind of sorry for the ditched ones, to be honest. They look like the losers of a dramatic, tumultuous race, sitting on the floor. If they were people, they'd each have their head in their hands.

First, I reach for *The Power and the Glory*. I read well into the night, and it's one o'clock before I look up from the pages. I have no clues yet, and I can feel frustration starting to creep in. *What if I've missed it?* I wonder, but I'm certain I'll know it when I see it. For all I know, the numbers on Glory Road might only go up to 20 or 30, but I read on. I feel I must. This is what it's all about. Quitting now would be a sin.

At 3:46 a.m. (it's burned into my memory), I find it.

Page 114.

At the bottom of the page, in the left corner, there's the symbol for spades, drawn in black. Next to it are the words *Nicely done, Ed*.

I collapse back onto the couch in triumph. It doesn't get much better than this. No stones. No violence. It's about time this all became civilized.

Now I go straight to *The Clowns of God* and flick through. I can't believe I didn't just do this to begin with. It's definitely much easier than trying to find the clues in every word on every page. *Simpler than you think*, I remind myself.

This time it's on page 23. Just the symbol. And in *The Bell Jar,* it's page 39. I have the addresses, and I have exhaustion.

The digging's over.

I sleep.

4♠ the benefits of lying

It's Tuesday evening and we're playing cards at my place. Ritchie's complaining of a sore collarbone from the Sledge Game, Audrey's enjoying herself, and Marv's winning. He's unbearable, as usual.

I've been to Glory Road, and I've seen number 114. It's a Polynesian family with a husband bigger than the guy from Edgar Street. He works in construction and treats his wife like a queen and his kids like gods. When he gets home from work he picks them up and throws them in the air. They laugh and carry on and look forward to him arriving.

Glory Road is long and isolated. The houses are all pretty old. All fibro.

I don't know what to do there yet, but I'm pretty confident by now. It'll come to me.

"Looks like I win again," gloats Marv. He's in good form, with a cigar jammed into the side of his mouth.

"I hate you, Marv," says Ritchie. He's only summing up what we're all thinking at times like this.

Marv's quick to organize a Christmas game.

"Who's turn is it this year?" he asks, though we all know it's his and he'll try to get out of it. Marv could never cook a Christmas dinner. Not because he's hopeless. He's just too tight. He wouldn't pay for a turkey to save his life. Breakfast on the day of the Sledge Game was a oncer.

"You." Ritchie points straight at Marv. "It's *your* turn, Marv."

"You sure about that?"

"Yes." Ritchie's emphatic. "I am."

"But you know, my folks'll be there, and my sister, and—"

"Stiff shit, Marv, we love your parents." Ritchie's in fine touch. We all know he couldn't care less where the party's on. He's just loving getting stuck into Marv. "And we love your sister, too. She's hot as summer sand, boy. She's raging."

"Summer sand?" Audrey asks. "Raging?"

Ritchie slams his fist on the table. "Damn right, girl."

The three of us laugh as Marv fidgets.

"It isn't like you don't have the money," I say. "Thirty grand, isn't it?"

"Just hit forty," he replies. This triggers a discussion of what

Marv intends to do with that kind of money. He tells us it's his business alone and we don't give it a lot more thought. I guess we don't give many things a lot of thought.

After a few more minutes, I relent.

"We'll just have it here," I say. I look over at Marv. "But you'll have to put up with the Doorman, mate."

Marv isn't happy, but he agrees.

I go for more.

"All right, Marv," I say. "I tell you what—I'll have the Christmas game right here under one condition."

"What?"

"You have to bring the Doorman a present." I can't help rubbing it in a little. With Marv, you have to get mileage, and I must say, this is turning out better than I'd hoped. I'm delighted with myself. "You can bring him a nice juicy steak, and"—this is where it gets even better—"you have to give him a big Christmas kiss."

Ritchie clicks his fingers. "Brilliant idea, Ed. Perfect."

Marv's stunned.

Outraged.

"That's disgraceful," he tells me, but still it's better than paying for a turkey and going to the effort of cooking. He finally makes up his mind. "All right, I'll do it." He points a finger at me now. "But you're one twisted bastard, Ed."

"Thanks, Marv, I appreciate it," and for the first time in many years, I find myself looking forward to Christmas.

Depending on my cab shifts, I continue going back to Glory Road, and though it's obvious this family is working hard to make ends meet, I still don't know what I have to do. One evening, when I'm standing behind the bushes, the father comes over to me. He's a very big boy and could strangle me with one hand behind his back. He doesn't look happy.

"Hey," he calls out. "You there. I seen you before." He moves fast toward me. "Get out of those bushes quick smart." His voice isn't loud. It sounds like it would be gentle and quiet in most situations. It's the size of him that concerns me.

Don't worry, I calm myself. *You need to be here. It'll take what it takes.*

I step out and face the man as the sun sets behind the house. He has smooth dark skin and black curly hair and eyes that threaten me.

"You been spying on my kids, boy?"

"No, sir." I lift my head. I need to look proud and honest.

Hang on, I remind myself. *I am honest. Well, pretty much.*

"Well, why are you here?"

I lie and hope.

"I used to live in this house," I say. *Shit. Good thinking, Ed.* I've actually impressed myself. "A lot of years ago—before we moved closer to town. Sometimes I like to come up here and look at the place." *And please,* I beg, *let these people not have lived here long.* "My dad died not long ago, and when I come here, I think of him. I think of him when I see you with your kids, throwing them in the air and over your shoulder. . . ."

The man softens slightly.

Thank you, God.

He comes a little closer as the sun falls on its hands and knees behind him.

"Yeah, it's a pretty shoddy old place"—he motions with his hand—"but it's the best we can do right now."

"It looks all right to me," I say.

We go on awhile longer, and in the end, the man asks me a surprising question. He moves back, thinks, then says, "Hey, would you like to come in to look around? We're about to have dinner. You're welcome to stay."

My gut instinct is to decline, but I don't. The harder decision is to go in.

I follow the man onto his front porch and into the house. Before we go in he says, "My name's Lua. Lua Tatupu."

"Ed Kennedy," I respond, and we shake hands. Lua crushes nearly every bone in my right hand.

"Marie?" he calls out when we're inside. "Kids?" He turns to me. "The place just like you remember it?"

"Sorry?" Then I remember. "Oh. Yeah, it is."

The kids come pouring out of the woodwork and start climbing all over us. Lua introduces me to them and to his wife. Dinner is mashed potatoes and frankfurts.

We eat, and Lua tells jokes and the kids laugh and laugh, even though they've heard the same jokes a thousand times, according to Marie. Marie has wrinkles under her eyes and looks worn down from life and kids and putting food on the table each night. She's got milder skin than Lua and dark brown wavy hair. She was beautiful once—even more beautiful than this. She works in one of the supermarkets.

There are five kids. All have trouble eating with their mouths closed, but when they laugh, you can see the world in their eyes. You can tell exactly why Lua treats them like he does and loves them that much.

"Can I have a piggyback from Ed, Dad?" one of the girls asks.

I nod to him, and Lua says, "Of course, darlin', but you have to put something else in that sentence." It reminds me of Father O'Reilly's brother, Tony.

The girl smacks herself on the forehead, smiling and saying, "Can he *please* give me a piggyback?"

"Sure, baby," Lua says, and I do.

I've given thirteen piggybacks by the time Marie rescues me from the youngest of the boys.

"Jessie, I think Ed's all tuckered out, okay?"

"O-kaaay." Jessie gives in, and I fall backward to the couch.

Jessie's about six, and while I'm sitting there he whispers something in my ear.

It's the answer.

He says, "My dad's putting up our Christmas lights soon—you have to come and have a look one day. I love those lights. . . ."

"I promise," I say. "I'll come."

I look around the house one last time, almost convincing *myself* that I used to live here. I even conjure up a whole lot of great memories with my dad inside these walls.

Lua's asleep when I leave, so it's Marie who sees me out.

"Thank you," I say, "for everything."

She only looks at me with her warm, genuine eyes and says, "No worries, Ed. Come back anytime."

"I will," I say. This time I'm not lying.

On the weekend, I go past during the day. The Christmas lights are up and they're very old and faded. Some of the lights are missing. They're the old-style lights. They're not the type to flash. They're just big bulbs in different colors, strung along the eaves above the front porch.

I'll come back later, I think, *to have a look.*

Sure enough, in the evening, when the lights are on, I see that only half the ones that are still there actually work. That translates to four globes in operation. Four globes to brighten up the Tatupu house this year. It's not a big thing, but I guess it's true — big things are often just small things that are noticed.

The first chance I get, I'll be back, during the day, when everyone's at school and work.

Something has to be done about those lights.

I go to Kmart and buy a brand-new set of lights, exactly the same as the existing ones. Nice big globes of red and blue and yellow and green. It's a hot Wednesday, and surprisingly there are no questions from the neighbors as I get on the Tatupus' front porch and stand on a large overturned pot. I dismantle the original lights, bending back the nails that hold the power cord. When the whole thing is down, I notice the plug goes inside (as I should have expected), so I can't do the job completely. Instead, I put the old lights back up and leave the new ones at the front door.

I don't leave a note.

There's nothing else to do.

At first, I'd wanted to write *Merry Christmas* on the box somewhere, but I decide against it.

This isn't about words.

It's about glowing lights and small things that are big.

5 the power and the glory

I'm eating ravioli in the kitchen that same night when a van pulls up in front of the shack. The engine growls to a halt, and I hear the car doors slam. Next I hear the sound of little fists on my front door.

The Doorman barks for a change, but I calm him down and open up.

Standing there are Lua, Marie, and every kid from that family.

"Hi, Ed," says Lua, and the rest of them echo him. He continues. "We looked you up in the local phone book but you weren't in it, so we rang all the other Kennedys around here. Your mother gave us the address."

There's quiet now as I wonder what Ma might have told them. Marie breaks it.

"Come with us," she says.

Riding in the van, squashed between all the kids, I sit there, and for the first time with this family, everyone's quiet. This, as you can imagine, makes me considerably uneasy. The streetlamps flick past, like pages of light, each coming toward me and then turning away. Closing. When I look forward, I catch Lua looking at me in the rearview mirror.

We arrive at the house within five or ten minutes.

Marie takes charge.

"Right, inside, kids."

She goes with them, and this leaves Lua and me in the van together.

Again he looks in the mirror and lets his eyes reflect backward to mine.

"Ready?" he asks.

"For what?"

He only shakes his head. "Don't give me that, Ed." He gets out and rams the door shut. "Well, come on," he calls in through the window. "Get out, boy."

Boy.

I didn't like the way he said that. Kind of foreboding. My big fear is that I've insulted him with the new lights. He might be taking it as a sign that he can't provide properly for his own family. He might think I'm saying, *This poor, inadequate fool can't even get a full set of lights to work properly*. I don't dare to look at the house as I follow him to where he stands at the edge of the road, looking back. It's dark there. Very dark.

We stand.

Lua watches me.

I watch the ground.

The next thing I hear is the sound of the flyscreen door opening and slamming several times. The kids come sprinting toward us, followed by Marie at a fast walk.

When I count the kids, I realize one of them's missing.

Jessie.

I search all the faces before looking again at the ground. The loud call of Lua's voice almost makes me jump.

"Okay, Jess!" he shouts.

A few seconds collect and fall, and when I look up, the old fibro house is lit up. The lights are so beautiful that they appear almost to hold the house up by themselves. The faces of the kids, Lua, and Marie are splashed with red, blue, yellow, and green. I can feel a red light shining over my own face and my own relieved smile. The kids are cheering and clapping and saying this will be the best Christmas ever. The girls start dancing together, holding hands. That's when Jessie comes running from the house to have a look.

"He insisted on turning the power on," Lua tells me, and when I look at him, Jessie's smile is the biggest and the best. The most alive. *This is his moment,* I think, *and Lua and Marie's.* "When we got those new lights, Jessie said he wanted you to be here when we turned them on. So what else could we do?"

I shake my head, looking into the colors shining across the yard.

They swim through my eyes.

To myself I say, *The power and the glory.*

6 a moment of beauty

As the kids dance around the front yard under the night sky and the lights, I see something.

Lua and Marie are holding hands.

They look like they're so happy, just inside this moment, watching the kids and the lights on their old fibro house.

Lua kisses her.

Just softly on the lips.

And she kisses back.

Sometimes people are beautiful.

Not in looks.

Not in what they say.

Just in what they are.

7 ♠ a moment of truth

Marie makes me come in for a cup of coffee. At first I knock it back, but she insists. "You have to, Ed."

I give in, and we go inside and drink and talk.

It's all comfortable for quite a while, until Marie's words stop and stand in the middle of the conversation. She stirs her coffee and says, "Thank you, Ed." The wrinkles around her eyes become a little unsettled and her eyes seem filled with sparks. "Thank you so much."

"For what?"

She shakes her head. "Don't make me say it, Ed. We know it was you—Jessie couldn't keep a secret if we glued his mouth shut. We know it was you."

I surrender completely. "You deserved it."

She's still not satisfied. "But why? Why us?"

"That," I tell her the truth, "I have no idea about." I sip the coffee. "This is all very long and almost unexplainable. All I know is that I was standing outside this old house and the rest just happened."

Now Lua walks in among the words and pushes them forward. He says, "You know, Ed, we've been living here close to a year now, and nobody—absolutely nobody—has ever lifted a finger to help us or make us feel welcome." He drinks. "We expect no more these days. People have enough trouble getting by on their own. . . ." His eyes hold on to mine for just a second. "But then you come along, out of nowhere. We just don't get it."

That's when a moment of clarity takes shape in front of me.

I say, "Don't even try—I don't understand it myself."

225

Marie accepts my statement but still takes it a little further. She says, "Fair enough, Ed, but we *do* want to thank you."

"Yes," says Lua.

Marie nods to him and he stands up and walks over to the fridge. Stuck to it with a magnet is an envelope. The name *Ed Kennedy* is on it, and he comes back and hands it to me.

"We don't have much," he says, "but this is the best we can do to thank you." He places it in my hands. "Somehow, I think you'll like it. Just a feeling."

Inside is a homemade Christmas card. All the kids have drawn on it. Christmas trees, bright lights, and kids playing. Some of the drawings are shockers, but still excellent. Inside are the words, also written by one of the kids:

Dear Ed,

have a happy cristmas! we hope you also have some beautiful lights like the ones you gave us.

From all the Tatupu family

It makes me smile and I stand up and go into the lounge room, where the kids are all sprawled out, watching the telly.

"Hey, thanks for the card," I say to them.

They all answer me, but it's Jessie who speaks loudest. "It's the least we could do, Ed." And within a few seconds they're all focused on the TV again. It's a video. One of those animal adventure things. They're all glued to a cat going down a stream in a cardboard box.

"See you all later," I say, but none of them hears. I only look contentedly at the pictures again and head back to the kitchen.

When I get there, the presentation isn't over.

Lua's standing there with a small dark stone that has a pattern on it like a cross.

He says, "A friend once gave this to me, Ed—it's for luck." He holds it out to me. "I want you to have it."

At first, we all look down at it, not speaking.

My voice takes me by surprise.

"No," I say. "I can't take it, Lua."

His quiet, gentle words are calm but urgent. His eyes are wild with sincerity. "No, Ed—you have to. You've given us so much. More than you'll ever know." He holds out the stone again and goes to the extent of putting it in my palm and closing my hand to hold it firmly. He holds my hand in both of his. "It's yours."

"Not only for luck," Marie tells me. "Also for remembering."

Now I accept the stone and look at it. "Thank you," I say to both of them. "I'll look after it."

Lua places his hand on my shoulder. "I know."

The three of us stand in the kitchen together.

When I leave, Marie kisses me on the cheek and we say goodbye.

"Remember," she says. "Come back anytime. You're always welcome here."

"Thank you," I reply, and head out the front door.

Lua wants to drive me home, but I refuse, mainly because I really do feel like walking tonight. We shake hands, Lua crushing me once again.

He walks me out to the edge of the front lawn and wants an answer to one final question.

"Let me ask you something, Ed." We're a few steps apart.

"Of course."

He moves a little further away as we stand in the dark. Behind us, the lights still glow proudly in the night. This is the moment of truth.

Lua says, "You never lived in our house, Ed. Did you?"

There's no hiding it now. No way out.

"No," I answer. "I didn't."

We observe each other, and I can see there are many things that Lua wants to know. He's about to ask when I see him pull back. He prefers not to ruin things with any more questions.

What it is is what it is.

"Bye, Ed."

"Goodbye, Lua."

We shake hands and walk in our different directions.

At the end of the road, just before I go around the corner, I turn one last time to see the lights.

8 ♠ clown street. chips. the doorman. and me

It's the hottest day of the year, and I've got a day shift in the city. The cab has air-conditioning, but it breaks down, much to the disgust of everyone I pick up. I warn them every time they get in, but only one gets back out. It's a man who still has his last lungful of a Winfield in his mouth.

"Bloody hopeless," he tells me.

"I know." I only shrug and agree.

The stone that Lua Tatupu gave me is in my left pocket. It

makes me happy in the festering city traffic, even when the lights are green and all the cars remain still.

Not long after I return the cab to base, Audrey pulls into the lot. She winds her window down to talk to me.

"Sweating like crazy in here," she says.

I imagine the sweat on her and how I'd like to taste it. With blank expression, I slide down into the visual details.

"Ed?"

Her hair's greasy but great. Lovely blond, like hay. I see the three or four spots of sun thrown across her face. Again she speaks. "Ed?"

"Sorry," I say, "I was thinking of something." I look back to where the boyfriend stands, expecting her. "He's waiting for you." When I return to Audrey's face, I miss it and catch a glimpse of her fingers on the wheel. They're relaxed and coated with light. And they're lovely. *Does he notice those small things?* I wonder, but I don't speak it to Audrey. I only say, "Have a good night," and step back from the car.

"You, too, Ed." She drives on.

Even later, as the sun goes down and I walk into town and onto Clown Street, I see all of Audrey. I see her arms and bony legs. I see her smiling as she talks and eats with the boyfriend. I imagine him feeding her food from his fingers in her kitchen, and she eats it, allowing enough of her lips to smudge him with her beauty.

The Doorman's with me.

My faithful companion.

Along the way I buy us some hot chips with lots of salt and vinegar. It's old-style, all wrapped in the racing section of today's newspaper. The hot tip is a two-year-old mare called Bacon

Rashers. I wonder how she went. The Doorman, on the other hand, cares little. He can smell the chips.

When we make it to 23 Clown Street, we discover that it's a restaurant. It's tiny, and it's called Melusso's. Italian. It's in a little shopping village and follows the small-restaurant ritual of being dimly lit. It smells good.

There's a park bench across the road and we sit there, eating the chips. My hand reaches down inside the package, through the sweaty, greasy paper. I love every minute of it. Each time I throw the Doorman a chip, he lets it hit the ground, leans over it, and licks it up. He turns nothing down, this dog. I don't think he cares too much about his cholesterol.

Nothing tonight.

Or the next.

In fact, time is wasting away.

It's a tradition now. Clown Street. Chips. The Doorman and me.

The owner is old and dignified, and I'm quite sure it isn't him I'm here to see. I can tell. Something's coming.

On Friday night, after standing outside the restaurant and going home after closing, I find Audrey sitting on my porch, waiting. She's wearing board shorts and a light shirt without a bra. She isn't big up there, Audrey, but she's nice. I stop for a moment, hesitate, and continue. The Doorman loves her and throws himself into a trot.

"Hey, Doorman," she says. She crouches down warmly to greet him. They're good friends, those two. "Hi, Ed."

"Hi, Audrey."

I open the door and she follows me in.

We sit.

In the kitchen.

"So where were you this time?" she asks. It's almost laughable because usually that question is asked with contempt to unreliable-bastard husbands.

"Clown Street," I answer.

"*Clown* Street?"

I nod. "Some restaurant there."

"There's actually a street called Clown Street?"

"I know."

"Anything happen there yet?"

"No."

"I see."

As she looks away I make my mind up. I say, "So why are you here, Audrey?"

She looks down.

Away.

When she finally answers, she says, "I guess I missed you, Ed." Her eyes are pale green and wet. I want to tell her it's barely been a week since we last got together, but I think I know what she means. "I feel like you're slipping away somehow. You've become different since all this started."

"Different?"

I ask it, but I know it. I am.

I stand up and look into her.

"Yes." She confirms it. "You used to just be." She explains this like she doesn't really want to hear it. It's more a case that she *has* to say it. "Now you're *somebody*, Ed. I don't know everything about what you've done and what you've been through, but I don't know—you seem further away now."

It's ironic, don't you think? All I've ever wanted was to get closer to her. I've tried desperately.

231

She concludes. "You're better."

It's with those words that I see things from Audrey's perspective. She liked me being *just Ed.* It was safer that way. Stable. Now I've changed things. I've left my own fingerprints on the world, no matter how small, and it's upset the equilibrium of us—Audrey and me. Maybe she's afraid that if I can't have her, I won't want her.

Like this.

Like we used to be.

She doesn't want to love me, but she doesn't want to lose me either.

She wants us to stay okay. Like before.

But it's not as certain anymore.

We will, I try to promise.

I hope I'm right.

Still in the kitchen, my fingers feel the stone from Lua in my pocket again. I think about what Audrey's been telling me. Maybe I truly am shedding the old Ed Kennedy for this new person who's full of purpose rather than incompetence. Maybe one morning I'll wake up and step outside of myself to look back at the old me lying dead among the sheets.

It's a good thing, I know.

But how can a good thing suddenly feel so sad?

I've wanted this from the beginning.

I head back to the fridge and get more to drink. I've come to the conclusion that we have to get drunk. Audrey agrees.

*   *   *

"So what were you doing," I ask later on the couch, "while I was at Clown Street?"

I see her thoughts swivel.

She's drunk enough to tell me, at least in a coy kind of way.

"You know," she embarrasses.

"No." I mock her a little. "I don't."

"I was with Simon at my place and we . . . for a few hours."

"A few *hours*." I'm hurt but keep it out of my voice. "How'd you manage the strength to get over here?"

"I don't know," she admits. "He went home and I felt empty."

So you came here, I think, but I'm not bitter. Not at this moment. I rationalize that none of the physical things matter so much. Audrey needs me now, and for old times' sake, that's good enough.

She wakes me a bit later. We're still on the couch. A small crowd of bottles is assembled on the table. They sit there like onlookers. Like observers at an accident.

Audrey looks me hard in the face, wavers, then hands me a question.

"Do you hate me, Ed?"

Still stupid with bubbles and vodka in my stomach, I answer. Very seriously.

"Yes," I whisper. "I do."

We both smack the sudden silence with laughter. When it returns, we hit it again. The laughter spins in front of us and we keep hitting it.

When it calms completely, Audrey whispers, "I don't blame you."

The next time I'm woken, it's by a cracking at the door.

I stammer there, open it, and there in front of me is the guy who jumped my cab. That feels like an eternity ago.

He looks annoyed.

As usual.

He holds his hand up for me to be quiet and says, "Just"—he waits, for effect—"shut up and listen." He actually sounds a touch more than annoyed as he continues. "Look, Ed." The yellow-rimmed eyes scratch me. "It's three in the morning. It's still humid as hell, and here we are."

"Yes," I agree. A cloud of drunkenness hangs over me. I almost expect rain. "Here we are."

"Now don't you mock me, boy."

I reel back. "I'm sorry. What is it?"

He pauses, and the air sounds violent between us. He speaks.

"Tomorrow. Eight p.m. sharp. Melusso's." He walks away before remembering something. "And do me a favor, will you?"

"Of course."

"Cut down on the chips, for Christ's sake. You're making me sick." Now he points at me, threatening. "And hurry up with all this shit. You might think I don't have better things to do, but as it happens, I do, all right?"

"All right. It's only fair." In my stupor, I try for something extra. I call out, "Who's sending you?"

The young man with the gold-rimmed eyes, black suit of clothes, and brutal disposition returns up the porch steps. He says, "How the hell would I know, Kennedy?" He even laughs and shakes his head. "You might not be the only one getting aces in the mail. Did you ever think of that?"

He lingers a little longer, turns, and trudges off, dissolving into the darkness. Blending in.

Audrey's behind me at the door now, and I've got something to think about.

234

I write down what he told me about Melusso's.

Eight p.m. tomorrow night. I have to be there.

After sticking the note to the fridge, I go to bed, and Audrey comes with me. She sleeps with her leg across me, and I love the feel of her breath on my throat.

After perhaps ten minutes, she says, "Tell me, Ed. Tell me about where you've been."

I've told her once before about the Ace of Diamonds messages, but not in any detail. I'm so tired now, but I do tell her.

About Milla. Beautiful Milla. As I speak, I see her pleading face as she begged me that she did right by her Jimmy.

About Sophie. The barefoot girl with—

Audrey's asleep.

She's asleep, but I go on speaking. I tell her about Edgar Street and all the others. The stones. The beatings. Father O'Reilly. Angie Carusso. The Rose boys. The Tatupu family.

Just for now, I find I'm happy, and I want to stay awake, but soon the night falls down, beating me hard into sleep.

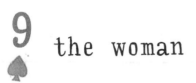

9 the woman

The yawn of a girl can be so beautiful it makes you cringe.

Especially when she's standing in your kitchen in her underpants and a shirt, yawning.

Audrey's doing this right now as I do the dishes. I rinse a plate and there she is, rubbing her eyes, yawning, then smiling.

"Sleep okay?" I ask.

She nods and says, "You're comfortable, Ed."

I realize I could take that comment badly, but it's a compliment.

"Have a seat," I say, and without thinking, I look at her shirt buttons and her hips. I follow her legs down to her knees, shins, and ankles. All in a brief second. Audrey's feet look soft and delicate. Almost like they could melt into the kitchen floor.

I make her some cereal and she crunches it. I didn't have to ask if she wanted some. Some things I know.

This is confirmed later, once Audrey's had a shower and dressed fully.

At the front door, she says, "Thanks, Ed." She pauses before speaking again. "You know, out of everyone, you know me the best, and you treat me the best. I feel most comfortable with you." She even leans close and kisses me on the cheek. "Thanks for putting up with me."

As she walks away, I still feel her lips on my skin. The taste of them.

I watch her all the way up the street, till she turns the corner. Just before she does, she knows I'm standing there, and she turns one last moment and waves. In answer, I hold up my hand, and she's gone.

Slowly.

At times painfully.

Audrey is killing me.

And do me a favor, will you? Cut down on the chips, for Christ's sake.

I hear the words of my friend from last night again.

All day they come back at me, along with the other statement he made.

You might not be the only one getting aces in the mail. Did you ever think of that?

Of course, there was a question mark at the end of his words, but I know it was a statement. It makes me think about all the people I've run into. What if they're *all* messengers, like me, and they're all threatened and desperate just to get through what they have to do to survive? I wonder if they, too, have received playing cards and firearms in their letter boxes or if they've had their own specific tools provided. *It would all be personal,* I think. *I got cards because that's what I do. Maybe Daryl and Keith were given the balaclavas, and my mate from last night was given his black outfit and his cantankerous demeanor.*

By quarter to eight I'll be back at Melusso's, minus the Doorman. This time I'm going in. I have to explain it to him before I go.

He looks at me.

What? he asks. *No chips tonight?*

"Sorry, mate. I'll bring you back something, I promise."

He seems happy enough by the time I leave because I've fixed him a coffee and thrown some ice cream in it as well. He almost jumps from paw to paw as I'm putting it down for him.

Nice, he tells me in the kitchen. We're still friends.

I must admit, I even miss him a little as I walk to Clown Street and Melusso's. It feels like we were in this one together, and now I have to finish it alone and take all the glory.

That is.

If there *is* glory.

I've almost forgotten that things can go wrong and be difficult. Exhibit A for that was Edgar Street. Exhibit B, the Rose boys.

Now I wonder what I'll deliver this time round as I walk

237

through the door of Melusso's restaurant into the all-consuming smell and warmth of spaghetti sauce, pasta, and garlic. I've kept my eyes open for anyone following me, but I haven't seen a soul who looks interested. There are just people going about what they always do.

Talking. Parking crooked.

Swearing. Telling their kids to hurry up and stop fighting.

All that kind of thing.

Now, in the restaurant, I ask the plump waitress to put me in the darkest corner.

"Over there?" she asks in amazement. "Near the kitchen?"

"Yes please."

"No one's ever asked to be seated there," she claims. "You sure, mate?"

"Positive."

What a strange fellow, I see her think, but she takes me over.

"Wine list?"

"Sorry?"

"Would you like some wine?"

"No, thanks."

She lashes the wine list from the table and tells me the specials. I order spaghetti and meatballs and lasagna.

"You expecting someone?"

I shake my head. "No."

"So you're going to eat *both*?"

"Oh, no," I answer. "The lasagna's for my dog—I promised to bring him home something."

This time she gives me a look that says, *What a poor, pathetic, lonely bastard,* which is understandable, I suppose. But she says, "I'll bring you that just before you go, okay?"

"Thanks."

"Any drinks?"

"No, thanks."

I refuse all drinks at restaurants because I figure I can buy a drink anywhere—it's the food I can't cook that I'm here for.

She leaves and I survey the restaurant, which is half full. There are people gorging themselves, others sipping wine, while a young couple kiss over the table and share their food. The only person of interest is a man on the same side of the restaurant as me. He's waiting for someone, drinking wine but not eating. He wears a suit and has wavy combed-back hair, black and silver.

Soon after I get the meatballs and spaghetti, the night's significance comes to fruition.

I nearly choke on my fork when the man's guest arrives. He stands up and kisses her and puts his hands on her hips.

The woman is Beverly Anne Kennedy.

Bev Kennedy.

Otherwise known as Ma.

Oh, bloody hell, I think, and I keep my head down.

For some reason, I feel like I'm going to throw up.

My mother's wearing a flattering dress. It's a shiny dark blue. Almost the color of a storm. She sits down politely, and her hair actually flanks her face very nicely.

In short, it's the first time she's ever looked like a woman to me. Usually she just looks like foulmouthed Ma, who swears at me and calls me useless. Tonight, though, she wears earrings, and her dark face and brown eyes smile. She wrinkles a bit when she smiles, but, yes, she looks happy.

She looks happy being a woman.

*   *   *

The man is very much the gentleman, pouring her some wine and asking what she'd like to eat. They talk with pleasure and ease, but I can't hear what they say. To be honest, I try not to.

I think of my father.

I think of him, and immediately it depresses me.

Don't ask me why, but I feel like he deserved more than this. He was, of course, a drunk, especially at the end of his life, but he was so kind, and generous, and gentle. Looking into my meatballs, I see his short black hair and his nearly colorless eyes. He was quite tall, and when he left for work, he always wore a flannel shirt and had a cigarette in his mouth. At home, he never smoked. Not in the house. He, too, was a gentleman, despite everything else.

I also remember him staggering through the front door and lurching for the couch after closing at the pub.

Ma screamed at him, of course, but it lost effect.

She nagged him all the time, anyway. He'd work his guts out, but it was never enough. Remember the coffee table incident? Well, my father had to put up with that every day.

When we were younger, he used to take us kids places, like the national park and the beach and a playground miles away that had a huge metal rocket ship. Not like the plastic vomit playgrounds the poor kids have to play on these days. He'd take us to those places and quietly watch us play. We'd look back and he'd be sitting there, happily smoking, maybe dreaming. My first memory is of being four years old and getting a piggyback from Gregor Kennedy, my father. That was when the world wasn't so big and I could see everywhere. It was when my father was a hero and not a human.

Now I sit here, asking myself what I have to do next.

My first order of business is to not finish the meatballs. I only watch Ma on her wonderful date. It's quite obvious that the two of them have been here before. The waitress knows them and stops for a brief exchange of words. They're very comfortable.

I try to be bitter about it, and angry, but I catch myself. What's the point? She is, after all, a person, and she deserves the right to be happy just like everyone else.

It's only soon after that I understand exactly why my first instinct is to begrudge her this happiness.

It's nothing to do with my father.

It's me.

In a sudden wave of nausea, I see the absolute horror, if you will, of this situation.

There's my ma, fifty-odd years old, hightailing around town with some guy while I sit here, in the prime of my youth, completely and utterly alone.

I shake my head.

At myself.

10 ♠ front-porch cyclone

The waitress takes away my meatballs and brings out the Doorman's lasagna in a cheap plastic box. He'll be very happy with that, I expect.

As I slip to the counter and pay, I look back at Ma and the man, cautious not to be seen, but she's totally engrossed in him.

241

She stares and listens with such intent that I don't even bother trying to hide myself from view anymore. I pay up and get out of there, except I don't go home. I walk to Ma's place and wait on the front porch.

It smells like my childhood, this house. I can even smell it from under the door as I sit here on the cool cement.

The night is alive with stars, and when I lie down and look up, I get lost up there. I feel like I'm falling, but upward, into the abyss of sky above me.

The next thing I feel is someone's foot nudging my leg.

I wake up and find the face that belongs to it.

"What are *you* doing here?" she says.

That's Ma.

Friendly as ever.

I rise to an elbow and decide not to dance around this. "I came to ask if you had a nice time at Melusso's."

An expression of surprise falls from her face, though she's trying to keep it. It breaks off and she seems to catch it and fidget with it in her hands. "It was very nice," she says, but I can tell she's stalling to go through her options. "A woman has to live."

I sit up now. "I guess that's fair."

She shrugs. "That the only reason you're here—to grill me about going out to dinner with a man? I have needs, you know."

Needs.

Have a listen to her.

She steps past me toward the door and inserts the key. "Now if you don't mind, Ed, I'm very tired."

Now.

The moment.

I nearly give in, but tonight I stand up. I know full well that out of all of her offspring, I'm the only one this woman won't invite into the house in this situation. If my sisters were here, she'd already be making coffee. If it was Tommy, she'd be asking him how university's treating him, offering him a Coke or a piece of cake.

Yet, with me, Ed Kennedy, every bit as much one of her kids as the others, she steps past and refuses friendliness, let alone an invitation to come in. Just once, I'd like her to be even the slightest bit affable.

The door's nearly shut when I stop it with my hand. The sound of a slapped face.

Her expression swells as I look at her.

I speak, saying the words hard.

"Ma?" I ask.

"What?"

"Why do you hate me so much?"

And now she looks at me, this woman, as I make sure my eyes don't give me away.

Flatly, simply, she answers.

"Because, Ed—you remind me of *him*."

Him?

It registers.

Him—my father.

She goes inside and the door slams.

I've had to take a man up to the Cathedral and attempt to kill him. I've had hit men eat pies in my kitchen and lay me out. I've been jumped by a group of teenage thugs.

This, however, feels like my darkest hour.

Standing.

Hurting.

On my mother's front porch.

*　　*　　*

The sky opens now, crumbling apart.

I want to hammer the door with my hands and my feet.

I don't.

All I do is sink to my knees, felled by the words that could deliver such a knockout blow. I try to make something good of it because I loved my father. Apart from the alcoholic section, I think it can't be totally shameful to be like him.

So why does this feel so awful?

I don't move.

In fact, I vow not to leave this shitty front porch until I get the answers I deserve. I'll sleep here if I have to and wait in the scorching heat all day tomorrow. I stand back up and call out.

"I'm not leaving, Ma!" Again. "You hear me? I'm not leaving."

After fifteen minutes the door pulls open again, but I don't look at her. I turn around and speak to the road, saying, "You treat everyone else so good—Leigh, Kath, and Tommy. It's like . . ." I can't allow myself to weaken. I pace. "But you speak to me with complete disrespect, and I'm the one who's *here*." Now I turn and look at her. "I'm the one who's here if you need something—and each time, I do it, don't I?"

She agrees. "Yes, Ed," but she also pounces. She assaults me with her own version of the truth. The words cut me through the ears so hard that I expect blood to ooze from them. "Yes, you're here—and that's exactly it!" She holds her arms out. "Look at this dump. The house, the town, everything." The voice is dark. "And your father—he promised me that one day we'd leave this place. He said we'd just pack up and go, and look where we are, Ed. We're still here. I'm here. *You're* here, and just like your old man, you're all promise, Ed, and no results. You"—she points at

244

me with venom—"you could be as good as any of them. As good as Tommy, even. . . . But you're still here and you'll still be here in fifty years." She sounds so cold. "And you'll have achieved nothing."

Fade to silence.

"I just want you"—she breaks it—"to make something of yourself." Slowly she makes her way to the front steps and says, "You have to realize something, Ed."

"What?"

Carefully now, her statement comes out. "Believe it or not— it takes a lot of love to hate you like this."

I try to understand.

She's still on the porch when I go down to the front lawn and turn back.

God, it's dark now.

As dark as the Ace of Spades.

"Were you seeing that man when Dad was still alive?" I ask her.

She looks at me, wishing she didn't have to, and although she says nothing, I know. I know it's not only my father she hates, but herself. That's when I realize she's got it wrong.

It's not the place, I think. *It's the people.*

We'd have all been the same anywhere else.

I speak again. One last question.

"Did Dad know?"

Long pause.

A pause that murders, until my mother turns away and cries,

and the night is so deep and dark that I wonder if the sun will
ever come up.

J♠ a phone call

"Ma?"

"Yeah?"

I look down at the Doorman, who's eating his lasagna with
what can only be described as the ultimate ecstasy. It's 2:03 a.m.,
and I hold the phone receiver against my ear.

"You okay, Ma?"

The voice shivers back but answers the way I expected.

"Yeah, I'm okay."

"That's good."

"Except you woke me, you useless—"

I hang up but smile.

I'd wanted to tell her I still love her, but maybe it's better this
way.

Q♠ the bell street theater

I can't help thinking about all the things Ma said last night.

It's Sunday morning, and I've hardly slept. The Doorman and

I each have a few coffees, but it doesn't wake me up much. I wonder if I'm done with Clown Street and my mother, but my feeling tells me I am. She needed to tell me those things.

Of course, the fact that my mother thinks I'm a complete loser is not pleasant.

The fact that she also considers herself one isn't much comfort, either, even if it should be. In a way, it has woken me a little. I realize I can't be a cabdriver all my life. It'll drive me crazy.

For the first time, a message has touched part of my own life in some way.

Who was it for?

For Ma or me?

Then I hear her words again. *It takes a lot of love to hate you like this.*

I think I saw some relief cross her face when she told me that.

The message was hers.

The Doorman and I go to the church to see Father O'Reilly, and he still has a fairly generous congregation.

"Ed!" he says excitedly afterward. "I was worried you weren't coming back. I've missed you the last few weeks." He pats the Doorman.

"I guess we've been busy," I say.

"The Lord been with you?"

"Not really," I answer. I think of last night and the idea of my mother committing adultery, hating my father for broken promises, and despising her only child who remains in town.

"Ah," he affirms. "Everything has its purpose."

I can only agree with that. Nothing has happened without reason, and I focus on the next message.

247

There's only Bell Street now, and I go there in the afternoon. Number 39 is an old, jaded cinema that you walk down into. There's an old terrace house above it, where a board sits glued to the awning. Today, the lettering says *Casablanca* 2:30 p.m. and *Some Like It Hot* 7 p.m. As you walk down, there are posters of old movies displayed in the window. The paper is yellow on the edges, and when I walk in, there are more inside.

The smell is of stale popcorn. It seems empty.

"Hello?" I call.

Nothing.

This place must have died years ago when the new Greater Union was put up across town. It's deserted.

"Hello?" I call again, louder this time.

I look into a back room and see an old man sleeping. He wears a suit and bow tie, like an old-style usher.

"You all right, mate?" I ask, and he jolts awake.

"Oh!" He leaps from his chair and straightens up his jacket. "What can I do for you?"

I look at the board above the counter and say, "Can I get a ticket to *Casablanca,* please?"

"God, you're my first customer in weeks!"

The lines around the man's eyes are enormous, and he has tremendously bushy eyebrows. His white hair is combed to perfection, and although he's balding, he doesn't execute a comb-over. His expression is genuine. The man's delighted. Quite frankly, he's chuffed to bits.

I hand him ten dollars and he gives me five change.

"Popcorn?"

"Yes, please."

He thrills himself as he scoops it up and puts it in the box. "On the house," he says, and winks at me.

"Cheers."

The cinema itself is small, but the screen is massive. I have to wait awhile, but the old man comes in at about 2:25. "I don't think anyone else is coming. Would you mind if we started early?" He's probably scared I'll piss off on him if I have to wait too long.

"No worries."

He rushes back up the aisle.

I'm sitting almost exactly in the middle of the theater. If anything, I'm a row closer than further back.

The movie begins.

Black and white.

A while through it, it cuts out and I look back up to where the projection window is. He's forgotten to change the reel. I call up.

"Hey!"

Nothing.

I think he's asleep again, so I walk out and find a door that says Staff Only and go in. It leads to the projection room, where the man snores quietly, leaning back in his chair and against the wall at his side.

"Sir?" I ask.

"Oh no!" he shouts at himself. "Not again!"

He's visibly upset, rushing around to get the new reel, castigating himself and apologizing.

"It's okay," I tell him, "calm down," but he won't have any of it.

He tells me over and over again. "Don't worry, son, you'll have your money back and I'll even give you a showing for free. Your choice." He continues on fervently. "Any movie you want."

I accept. I have no other option.

He rushes forward and says, "Now if you hurry down, you'll be there in time not to miss anything."

Before I head back to the theater, I feel compelled to introduce myself. I say, "My name's Ed Kennedy," and hold out my hand.

He stops and shakes it, looking into my face. "Yes, I know who you are." Momentarily, he forgets about the reel and looks me directly in the eye with total friendliness. "I was told you were coming."

He carries on with his work again now.

I stand there.

This keeps getting better and better.

I watch the rest of the movie and tell myself, *I'm not walking out of here until I find out who informed the old man I'd be coming.*

"Enjoy that?" he asks as I come out, but I don't allow him any room for that kind of discussion.

I say, "Who told you I was coming?"

He tries to shrug away.

"No." He's almost panicking. "I can't." He's moving off now. "I promised them, and they were such nice fellows. . . ."

I pull him back now to face me. "Who?"

He appears even older now, inspecting his shoes and the carpet.

"Was it two men?" I ask.

He looks at me like yes.

"Daryl and Keith?"

"Who?"

I try another angle. "Did they eat your popcorn?"

Again a yes.

"It was Daryl and Keith," I confirm. The greedy bastards. "They didn't hurt you, did they?"

"Oh no. No, they were very nice. Genial. They came in about a month ago and watched *Mister Roberts*. Before they left they told me a guy named Ed Kennedy would be coming and that you'd get a delivery when you're finished."

"And when am I finished?"

He holds out his hands. "They told me *you'd* know." His face tilts, almost in sorrow. "*Are* you finished?"

I shake my head. "No, it doesn't feel like it." I look away and back at him. "I have to do something for you. Something good, I'd say, in your case."

"Why?"

I almost tell him I don't know, but I refuse to lie. "Because you need it."

Does he need a good turnout like Father O'Reilly?

I doubt it. Not twice.

"Maybe"—he comes closer—"you'll finish when you come back to see that free movie."

"All right," I agree.

"You can bring your girlfriend," he suggests. "You got a girl, Ed?"

I indulge the moment.

"Yes," I say. "I got a girl."

"Well, bring her along." He rubs his hands together. "Nothing like just you and your girl in front of the big screen." A mischievous laugh jumbles from his mouth now. "I used to love bringing the girls here myself when I was a kid. That's why I bought this place when I retired from building."

"Did you ever make any money out of it?"

"Oh, Christ no, I don't need it. I just like putting them on, watching them, sleeping a bit. The wife says if it keeps me out of strife, why not?"

"Fair enough."

"So when you think you'll make it back?"

"Tomorrow, maybe."

He gives me a catalog the size of an encyclopedia to look through and suggest a movie, but I don't need it.

"No, thanks," I explain to him. "I know what I want."

"Really? Already?"

I nod. *"Cool Hand Luke."*

He rubs his hands together again and grins. "Lovely choice. A great film. Paul Newman's outstanding, and George Kennedy, your namesake—unforgettable. Seven-thirty tomorrow?"

"Beautiful."

"Great, I'll see you and your girl tomorrow then. What's her name, this girl of yours?"

"Audrey."

"Ah, lovely."

I'm about to leave when I realize I have no idea of this man's name.

He apologizes. "Oh, I'm very sorry, Ed. My name's Bernie. Bernie Price."

"Well, nice to meet you, Bernie." I make my way out.

"Same here," he says. "I'm glad you came."

"Me, too."

I step out into the hot air of late afternoon and summer.

Christmas Eve's on Thursday this year, which is when everyone's coming over for cards, turkey, and Marv's big kiss with the Doorman.

252

I ring Audrey about tomorrow and she cancels a date with the boyfriend. I think she could tell by the urgency in my voice that I needed her to come out with me.

As soon as we've sorted that out, I go for a walk to Milla's place, on Harrison Avenue.

She opens the door, and it seems frailty has overcome her in the past weeks. It's been a while since I've visited, and she glows upon my arrival. She stands crookedly at first but straightens when she sees my face.

"Jimmy!" Her voice soars. "Come in, come in!"

I do as she says, and when I enter the lounge room, I see she's been trying to read *Wuthering Heights* on her own, but she hasn't made it far.

"Oh yes," she says when she comes in with the tea. "I've been trying to read it without you, but it's not quite working."

"You want me to read you some now?"

"That would be nice." She smiles.

I love that old woman's smile. I love the patches of human wrinkles on her face and the joy in her eyes.

"Would you like to come to my place on Christmas Day?" I ask her.

She puts the tea down and answers. "Yes, of course, I'd love to. It's"—she lets herself look at me—"it's getting lonelier and lonelier without you, Jimmy."

"I know," I say. "I know."

I put my hand on hers and rub it gently. It's times like this I pray that souls can find each other after death. Milla and the real Jimmy. I pray for that.

"'Chapter six,'" I read. "'Mr. Hindley came home to the funeral; and—a thing that amazed us, and set the neighbors gossiping right and left—he brought a wife with him. . . .'"

253

Monday is a full day working in the city. I pick up a lot of people and seem able to weave nicely through the traffic for once. Often my goal as a cabdriver is simply not to annoy other drivers. Today it's working.

I'm home just before six, eat with the Doorman, and pick up Audrey around seven. I'm wearing my best jeans, my boots, and an old red shirt that's faded to orange.

Audrey answers the door, and I can smell perfume.

"You smell good," I say.

"Well, thank you, kind sir," and she allows me to kiss her hand. She wears a black skirt, nice tall shoes, and a sandy-colored blouse. It all matches well, and her hair is tied back into a plait with a few strands falling down the side.

We walk the street, and she has her arm linked to mine.

When we look at ourselves, we laugh. We can't help it.

"But you smell so good," I tell her again, "and you look great."

"So do you," she replies, and thinks a moment. "Even in that atrocious shirt."

I look down.

"I know, it's a shocker, isn't it?"

But Audrey doesn't mind. She almost skips or dances as she walks, and she says, "So what movie are we seeing?"

I try to hide my look of self-congratulation because I know it's a favorite of hers. *"Cool Hand Luke."*

She stops, and her expression reaches such a point of beauty that I nearly cry. "You've outdone yourself, Ed." The last time I heard that phrase was Marv speaking to Margaret, the waitress. This time it isn't sarcastic.

"Thank you," I reply, and we keep walking. We turn onto Bell

Street, and Audrey's arm is still linked with mine. I wish the cinema was further away.

"Here they are!" says Bernie Price when we arrive. He's excited. I'm actually surprised he's not asleep.

"Bernie," I say politely. "This is Audrey O'Neill."

"The pleasure's mine, Audrey." Bernie grins. When she goes to the bathroom, he pulls me aside excitedly and whispers, "Well, she's a bit of all right, isn't she, Ed?"

"She is," I agree. "She certainly is."

I buy the stale popcorn, or at least try (because Bernie, in his words, won't have it), and we go through and sit down near where I watched from yesterday.

He's given us a ticket each.

Coool Hand Luke: 7:30 p.m.

"Has your *cool* got three *o's*?" Audrey inquires.

I look down at it, amused. It has and it seems perfect for this night.

We sit and wait, and soon there's a knocking from above, at the projection window. We hear a muffled voice. "You two ready?"

"Ready!" we both call back, and turn again toward the screen.

The movie begins.

I hope as we watch that Bernie's up there, happy, remembering what it was like when he came here himself at my age.

I hope he still believes that Audrey really is my girl as he looks at the two figures sitting in front of the big screen—just two silhouettes.

This message is at the back of me.

It's delivered, but I don't see the look on Bernie's face. I try to catch it in the people on the screen.

Yes, I hope Bernie's happy.

I hope he remembers well.

Audrey lightly hums with the music on-screen, and at this moment she's my girl. I can make myself believe it.

Tonight's for Bernie, but I also take a small piece of it for myself.

We've both seen this movie a few times. It's a definite favorite. We can almost speak the words with the characters in some places, but we never do. We only sit there and enjoy it. We enjoy the empty theater, and I enjoy Audrey. I love the fact that it's only her and me in here alone.

Just you and your girl, I hear Bernie say from yesterday, and I realize that Bernie really deserves more than sitting up in the projection room tonight. I whisper to Audrey.

"Would you mind if I ask Bernie to come down and sit with us?"

She answers as I expect. "Not at all."

I climb over her legs and walk out up to the projection room. Bernie's asleep up there, but I wake him gently with my hand.

"Bernie?" I ask.

"Oh—yes, Ed?" He pulls himself from his tiredness.

"Audrey and I . . . ," I say, "we were wondering if you'd like to come down and watch the movie with us."

He protests, sitting forward. "Oh no, Ed, I could never do that. Never! I've got a lot to do here, and you young folks should be alone down there. You know," he says, "to get up to some mischief."

"Come on, Bernie," I say. "We'd love to have you."

"No, no, no." He's adamant. "I can't."

After another minute or so of arguing, I give up and head back down to the cinema. When I sit next to Audrey again she asks where he is.

"He didn't want to interrupt us," I tell her, but as I make myself comfortable in my seat, the back door opens and Bernie stands there in the light. He walks slowly down toward us and sits on the other side of Audrey.

"Glad you could make it," she whispers.

Bernie looks across at both of us. "Thank you." His exhausted eyes blink with gratitude, and he faces the screen, alive.

Maybe fifteen minutes later, Audrey finds my hand on the armrest. She slips her fingers onto mine and takes them. When she softly squeezes me I look across and discover that she holds Bernie's hand as well. Sometimes Audrey's friendship is enough. Sometimes she knows exactly what to do.

Her timing can be perfect.

Everything's going fine until the reel needs to be changed.

Bernie's asleep again. We wake him.

"Bernie," says Audrey quietly. She shakes him a little.

When he wakes up, he jumps from his chair and shouts, "The reel!" He moves quickly toward the aisle, and when I turn to look up at the projection room, I notice.

There's already someone in there.

"Hey, Audrey," I say. "Look," and we both stand and fix our eyes on the window. "There's someone up in the room." It feels like the air holds its breath around us until I finally get moving. I push past and head for the aisle.

At first Audrey doesn't know what to do, but soon I hear her feet behind me. I run up the aisle with my eyes gripped to the shadow in the projection room. It sees us, and its movements quicken accordingly. It exits the room almost frantically when we're halfway to the cinema door.

Out in the foyer, I can smell tension among the stale popcorn and carpet. The smell of someone been and gone. I head for the Staff Only door. Audrey's right behind me.

When we get to the room, the first thing I see is Bernie's shaking hands.

Shock flows down his face.

Across his lips to his throat.

"Bernie?" I ask. "Bernie?"

"He gave me an awful surprise," he says. "Nearly knocked me over as he was running out." He sits down. "I'm fine, Ed." Soon he points over at a pile of reels.

"What?" says Audrey. "What is it?"

"The one on top," Bernie answers. "That isn't one of mine."

He goes over and picks it up. He studies it. There's a small label on it with scuffed lettering. It says one word: *Ed.*

"Should we put it on?"

I remain still for a while but answer yes.

"You better get down to the theater," Bernie suggests. "You'll see it much better from there."

Before I go, I ask a question I have a feeling Bernie can answer.

"Why, Bernie?" I ask. "Why do they keep doing this to me?"

But Bernie only laughs.

He says, "You still don't understand, Ed, do you?"

"Understand what?"

He looks up at me and takes his time. "They do it because they can." The voice is tired but true. Determined. "It's all been worked out long ago. At least a year."

"Did they tell you that?"

258

"Yes."

"In those words?"

"Yes."

We stand there a good few minutes, thinking, till Bernie dismisses us. "Come on," he says, "you kids get back down there. I'll have this reel up and running in a minute."

Back in the foyer, I lean against the door, and Audrey speaks.

"Is it always like this?"

"Pretty much," I answer, and she can only shake her head and stay silent. "We better go," I tell her, and after a few attempts, I convince her to go back into the cinema. "It's nearly over," I say, and for some reason I assume Audrey thinks I'm talking about the movie.

But me?

I don't think about movies anymore.

I don't think about anything.

Except cards.

Except aces.

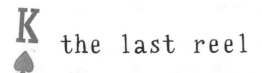 the last reel

The screen is still blank as we walk down the aisle.

When it comes alive, the scene is dark and I see the feet of some young men. They're walking.

Ahead, they approach a lone figure on the street.

It's a street of *this* town.

The figure is also of this town.

I stop walking.

Immediately.

Audrey goes a little further until she turns and sees me with my eyes transfixed on the screen.

I only point at first.

Then I say, "That's me there, Audrey."

On the screen, we watch the footage of the Rose boys and their friends leaping onto me and mauling me on the street.

Standing in the aisle, I feel the scars on my face.

My fingers turn and burn on my healing skin.

"That's me," I say again. It's a whisper this time, and next to me, Audrey's eyes collapse and cry in the dark, dark theater.

The next scene shows me walking out of the library, carrying all those books. After that it's the lights on Glory Road. It's just a shot of them alone at night—the power and the glory. There's darkness, until they flick on and glow through the theater. Next is the scene of the front-porch cyclone, silent. I see my mother delivering her painful words, almost gouging my face with them, until slowly I walk away, nearly right into the camera. We watch me walking toward the Bell Street Cinema.

The last thing we see are some words written directly on the reel. They say: *Trying times for Ed Kennedy. Well done, Ed. Time to move on.*

And it's black again.

All black.

I still can't move my feet. Audrey attempts to pull me along, but there's almost no point. I stand motionless, staring at the screen.

"Let's get to our seats," she says, and I can hear the worry in her voice. "I think you'd better sit down, Ed."

Slowly, I lift one foot.

Then the other.

"Can I play the movie again?" Bernie calls down.

Audrey looks at me with asking eyes.

I lift my head slightly and bring it down to agree.

"Yes, Bernie!" To me, she says, "Good idea. It'll take your mind off it."

For a few seconds, I consider running back out and searching the whole place for whoever's been here. I want to ask Bernie if it was Daryl and Keith again. I want to know why Bernie's been told what he has and why they keep *me* in the dark.

Yet I know it's futile.

They do it because they can.

Those words lap me a few times, and I know that this is exactly where I'm supposed to be. For spades, this is the final trial I need to dig myself out of. We have to stay.

When the screen blinks on, I'm awaiting the famous scene in *Cool Hand Luke* when Luke finally breaks and everyone deserts him. *"Where are you now?"* I wait for him to scream very soon from his bunk.

As we walk back to our seats, Luke begins dragging himself across the screen with complete, desolate desperation. He turns and falls near his bunk. "Where are you now?" he says quietly.

Where are you now? I ask, and I turn, expecting to see a figure standing somewhere in the theater. I anticipate some footsteps scattering across the floor behind us. I jerk my head around to look. There are people everywhere, but nowhere. In each black space I find, I think I locate someone, but each time, the darkness thickens and that's all there is. Darkness.

"What is it, Ed?" Audrey asks.

"They're here," I answer, although I can't be sure of anything. This whole experience has taught me that. "They *have* to be," but as my eyes scour the whole theater I see nothing. If they're here, I can't see them.

Soon, I realize.

I realize when we get back to our seats that they're not here at all now—but they've been.

They've been here all right because sitting on my seat, in my place, is the Ace of Hearts.

"Where are you now?" screams Luke on the screen, and it's my heartbeat that answers. It shakes the inside of me like the giant clanging of a bell. It swells and ignites as I swallow.

I pick the card up and hold it in my hand.

"Hearts," I whisper.

That's where I am.

I'm tempted to read what's on the card, but I manage to watch the rest of the movie just holding it.

I watch the movie.

I watch Audrey and enjoy the moment, or at least what's left of it.

In my hand, I can almost feel the pulse of the heart card as it sits there and waits.

part four: **The Music of Hearts**

The Suitcase
Cat Ballou
Roman Holiday

A the music of hearts

There's music in my head, and it's the color of red and black.

It's the morning after.

The morning after the Ace of Hearts.

I feel it like a hangover.

After making sure Bernie was okay (we left him asleep in the projection room), we walked back up onto Bell Street and into the night. It was warm and humid, and the only person around was a young man facing the other way. He was sitting on an old, scabby bench.

At first, I was lost in the thoughts of all that had happened, and when I turned around to see him again, he was gone.

He'd vanished.

Audrey's voice asked a question, but I didn't hear it. It was on the periphery of the wide blast of noise inside my ears. At first I wondered what it was, but then, without question, I was sure. It was red hearts and black words. Beating.

The sound of hearts.

Without question, I knew that the young man back there was the one sent to the theater.

Maybe he could have led me to the person sending the cards.

Maybe many things.

As we walked on, the giant noise inside my ears subsided. Footsteps and Audrey's voice became clear again.

Now it's morning and I hear that sound again.

The card is on the floor.

The Doorman lies next to it.

I shut my eyes, but everything's red and black.

This is the last card, I tell myself, but I roll over into sleep again, despite the music of hearts beating in my bed.

I dream of running.

In a car.

With the Doorman in the front seat.

That probably comes from smelling him next to my bed.

It's a beautiful dream, like the end of an American movie, where the protagonist and his girl drive off into the rest of the world.

Except I drive alone.

No girl.

Just me and the Doorman.

The tragedy is that as I sleep, I believe it. Waking up is a rude shock because I'm no longer on the open road. Instead, the Doorman's snoring and his back leg is stretched across the card on the floor. I couldn't get my hands on it now even if I wanted to. I don't like moving the Doorman when he's asleep.

In my drawer, the other cards wait now for the last one.

Each is complete in its own right.

Just one more, I think, and I get to my knees on the bed, bury-ing my head deep in the pillow.

I don't pray, but I come close.

When I get up, I shift the Doorman and read the card again. The black lettering is the same as all the other words I've been given. This time they say the following titles:

The Suitcase
Cat Ballou
Roman Holiday

I'm quite confident that they're all movie titles, though I haven't seen any of them. I recall that *The Suitcase* was a fairly recent one. It wouldn't have been on at the Bell Street Cinema, but I'm sure it got a run at one of those obscure yet popular the-aters in the city. I remember seeing some poster ads. It was a Spanish remake, I think—a comedy-gangster movie, full of hit men, bullets, and a suitcase full of stolen Swiss francs. The other two films are unknown to me, but I'm sure I know the man who can help.

I'm ready to begin, but in the few days leading up to Christmas I allow work to get in the way. It's always busy around this time, so I take on some extra shifts and drive a lot of nights. I keep the Ace of Hearts in my shirt pocket. It travels with me wherever I go, and I won't let go of it until this is finished.

But will it end with this? I ask myself. *Will* it *let go of me?* Already, I know that all of this will stay with me forever. It'll haunt me, but I also fear it will make me feel grateful. I say *fear* because at times I really don't want this to be a fond memory until it's over. I also fear that nothing really ends at the end. Things just keep going as long as memory can wield its ax, always finding a soft part in your mind to cut through and enter.

For the first time in years, I give out Christmas cards.

The only difference is that I don't give out cards with little Santas or Christmas trees on them. I find a few old packs of playing cards and pull out all the aces. I write a short note on the card for each place I've visited, stick it in a small envelope, and write *Merry Christmas from Ed.* Even for the Rose boys.

It's before a night shift that I drive around and deliver them, and at most places I escape unnoticed. It's at Sophie's that I'm seen, and I must confess, I kind of wanted her to find me.

For some reason, there's something special in me for Sophie. Maybe a part of me loves her because she's the eternal also-ran, a lot like me. But I also know it's more than that.

She's beautiful.

In the way she is.

When I put the envelope in her letter box, I turn and walk purposefully away, just like everywhere else, but her voice finds me from up above, at her window.

"Ed?" she calls down.

When I turn back around, she calls again for me to wait, and she's soon out the front door. She wears a white T-shirt and a pair of small blue running shorts. Her hair's tied back, but her fringe floats to her face.

"Just brought you a card," I say, "for Christmas." A sudden stupidity overcomes me, and I feel awkward standing there on her driveway.

She opens the envelope and reads the card.

On hers, I wrote something extra below the diamond.

You've got beauty, I wrote, and I see her eyes melt a little as she reads it. It's what I said to her on the day of the bare feet and the blood at the athletic field.

"Thank you, Ed," she says, and she looks intently at the card. "I've never been given a card like this before."

"They were all out of Santas and Christmas trees," I answer.

It feels strange delivering the cards to these people. They'll never really know what it means and in some cases will have no idea who in the hell this Ed person is. In the end, I decide it doesn't matter, and Sophie and I say our goodbyes.

"Ed?" she asks.

I'm in the cab now and wind down the window. "Sophie?"

"Could you?" Her voice steps politely from her mouth. "Could you tell me what I can give to you? You've given me so much."

"I've given you nothing," I tell her.

But she knows me well enough.

Nothing was an empty shoe box, but we'd never trade it.

We both know.

The steering wheel's warm as I drive off.

The last card I deliver is to Father O'Reilly, who seems to be having a party at his place for all the hopeless cases on his street. Those guys who tried to get my jacket and my nonexistent money and cigarettes are there, all eating sausage sandwiches with lots of sauce and onions.

"Hey, look." One points me out. I think it's Joe. "It's Ed!" He tries to find the father. "Hey, Father!" he calls, spitting out half his sandwich with the words. "Ed's here!"

Father O'Reilly comes hurrying over and says, "And here he is — the man who made all the difference to the year. I've been trying to call you."

269

"I've been a bit busy, Father."

"Ah yes." He nods. "Your mission." He pulls me aside and says, "Look, I just want to thank you again, Ed."

I know I should feel good about that, but I don't. "I'm not here to be thanked, Father. I was just bringing you a lousy Christmas card."

"Well, I thank you anyway, boy."

I'm frustrated because of my final ace.

Hearts, of all things to be last.

I expected spades.

I got hearts, and for some reason, this feels the most dangerous of them all.

People die of broken hearts. They have heart attacks. And it's the heart that hurts most when things go wrong and fall apart.

When I walk back onto the street, the father intuits my apprehension. He says, "It's still not over, is it?" He knows he was just one piece of what I have to do. One message of the given hand.

"No, Father," I reply. "It's not over."

"You'll be all right," he says to me.

"No," I tell him, "I won't. I won't be okay just for the sake of it. Not anymore."

It's true.

If I'm ever going to be okay, I'll have to earn it.

The card still sits in my pocket as I wish the father a merry Christmas and move on into the evening. I feel the Ace of Hearts sway inside my pocket. It leans forward, trying to get closer to the air and the world I have to face.

"Where to?" I ask my first pickup the next day, but I can't hear the answer. All I can hear is the sound of the hearts again, shouting and screaming and beating through my ears.

Faster.

Faster.

There is no engine.

There's no ticktock of the blinker, no voice of the customer, and no sizzle of the traffic. Only hearts.

In my pocket.

In my ears.

In my pants.

On my skin. On my breath.

They're in the inside of the inside of me.

"Just hearts," I say, "everywhere," but my customer has no idea what I'm talking about.

"Here'll do," she says.

She's about forty and wears deodorant that smells like sweet smoke and makeup the color of roses. When she hands me the money, she speaks, looking at me in the mirror.

"Merry Christmas," she says.

Her voice sounds like hearts.

2
♥ the kiss, the grave, the fire

I've bought everything I need to buy. More alcohol than food, of course, and by the time everyone shows up for Christmas Eve, my shack smells like turkey, coleslaw, and, of course, the

271

Doorman. For a while, the turkey overpowers him, but the smell of that dog can get to anything.

First to show up is Audrey.

She brings a bottle and some biscuits she's made.

"Sorry, Ed," she tells me as she comes in. "I can't stay too long." She kisses me on the cheek. "Simon's got this thing on with his mates and he wants me to go."

"Do *you* want to go?" I ask, though I know she does. Why would you prefer to stay with three positively pointless blokes and a filthy dog? She'd be crazy to stay with us.

Audrey answers. "Of course. You know I wouldn't do anything I don't want to."

"That's true," I reply. It is.

We start to drink as Ritchie comes in next. We hear his bike from the top of the street, and when he pulls in, he calls out for us to open the door for him. He carries in a big cooler stocked with prawns, salmon, and sliced lemons.

"Not bad, huh?" He drops it. "The least I could do."

"How'd you get it here?" I ask.

"What?"

"The cooler? You know, with the bike?"

"Oh—I strapped it on back. I was practically standing up the whole way. The cooler took up half my seat." Ritchie winks at us, generously. "It was worth it, though." Half his dole check would have gone into the contents of that cooler.

Now we wait.

For Marv.

"I bet he doesn't show up," Ritchie says once he's settled in. His hand feels at the scratchy whiskers on his face, and his muddy hair is as unwashed and coarse as ever. Amusement is his overriding expression. He's looking forward to this. Sipping a beer and sitting on the couch, he uses the Doorman as a footstool. He's lazy and lanky, Ritchie, lying there with his feet extended in comfort. Somehow, he looks gracious.

"Oh, he's showing up all right," I affirm. "If he doesn't, I'll drag the Doorman to his doorstep and make him kiss him right there and then." I put down my drink. "I haven't looked forward to Christmas like this for years."

"Me, too," Ritchie replies. He can barely wait.

"Plus, it's a free feed," I continue. "Marv might have forty grand in the bank but he still can't keep himself from freeloading. Believe me. He'll come."

"The tight arse," Ritchie affirms. This is Christmas spirit in its purest form.

"Should we call him?" Audrey suggests.

"No. Let him come to us," Ritchie says with a smirk, and I can smell it. This is going to be great. He looks down at the dog and says, "You all pumped up for the big one, Doorman?" The Doorman looks up as if to say, *Just what the hell are you on about, mate?* No one's told him about what's still to come tonight. The poor dog. Nobody asked *him* if it was okay.

Finally, Marv walks in, empty-handed.

"Merry Christmas," he says.

"Yeah, yeah," I say. "Same to you." I point now to his empty hands. "Jeez, you're a generous bastard, aren't you?"

But I know how Marv thinks.

He's decided that if he has to kiss the Doorman, that's more than enough for him to do this year. I can also tell he's still clinging to a faint hope that we all might have forgotten.

Ritchie destroys all notions of that immediately.

He stands up and says, "Well, Marv?" He's grinning.

"Well what?"

"You know," Audrey chimes in.

"No," Marv persists, "I don't."

"Now, don't you give me the shits." Ritchie lays down the law. "You know it. We know it." He's enjoying this. I almost expect him to rub his hands together with delight. "Marv," he announces, "you will kiss this dog." He motions to the Doorman. "And when you kiss him, you're going to like it. You're going to do it with a big bloody smile on your face or else we'll make you do it again, and again, and—"

"All right!" Marv snarls. He reminds me of a little kid not getting his own way. "On top of the head, right?"

"Ohh no," Ritchie asserts. He stands up, relishing every minute of this. "I believe the agreement was that you'd kiss him right on the lips, and that's just"—he points his finger at Marv—"where you're going to do it."

The Doorman looks up.

He looks uneasy as we all watch him.

"You poor fella," Ritchie states.

Marv sulks. "I know."

"Not you," Ritchie charges. "Him!" And he throws his head toward the dog.

"All right," Audrey says. "No messing about now." She hands me my camera. "Off you go, Marv. He's all yours."

With the weight of the world on his shoulders, Marv bends down in horror and finally brings himself to get close to the Doorman's face. The Doorman looks nervous enough to cry— black and gold fur and watery eyes.

"Does he have to have his tongue out like that?" Marv asks me.

"He's a dog," I say. "What more do you want from him?"

Copiously disgruntled, Marv eventually does it. He leans in and kisses the Doorman on the snout, just long enough for me to take the photo and for Audrey and Ritchie to cheer, clap, and crack up.

"That wasn't so hard now, was it?" Ritchie says, but Marv's gone straight to the bathroom.

The poor Doorman.

I give him a kiss myself, on the forehead, and a prime piece of turkey.

Thanks, Ed. He smiles.

The Doorman's got a nice smile.

We manage to get Marv to loosen up and laugh a bit later, though he still complains of tasting the Doorman on his lips.

We all eat and drink and play some cards until a knock at the door brings the boyfriend in. He drinks with us awhile and eats some prawns. He's a nice guy, I decide, but I can tell by looking. Audrey doesn't love him.

I guess that's the point.

After Audrey's gone, we decide not to cry in our beer. Ritchie, Marv, and I eat up, drink up, and go wandering through town. There's a bonfire lighting up the top of Main Street, and that's the way we head.

For a while, it's hard to walk straight, but by the time we make it, we're all pretty sober.

It's a good night.

People dancing.

Loud talking.

A few people fighting.

It's always the way at Christmas. The whole year's tension comes to a head.

At the fire, I see Angie Carusso and her kids, or rather, they come over to me.

There's a tap on my leg and when I look down I see one of her boys. The one that always cries.

"Hey, mister?" he says.

When I turn around, I see Angie Carusso holding an ice cream. She offers it to me and says, "Merry Christmas, Ed." I take it.

"Thanks," I say. "Just what I needed."

"Sometimes we all do." Her happiness at being able to return a small favor is obvious.

I take a bite and ask, "So how are you, Angie?"

"Ah . . ." She looks at the kids and now back at me. "I'm surviving, Ed. Sometimes that's enough." She recalls something. "Thanks for the card, by the way." Slowly, Angie begins to move on.

"No worries," I call after her. "Enjoy the night."

"Enjoy the ice cream," she answers. She walks alongside the fire.

"What was all that about?" asks Marv.

"Just a girl I know."

I've never been given an ice cream for Christmas before.

Watching the fire, I let the sweet cool of it soak into my lips.

Behind me, I hear a father talking to his son.

"Do that again," he says, "and I'll kick your arse so hard you'll fall into the fire." His voice sweetens sardonically. "And we wouldn't want that now, would we? Santa won't be too impressed with *that,* will he now? No, he won't."

Marv, Ritchie, and I all enjoy hearing that.

"Ahhh," Ritchie sighs happily. "This is what Christmas is all about."

We've all heard that from our fathers. At least once.

I think of my own father, dead and buried. My first Christmas without him.

"Merry Christmas, Dad," I say, and I make sure to keep my eyes out of the fire.

The ice cream melts to my fingers.

As the night moves on and blurs toward Christmas morning, Marv, Ritchie, and I become separated. The crowd's thick, and once we lose each other, it's all over.

I go back through town and visit my father's grave and stay there a long time. From the cemetery, I see a small glow that's the fire, and I sit there, looking at the gravestone with my father's name on it.

I cried at his funeral.

I let the tears trample my face in complete silence, guilty that I couldn't even summon the courage to speak about him. I knew everyone there was only thinking about what a drunk he was, while I was remembering the other things as well.

"He was a gentleman," I whisper now.

If only I could have said that on the day, I think, because my father never had a bad word for anybody or a true act of unkindness. Certainly, he never achieved much, and he disappointed my mother with broken promises, but I don't think he deserved not a word from anyone in his family that day.

"I'm sorry," I tell him now as I get up to leave. "I'm so sorry, Dad."

I walk away, afraid.

Afraid because I don't want my own funeral to be that forlorn and empty.

I want words at my funeral.

But I guess that means you need life in your life.

Walking now.

Just walking.

When I make it home, I find Marv asleep in the backseat of his car and Ritchie sitting on my porch. His legs are out straight, and he leans back against the fibro. On closer inspection, I find that Ritchie's also asleep. I tug at his sleeve.

"Ritchie," I whisper. "Wake up."

His eyes slap open.

"What?" he says, almost in panic. "What?"

"You're asleep on my porch," I tell him. "You better get home."

He shakes himself awake now, looks at the half-moon, and says, "I left my keys on your kitchen table."

"Come on." I drop my hand, he takes it, and I help him up.

Inside, I find it's a few minutes past three o'clock.

Ritchie's fingers curl around the keys.

"You want anything?" I ask. "Drink, food, coffee?"

"No, thanks."

But he doesn't leave, either.

For a moment, we stand awkwardly, until finally Ritchie looks just past me and says, "I don't feel like going home tonight, Ed."

I catch a dent of sadness in his eyes, but it disappears immediately as Ritchie quickly smooths it over. He only looks at the keys now, and I wonder what lurks beneath the cool, calm exterior of my friend. I wonder tiredly what could ever bother someone as laid-back as Ritchie.

His eyes drag themselves up again to mine.

"Sure," I tell him. "Stay here the night."

Ritchie sits down at the table.

"Thanks, Ed," he says. "Hey, Doorman."

The Doorman has walked into the kitchen as I go out to get Marv.

For a moment I consider leaving him out in the car, but Christmas spirit can even make its way to someone like me.

I attempt to knock on the window, but my hand goes right through.

Of course.

There is no window.

Marv *still* hasn't had it fixed since the bungled bank robbery. I think he got a quote for it, but the guy said the window would end up being worth more than the car.

He sleeps with his head twisted in his hands, and the mosquitoes are queuing up for his blood.

The front door's unlocked, so I open it and matter-of-factly blow the horn.

"Christ!" Marv shrieks.

"Come inside," I tell him. Soon after, I hear the car door open and slam and the scuffing of his feet behind me.

Ritchie gets the couch, Marv takes my bed, and I decide to stay in the kitchen. I tell Marv I wouldn't have slept anyway, and he's quite gracious in accepting the bed.

"Thanks, Ed."

Before he goes in, I take my opportunity, walk inside the room, and retrieve all the cards from the drawer next to the bed. The Tatupu stone is also there.

In the kitchen, I go through them, reading them all again, though the fatigue in my eyes makes the words swap and turn and juggle. I feel eroded.

In moments of awakeness, I remember the diamonds, relive the clubs, and even smile about the spades.

I worry about the hearts.

I don't want to sleep in case I dream them.

3 ♥ the casual suit

Tradition can be a dirty word, especially around Christmas.

Families all over the globe get together and enjoy each other's company for all of a few minutes. For an hour, they endure each other. After that, they just manage to stomach each other.

I go over to Ma's place after an uneventful morning with Ritchie and Marv. All we did was eat leftovers from the night before and play a few games of Annoyance. It wasn't the same without Audrey, and it didn't take long for us to pack up and for the other two to leave.

The usual agreement with my family is for a twelve o'clock meeting time at Ma's place.

My sisters are there with their kids and husbands, and Tommy's shown up with a stunning girl he's managed to pick up at university.

"This is Ingrid," he introduces her, and I must say, Ingrid is calendar-worthy. She has long brown hair, a lovely tanned face, and a body I'd let myself dissolve in.

"Nice to meet you," she says. Lovely voice, too. "I've heard a lot about you, Ed." She's lying, of course, and I decide not to go along with it. This year I simply don't have the strength.

I say, "No you haven't, Ingrid," but I remain pleasant as I say it. I'm almost shy. She's too beautiful to get annoyed with. Beautiful girls get away with murder.

"Oh, *you're* here," says Ma when she sees me.

"Merry Christmas, Ma!" I shout excitedly, and I'm sure everyone picks up on the sarcasm in my voice.

We eat.

We give presents.

I give Leigh's and Katherine's kids a hundred airplane rides and piggybacks, or at least until I can't stand up anymore.

I also catch Tommy with his hands all over Ingrid in the lounge room. Right near the famous cedar coffee table.

"Shit—sorry," and I back away from the room.

Good luck to him.

By quarter to four, it's time to go and pick up Milla. I kiss my sisters, shake the hands of my brothers-in-law, and say a final goodbye to the kids.

"Last to get here, first to leave," says Ma, blowing out some cigarette smoke. She smokes a lot at Christmas. "And he lives the closest," which nearly makes me throw my temper from my skin and hurl it at her.

Cheating on Dad, I think. *Insulting me at every turn.*

I want so much to verbally abuse this woman standing there in the kitchen, sucking in smoke, and pouring it out from her lungs.

Instead, I look right at her.

I speak through the warm mist.

"The smoking makes you ugly," I say, and I walk out, leaving her stranded among the haze.

*   *   *

On the front lawn as I leave, I'm called back twice. First by Tommy, then Ma.

Tommy comes out and says, "You doing all right, Ed?"

I walk back. "I'm doing fine, Tommy. It's been a crazy year but I'm doing fine. You?"

We sit on the front steps, which are half in shadow, half in the sun. As it happens, I sit in the darkness and Tommy sits in the light. Quite symbolic, really.

It's the first time I've felt comfortable all day as my brother and I talk and answer each other's brief questions.

"University okay?"

"Yeah, the marks have been good. Better than I hoped."

"And Ingrid?"

There's a silence before we can't contain it anymore. It breaks between us and we both laugh. It feels very boyish but I'm congratulating him, and Tommy's congratulating himself.

"She's not bad," he says, and genuinely I tell my brother that I'm proud of him—and not for Ingrid. Ingrid means nothing in comparison to what I'm talking about.

I say, "Good for you, Tommy," plant my hand on his back, and stand up. "Good luck."

As I walk down the steps, he says, "I'll call you sometime. We'll get together."

But again, I can't go along with it. I turn and speak with a quietness that surprises even me. I say, "I doubt you will, Tommy," and it feels good. It feels nice to emerge from the lies.

Tommy agrees.

He says, "You're right, Ed."

We're still brothers, and who knows? Maybe one day. One day, I feel certain, we'll get together and remember and tell and speak many things. Things bigger than university and Ingrid.

Just not soon.

For now, I walk across the lawn and say, "Bye, Tommy, thanks for coming out," and I'm satisfied with just one thing.

I'd wanted to stay on that porch with him until the sun shone bright on both of us, but I didn't. I stood up and walked down the steps. I'd rather chase the sun than wait for it.

As Tommy goes in and I leave again, Ma comes out.

"Ed!" she calls.

I face her.

She walks closer and says, "Merry Christmas, all right?"

"Same to you." Then I add, "It's the person, Ma, not the place. If you left here, you'd have been the same anywhere else." It's truth enough, but I can't stop now. "If I ever leave this place"— I swallow—"I'll make sure I'm better *here* first."

"Okay, Ed." She's stunned, and I feel sorry for the woman standing on the front porch of a poor street in an ordinary town. "That sounds fair."

"See you later, Ma."

I'm gone.

That had to be done.

I drop in at home for a quick drink and go to Milla's. When I get there, she's waiting eagerly, wearing a light blue summer dress and holding a present. She also holds an excitement across her face.

"For you, Jimmy," she says, handing me the big, flat box.

I feel bad because I don't have a gift for her. "I'm sorry," I begin to say, but she shuts me up quickly with a wave of her hand.

"It's enough that you came back for me," she says. "Are you going to open it?"

"No, I'll wait," and I offer the old lady my arm. She takes it and we leave her house, heading over to my place. I ask if we should get a cab, but she's happy to walk, and halfway there, I'm not sure if she's going to make it. She coughs hard and struggles for air. I imagine myself having to carry her. She makes it, though, and I give her some wine when we get there.

"Thank you, Jimmy," she says, but she sinks into the armchair and falls asleep almost straightaway.

As she remains there, I come back a few times to check she's still alive, but I can always hear her breathing.

In the end, I sit in the lounge room with her as the day dies outside the window.

When she wakes up, we eat turkey from last night and some bean salad.

"Marvelous, Jimmy." The old lady beams. "Just marvelous." Her smile crackles.

In normal circumstances, I'd prefer to shoot someone who uses the word *marvelous,* but it suits Milla down to the ground. She wipes her mouth and mutters "Marvelous" several times, and I feel like Christmas is complete.

"Now." She slaps the arms of the chair. She seems much more alive now that she's slept a little. "Will you open your present, Jimmy?"

I give in.

"Of course."

I go over to the gift-wrapped box and lift the lid. Inside is a casual black suit and an ocean blue shirt. It's probably the first and last suit anyone will ever buy me.

"You like?" she asks.

"It's great." I fall in love with it instantly, despite knowing I'll rarely, if ever, get a chance to wear it.

"Put it on, Jimmy."

"I'm going," I say. "I'm going." And once I've disappeared to the bedroom to put it on, I find an old pair of black shoes to match. The suit doesn't have big shoulders, which is a relief. I'm excited to get back out there to show her, but when I come out, Milla's asleep again.

So I sit.

In the suit.

When she wakes up, the old lady says, "Oh, that's a *nice* suit, Jimmy." She even touches it to feel the fabric. "Where'd you get it from?"

I stand a moment, confused, before realizing that she's completely forgotten. I give the old lady a kiss on the cheek.

"A beautiful woman gave it to me," I say.

The old lady's marvelous.

"That's lovely," she says.

"It is," I agree.

She's right.

After we've had coffee, I call a cab and go home with her. The driver's actually Simon, the boyfriend, earning some double time on Christmas Day.

Before I take Milla inside, I ask him to wait. It's laziness, I know, but I've got the money today and can afford the trip home.

"Well, thanks again, Jimmy," Milla says, and she walks shakily to the kitchen. She's so frail, yet so beautiful. "It's been a great day," she tells me, and I can't help but agree. It has. It hits me that all along I thought I was doing this old lady a favor by spending Christmas Day with her.

Walking out again in my casual black suit, I realize it's the opposite.

I'm the privileged one, and the old lady will always be marvelous.

"Back home?" the boyfriend asks me when I return to the cab.

"Yes please."

I sit in the front seat, and the boyfriend initiates conversation. He seems intent on discussing Audrey, though I wish he wouldn't.

He says, "So you and Audrey been friends for years, huh?"

I look at the dash. "Probably more than years."

He comes at me. "Do you love her?"

I'm taken aback by the frankness of his question, especially so early in the dialogue. I come to the conclusion that he knows it's only a short drive. He wants to maximize outcomes quickly, which is fair enough. He asks again. "Well?"

"Well what?"

"Now, don't start on me, Kennedy. Do you love her or not?"

"Well, what do you think?"

He rubs his chin and says nothing, so I continue.

I say, "Whether I love her isn't the question at all. Whether she loves you is what you want to know." My voice trounces him. I'm all over the poor guy. "Isn't it?"

"Well . . ." He trips about as he drives, and I see he deserves at least some form of an answer.

"She doesn't *want* to love you," I tell him. "She doesn't want to love anyone. She's had a rough life, Audrey. The only people she ever loved she hated." I get some flashbacks of when we were growing up. She was hurt a lot, and she vowed it wouldn't continue that way. She wouldn't let it.

The boyfriend says nothing. He's handsome, I decide. More

handsome than me. He has soft eyes and a solid jaw. The whiskers on his face give him that male-model look.

We're silent till we pull up back at my place, and the boyfriend speaks again. He says, "She loves *you,* Ed. . . ."

I look at him. "But she wants you."

And that's the problem.

"Here."

I pass him the money but he waves it away.

"On the house," he says, but I try again, and this time he takes it.

"Don't put it in the till," I suggest. "I think you've earned it for your own pocket today." We share a moment before I get out.

"Nice talking to you," I say, and we shake hands. "Merry Christmas to you, Simon."

I guess he's Simon now, not the boyfriend.

Once inside, I sleep on the couch in my casual black suit and the ocean blue shirt.

Merry Christmas, Ed.

4 ♥ to feel the fear

I work on Boxing Day and visit Bernie at the Bell Street Cinema the next day.

"Ed Kennedy!" he cries out when I get there. "Back for more, ay?"

"No," I tell him. "I need your help, Bernie."

Immediately he comes closer and asks, "What can I do for you?"

"Well, you know your movies, right?"

"Of course. You can watch anything you—"

"Shh—just tell me, Bernie. Tell me everything you know about these titles." I pull out the Ace of Hearts although I could easily recite them without it. "*The Suitcase, Cat Ballou,* and *Roman Holiday.*"

Bernie clicks into business straightaway. "*Roman Holiday* I have, but the other two I don't." He inundates me with facts. "*Roman Holiday* is widely considered one of the best movies starring Gregory Peck, made in 1953 and directed by William Wyler, of *Ben-Hur* fame. It was filmed with breathtaking beauty in Rome and was famous for the glorious performance of Audrey Hepburn, who Peck insisted have equal billing. He claimed that if she didn't, he would be a laughingstock—such was the strength of her performance. This was backed up when she pocketed an Oscar for her troubles. . . ."

He talks on at a very fast pace, but I rewind to one word that Bernie has spoken.

Audrey, I think.

"Audrey," I say.

"Yes." He looks at me, disoriented by my ignorance. "Yes, Audrey Hepburn. And she was absolutely marv—"

No, don't say marvelous, I beg. *That word belongs to Milla.*

"Audrey Hepburn!" I almost shout. "What can you tell me about the other two?"

"Well, I've got a catalog," Bernie explains. "It's even bigger than the one I showed you last time. It contains just about every movie ever released. Actors, directors, cinematographers, sound tracks, musical scores, the lot."

He brings back the thick book and offers it to me. First up, *Cat Ballou*. I read aloud as soon as I find the page.

"'Starring Lee Marvin in one of his most famous roles. . . .'" I stop because I've found it. I go back and read the name again. "'Lee *Marvin*.'"

Now I move on to *The Suitcase*.

As soon as I find it, I read the cast list and the director. The director of *The Suitcase* is someone called Pablo Sanchez. He and Ritchie share the same last name.

And I have my three addresses.

Ritchie. Marv. Audrey.

There's an express exhilaration that is quickly replaced by anxiety.

I hope the messages are good, I think, but something tells me this won't be easy. There must be good reason these three were left till last. As well as being my friends, they'll also be the most challenging messages I have to deliver. I can feel it.

I hold the card and drop the catalog book to the counter.

Bernie's concerned. "What is it, Ed?"

I look at him and say, "Wish me luck, Bernie. Wish me the heart to get through this."

He does.

Still holding the card, I walk out onto the street. Outside, I meet the darkness and uncertainty of what will come next.

I feel the fear, but I walk fast toward it.

The smell of street struggles to get its hands on me, but I shrug it off and walk on. Each time a shudder makes its way to my arms and legs, I walk harder, deciding if Audrey needs me, and Ritchie and Marv, I have to hurry.

Fear is the street.

Fear is every step.

The darkness grows heavier on the road and I begin.

To run.

My first instinct tells me to go straight to Audrey's.

I want to make it there as fast as possible to ease whatever problem she has. I don't even dare to contemplate the fact that I might need to perform something unpleasant.

Just get there, I tell myself, but then it's another instinct that takes control.

I walk on but pull the card up and hold it in front of my eyes. I check the order.

Ritchie. Marv. Audrey.

A strong feeling reaches out in front of me and drags with it a knowledge that I have to go in order. Audrey's last for a reason, and I know it. First up's Ritchie.

"Yes," I agree with my thoughts, and I keep walking hard. I make my way to Ritchie's place, on Bridge Street. I work out the quickest way there, and my feet move further and faster.

Am I hurrying so I can make it quicker to Audrey? I ask, but I give no answer.

I focus on Ritchie.

A vision of his face comes to me as I pass under the branches of a tree. I brush through the leaves and wipe him from my sight, hearing his voice and the constant remarks during cards. I remember his Christmas joy at Marv's kiss with the Doorman.

Ritchie, I wonder. *What message do I deliver to Ritchie?*

I'm nearly there now.

The corner of Bridge Street is up ahead.

My pulse goes into spasm and gains momentum.

As I round the bend I see Ritchie's place immediately. A question of shock stands beside me and breathes at my face.

I see the lights in Ritchie's kitchen and in the lounge room, but my path is distracted by one thought. It refuses to leave. *What do I do now?* it asks me.

Every other place was relatively easy because I didn't really know the people (excluding Ma—and when I was sitting in that Italian restaurant, I had no idea I was waiting for *her*), so there wasn't much choice. I just waited for the opportunity to arise. But with Ritchie, Marv, and Audrey, I know them all far too well to loiter around their houses. It's the last thing I would ever do.

Still, I weigh it up for close to a minute and eventually decide to cross the road and sit against an old oak tree to wait.

I'm there nearly an hour, and to be perfectly honest, not a whole lot's happening. I notice that Ritchie's folks are home from their holiday. (I saw his ma doing the dishes.)

It's getting late, and soon it's only the kitchen that's lit up. House lights across the whole street are being cut down at the knees, and all that's left are the streetlights.

In the Sanchez house, a lone figure has walked in and sits at the kitchen table.

I know, without question, that it's Ritchie.

For a moment, I consider going in, but before I get a chance to rise to my feet, I hear some people moving in my direction from down the street.

Soon there are two men standing above me.

They're eating pies.

One of them looks down and speaks at me. He looks at me with a kind of familiar, indifferent disdain and says, "We were

291

told we might find you here, Ed." He shakes his head and throws down a pie, obviously bought from a local service station. As it drops to the ground, he says, "You're a dead-set shocker, aren't you?"

I look up, completely lost for words.

"Well, Ed?" It's the other one talking now, and as ludicrous as it sounds, it's actually quite hard to recognize them without their balaclavas.

"Daryl?" I ask.

"Yes."

"Keith?"

"Correct."

Daryl sits down now and gives me the pie. "For old times' sake," he explains.

"Right," I reply, still in shock. "Thanks." Memories of their last visit start to hurry me. Crowded thoughts of blood, words, and the dirty kitchen floor. I have to ask it. "You're not going to . . ." It's still a little hard to speak.

"What?" says Keith this time, sitting at my other side. "Lean on you a little?"

"Well," I say, "yes."

As an act of good faith, Daryl opens the plastic wrapper of my pie and hands it back to me. "Oh no, Ed. No touch-ups today. Nothing of the sort." He allows a nostalgic laugh to exit his lips. He makes it sound like we're old war buddies or something. "Mind you, if you get smart on us . . ." He gets comfortable on the ground. He has pale skin and a face infested with fight scars, but he somehow still manages to be handsome. Keith, on the other hand, has a face bulleted with old acne, a pointy nose, and a crooked chin.

I look over at him and say, "Jesus, mate, I think I liked you better with the mask on." Daryl lets out a shot of laughter. Keith, by comparison, is not impressed, or at least not to begin with. Soon he calms down, and the feeling among us is good. I guess it really is because we've been through something together, even if from totally different sides.

For a minute or so, we sit and eat.

"Any sauce?" I ask.

"I told you!" Keith accuses Daryl.

"What?"

"Well, *I* said we should get you some sauce, Ed," Keith explains, "but tight arse over there wouldn't hear of it."

Daryl throws back his head before answering.

"Look," he begins, "sauce is too dangerous." He points a finger at my shirt. "Look what Ed's wearing there, Keith, huh? Tell me. What color is it?"

"I *know* what color it is, Daryl. There's no need to get all condescending again."

"Again? When the hell am I ever condescending?"

They're almost shouting across me now as I take another bite of the half-cold pie.

"Right now," continues Keith. He attempts to bring me into it, asking, "What about you, Ed? What would you say?" His eyes are pointed right at me. "Is Daryl being condescending?"

I decide to answer Daryl's original question.

"I'm wearing a white shirt," I say.

"Exactly," Daryl responds.

"Exactly what?"

"Exactly, *Keith,* it is simply far too dangerous for Ed to even *contemplate* eating that pie with sauce." His tone is definitely condescending now. "It'll drip off, land on that lovely white shirt, and the poor bastard'll end up having to wash the bloody thing. And we don't want that now, do we?"

"It's not going to *kill* him to wash it!" Keith's particularly vehement on this point. "He can put a load on while he's washing that shitheap dog of his—that'll take at least a few hours or so."

"Now, there's no need to bring the Doorman into it," I protest. "He hasn't done anything."

"Exactly," Daryl agrees. "That was uncalled for, Keith."

Keith cools down a moment and admits it. His head drops. "I know." He even apologizes, "Sorry, Ed." And I can tell that this time they've been ordered to be on their best behavior toward me. That's probably why they're having double the arguments with each other.

They go on awhile longer, until they've both apologized, and for a while, we talk among the night that has dripped upon us with silence.

We're all quite happy, with Daryl telling jokes about men walking into bars, women with shotguns, and then wives, sisters, and brothers who would all sleep with the milkman for a million dollars.

Yes, we're all quite happy, until the light goes off in Ritchie's kitchen.

That's when I stand up and say, "Great." I turn to the two best arguers I've ever met and tell them I've missed my chance.

They seem unconcerned.

"Your chance at what?" Daryl asks.

"You know," I tell him.

But he only shakes his head.

He says, "No, Ed, as a matter of fact, I don't. I only know that this is your next message and you still don't seem to be thinking clearly about what you're supposed to be doing." His voice is so casual, but so heavy with something else.

Truth, I think.

That's what the voice weighs in with.

He's right. I really don't know what I'm doing. I'm still guessing as I stand here hoping that the answers will simply come.

Daryl and Keith stand up next to me under the oak.

It's Keith who deals the last questions from my left side.

He feeds the words into my ears with a coarse, gentle, knowing voice.

Close, so close to me, he says, "What are you even doing here, Ed?" The words loom nearer still and crawl into my ear. "Why are you standing here waiting? You should *know* what to do. . . ." He rests a moment before delivering the final deluge of words. They enter me like a flood. "Ritchie's one of your best friends, Ed. You don't need to *think* about anything, or wait, or decide what to do. You *know* already, without any question or doubt. Don't you?" He repeats it now. "Don't you, Ed?"

I stagger back and slide down the tree to where I was sitting.

The two figures still stand, looking at the house.

My voice trips forward, landing on the ground at their feet.

You know what to do, I think.

"Yes," I answer. "I know."

Visions tear me up.

There are pieces of me on the ground.

Keith and Daryl walk off.

"Hooray," says one of them, but I don't know which.

I want to stand up and chase them and ask them and beg them to tell me who's behind this and why, but.

I can't.

All I'm able to do is sit there and collect the shredded pieces of everything I just saw.

I saw Ritchie.

I saw myself.

Now, with the tree above me, I attempt to deny it and stand up, but my stomach drops and I sit down again.

"I'm sorry, Ritchie," I whisper, "but I have to."

If my stomach was a color, I think, *it would be black, like tonight,* and I steady myself and begin what feels like an endless walk home.

When I get there, I do the dishes.

They're piled up on the sink, and the last thing I wash is a clear, flat knife. It reflects the kitchen light and I catch my own face, lukewarm, inside the metal.

I'm oval and distorted.

I'm cut off at the edges.

The last things I see are the words I need to speak with Ritchie. At that, I place the knife on the rack, on top of the mountain of clean dishes. It slips and clangs to the floor, then spins like a clock hand.

My face appears in it three times as it circles the room.

The first time, I see Ritchie in my eyes.

Then I see Marv.

Then Audrey.

I pick it up and hold it in my hand.

I wish I could hold up that knife and tear open the world. I'd slice it open and climb through to the next one.

In bed, I cling to that thought.

There are three cards in my drawer and one in my hand.

As sleep stands above me, I gently press my finger to the edge of the Ace of Hearts. The card is cool and sharp.

I hear a clock ticking.
Everything watches impatiently.

5 ♥ ritchie's sin

Name: David Sanchez.
Also known as: Ritchie.
Age: Twenty.
Occupation: None.
Achievements: None.
Ambitions: None.
Likelihood of ever attaining answers to
the previous three questions: None.

The next time I go to Ritchie's house on Bridge Street, I find the place completely dark. I almost leave, until the light jump-starts on in the kitchen. It flicks and dies several times before forcing itself alive.

A silhouette arrives and sits at the kitchen table. It's Ritchie for sure. I can tell by the shape of the hair and the way he moves and sits down.

When I move closer I discover he's listening to the radio. It's mostly talkback, with a few songs thrown in. Faintly, I hear it.

I hide myself as close as I can without being caught out and listen.

The voices from the radio blur and reach out. Words like arms that land and rest heavily on Ritchie's shoulders.

I imagine the whole scene of the kitchen.

A toaster with crumbs around it.

Half-dirty oven.

White but fading Laminex.

The red, plastic-covered chairs with holes picked in them.

Cheap lino floor.

And Ritchie.

I try to imagine his face as he sits there, listening. I remember Christmas Eve and Ritchie's words. *I don't feel like going home tonight.* I see the eyes that dragged themselves toward me, and I see now that anything would be better than sitting alone in his kitchen.

With Ritchie, it's always hard to imagine a pained look on his face because of his relaxed manner. I saw a glimpse that Christmas Eve, though, and I revisit it again now.

I also imagine his hands.

They sit on the kitchen table, wrapped together, gently moving and pushing down. They're half pale and frustrated. They have nothing to do.

The light smothers him.

He sits there for nearly an hour, and the radio seems to fade out more than anything else. When I look to the window, he's resting his head on the kitchen table, sleeping. The radio's up there, too, next to him. I walk away; I can't help it. I know I'm supposed to go in there, but tonight doesn't feel quite right.

I walk home without looking back.

We play cards the next two nights. Once at Marv's and once at my place. At my place, the Doorman comes and sits under the table. I pat him with my feet and study Ritchie all night. The previous night when I stood outside his house the same thing happened. He woke up, entered the kitchen, and listened to the radio.

The Hendrix tattoo stares at me as Ritchie throws down the Queen of Spades and wrecks me.

"Thanks a lot," I tell him.

"Sorry, Ed."

His existence consists of these late, lonesome nights, waking up at ten-thirty in the morning, being up at the pub by twelve and across at the betting shop by one. Add to that the odd dole check, playing a card game or two, and that's it.

There's a lot of laughter at my place because Audrey's telling the story of a friend of hers who's been looking for a job in the city. She went through one of those recruiting agencies, and they have a policy of giving people a small alarm clock when they get a job. When she got the position, she turned up on the same day to thank the people who hired her and forgot about the clock. She left it on the counter in the main office when she left.

The clock was sitting there in the box.

Ticking.

"See, and no one wants to touch it," Audrey explains. "They think it's a bomb." She throws down a card. "They call the head honcho of the company, and he practically *shits* himself because he's probably getting it off with one of his secretaries and his wife's finally got the better of him for it." She lets her words pause to keep us listening. "Anyway, they evacuated the whole building, called the bomb squad, the police, the lot. The bomb squad arrives and opens the box when it starts ringing." Audrey shakes her head. "She got fired before she even started. . . ."

When the story ends, I watch Ritchie.

I want to move on him.

I want to make him uncomfortable, to rip him from where he is and put him in his kitchen at one a.m. If I can achieve that somehow, I might see a longer version of what he looks like and how he feels. It's just a matter of timing.

The time comes half an hour later when he suggests we play cards at his place in a few days' time.

"About eight?" he asks.

When we've all agreed and are about to say goodbye, I say, "And maybe you can show me what radio station you've got there." I force myself to be brutal and calculated. "The late show must be excellent."

He looks at me. "What are you talking about, Ed?"

"Nothing," I say, and I leave it at that because I've seen the look on his face again now and I know what it is. I know exactly how Ritchie looks and feels when he sits there in the paralyzed kitchen light.

I go into the blackness of his eyes and find him somewhere far inside, searching through a maze of anonymous, empty avenues. He's walking alone. The streets shift and turn around him, but never does he change step or mood.

"It's waiting for me," he says as I take my place next to him, deep inside.

I have to ask it. "What is, Ritchie?"

At first he only continues walking. Only when I look down at our feet do I realize that we're actually going nowhere. It's the world that moves—the streets, the air, and the dark patches of inner sky.

Ritchie and I are still.

"It's out there," I imagine him saying. "Somewhere." He walks with more purpose now. "It wants me to come for it. It wants me to take it."

300

Everything stops now.

I see it so clearly in Ritchie's eyes.

Inside them, where we stand, I say, "What's waiting, Ritchie?"

But I know.

Without question, I know.

I only hope he can find it.

When everyone's left, I share another coffee with the Doorman. After about half an hour, we're interrupted by a knock at the door.

Ritchie, I think.

The Doorman seems to nod in agreement as I walk over and open it.

"Hey, Ritchie," I greet him. "You forget something?"

"No."

I let him in and we sit at the kitchen table.

"Coffee?"

"No."

"Tea?"

"No."

"Beer?"

"No."

"You're picky, aren't you?"

He answers that one with silence but soon looks at me. He asks, with penetration, "You been following me?"

I look straight back and say, "I follow everyone."

He pockets his hands. "You a pervert or something?"

It's funny—that's what Sophie asked me as well. I shrug. "No more than anyone else, I s'pose."

"Well, could you stop?"

"No."

His face edges closer. "Why not?"

"I can't."

He looks at me as if I'm trying to pull one over him. His black eyes say, *Why don't you enlighten me, Ed?* so I do.

I go into my bedroom and pull the cards out from the drawer and return to the table. My hand drops them down in front of my friend and I say, "Remember when I got that first card in the mail, back in September? I told you I threw it away, but I didn't." It flows out of me quickly. I face him. "And now you're on one of the cards, Ritchie. You're one of the messages."

"Are you sure?" He attempts to point out that it might be a mistake, but I hear nothing of it. I only shake my head and feel some sweat gather under my arms.

"It's you," I tell him.

"But why?"

Ritchie's pleading with me, but I don't let it get in the way. I can't let him slink off to that darkness place inside him, where his pride is strewn all over the floor in some hidden room. In the end I talk completely devoid of emotion.

I say, "Ritchie—you're an absolute disgrace to yourself."

He looks at me like I just shot his dog or told him his ma died.

He sits in that kitchen every night, and no matter what the voices on the radio say, the words are always the same. They're the words I just spoke and we both know it.

Ritchie stares at the table.

I stare over his shoulder.

We both pore over what was just said. Ritchie sits there like an injury.

This goes on for a long time, until a certain smell arrives—the Doorman walks in.

"You're a good friend, Ed," Ritchie finally says, and returns to his usual easygoing expression. He fights to keep it there. "And you," he says to the Doorman, "smell like the sewer."

He stands up and leaves.

The words repeat themselves around me as the Kawasaki starts up and meanders down the dark, motionless street.

That was a bit harsh, Ed, the Doorman says.

We stand awhile in mutual silence.

The next night, I'm there again, outside Ritchie's. Something tells me I can't relent on him.

The figure of him becomes visible in the kitchen, but this time he comes out the front door with the radio in one hand and a bottle in the other. His feet fall and his voice calls out to me.

"Hey, Ed."

I step out.

He says, "Let's go to the river."

The river runs past town, and we sit there, having walked from Ritchie's place. We hand the bottle back and forth. The radio talks quietly.

"You know, Ed," Ritchie says after a while, "I used to think I had that chronic fatigue syndrome. . . ." He stops, like he's forgotten what he's going to say.

"And?" I ask.

"What?"

"Chronic fatigue—"

"Oh, yeah." He regathers it. "Yeah, I thought I had it, but then I realized that in actual fact, I just happen to be one of the laziest bastards on earth." It's quite funny, really.

"Well, you're not the only one."

"But most people have jobs, Ed. Even Marv's got a job. Even you've got one."

"What do you mean, even me?"

"Well, you're not the most motivated person I know, you know."

I admit it. "That's pretty accurate." I swig. "And I wouldn't call driving a taxi a real job."

"What would you call it?" Ritchie asks.

I think awhile before speaking. "An excuse."

Ritchie says nothing because he knows I'm right.

We drink on and the river rushes by.

It's been a good hour now.

Ritchie stands up and walks into the river. The water rises above his knees. He says, "This is what our lives are, Ed." He's picked up on the idea of things rushing past us. "I'm twenty years old, and"—the Hendrix-Pryor tattoo winks at me under the moonlight—"look at me—there isn't a thing I want to do."

It's impeccable how brutal the truth can be at times. You can only admire it.

Usually, we walk around constantly believing ourselves. "I'm okay," we say. "I'm all right." But sometimes the truth arrives on you, and you can't get it off. That's when you realize that sometimes it isn't even an answer—it's a question. Even now, I wonder how much of my life is convinced.

I get to my feet and join Ritchie in the river.

We both stand there, knee-deep in water, and the truth has well and truly pulled our pants down.

The river rushes by.

"Ed?" Ritchie says later. We're still standing in the water. "There's only one thing I want."

"What's that, Ritchie?"

His answer is simple.

"To want."

6 god bless the man with the beard, the missing teeth, and the poverty

Ritchie bypasses the pub and the betting shop the next day and actually starts looking for a job. As for me, I've also thought a lot about what was said last night at the river.

I'm driving people around the city, being told what to do and where to go. I watch the people. I speak with them. The weather's nice today. The weather's always something.

Am I whingeing?

Complaining?

No.

This is what I chose to do.

But is it what you want? I ask.

For a few kilometers, I lie that, yes, it is. I try to convince myself that this is *exactly* what I want my life to be, but I know it isn't. I know that driving a cab and renting a fibro shack can't be the final answer of my life. It can't be.

I feel like I just sat down at some point and said, "Right, this is Ed Kennedy."

Somewhere along the line, I feel like somehow I introduced myself.

To myself.

And here I am.

"Hey, is this the right way?" my plump, suited customer questions from the backseat.

I look in the mirror and say, "I don't know."

The next few days are quiet. We play cards one night and I realize I need to get started on Marv. With Ritchie on his way, Marv is next in line.

I watch him from the corner of my eye, wondering, *What the hell do I do with Marv?* He works. He's got money. Certainly, he owns the worst car in living history, but he seems satisfied enough, considering he won't spend any of that money of his to buy a new one.

So what could Marv want?

What could he need?

With every other message I waited for the solution to come.

With Marv, I'm not sure. For him, I have a different feeling. It moves close and resides somewhere I seem to walk past all the time but never notice. I must see it every day, but there's a big difference between seeing and finding.

In some way, Marv needs me.

I don't know what to do.

It goes on for the next twenty-four hours, this complete indecision. New Year's Eve has come and gone. The fireworks have swept the sky in the city. Drunken louts have decorated my cab, shrieking happiness that can only end in bedsheets soaked with the breath of beer and the weight of tomorrow.

Everyone went to Ritchie's place this time, and I made sure to drop in around midnight. His folks were having a party. I shook Marv's, Ritchie's, and Simon's hand. I kissed Audrey on the cheek and asked her how she managed to get the night off. Pure luck, apparently.

After that it was back to work and home to the Doorman in the early hours of morning. That's where I am now. We share a prolonged celebratory drink, and I say, "Here's to you, Mr. Doorman. May you live another year." He drinks up, heads over to the door, and lies down.

I'm pretty circumspect for New Year's Eve. I guess I'm not really in the mood for celebrating this year. Part of it's thinking of my father, as he's not here anymore for these kind of days and nights. Christmas. New Year's. Not that he was ever sober enough to really have an impact, but it affects me nonetheless.

I take the towels in the bathroom down as well as the fairly scungy tea towel in the kitchen. That was one of my father's idiosyncrasies, or superstitions. Never leave anything out to dry as the sun comes up for the new year. A hell of a legacy, I know, but better than nothing.

The other reason for my mood is the thought of Marv and what to do.

I sift through many things—what he's said lately and what he's done.

I think of the Sledge Game and the sheer patheticness of his car. And his preference for kissing the Doorman rather than forking out for the Christmas card game at his place.

Forty grand in the bank, but always pulling back when it comes to money.

Always, I think, and the question strikes me a few nights later as I watch an old movie.

307

What is it that Marv intends to do with forty thousand dollars?

Yes.
I have it.

The money.
What does Marv need to do with the money?
That's the message.

I remember what Daryl and Keith told me about Ritchie. They said I should know because he was one of my best friends. This nearly cajoles me into thinking I should also know what Marv needs with the money. *Maybe it's right under my nose,* I wonder, but nothing is immediately apparent, and I understand that with Marv, my knowledge of him is what I have to use to get the message out of *him*.

I might not know the message, but I know Marv and the options I can go through to figure this out.

On my front porch, I sit with the Doorman and the setting sun. I consider three tactics for Marv.

Tactic 1: argue with him.

This could be done quite easily by bringing up the subject of his car and why he refuses to buy a new one.

The danger here is that Marv could become so heated that he'll just storm out of the room and I won't learn anything. This would be nothing short of disastrous.

The advantage of this option is, first of all, that it could be fun, and it might actually make him buy a new car.

*　　*　　*

Tactic 2: get him so mind-numbingly drunk that he spills the message without even thinking.

Dangers: in coercing Marv into a drunken stupor, I might need to put myself in the same condition. This will leave me in no state to comprehend, let alone remember, what I have to do.

Advantages: no actual message extraction involved. I'd be hoping he just comes out with it. Highly unlikely, I realize, but perhaps worth a shot.

Tactic 3: come straight out and ask.

This is the most dangerous option because it can result in Marv becoming completely obstinate (as we know very well he can be), refusing to tell me anything. If Marv feels discomfort at my sudden extra concern for him (well, let's face it—I usually act like I couldn't care less about him), all other hopes and opportunities could be lost.

The advantages are that it's honest, up-front, and considerably low-maintenance. It either works or it doesn't, largely depending on timing.

Which tactic do I pursue first?

It's a difficult question, and only when I've turned it over several times do I find the right answer.

The unthinkable happens.

A fourth avenue stretches out and places itself in my hand.

Where?

The supermarket.

When?

Thursday night.

How?

Like this.

I walk in and buy a good fortnight's worth of groceries and come out struggling with my bags. They're already cutting into my hands as I walk out the doors, so I put them down for vital repositioning.

An old homeless man confronts me quietly with his beard, his missing teeth, and his poverty.

His expression bleeds.

He begs me timidly if I might have some change to spare. He speaks with humility on his lips.

As soon as he's said it, his eyes buckle to the ground with shame. He's broken me but doesn't know it until he finds me searching my jacket for my wallet.

At that exact moment, as my fingers feel for the money, the answer comes to me. It falls down at my feet, staring up.

Of course!

The inner voice rises up and reports the answer in an instant, perfect thought. I even speak it to believe it. To remember it.

"Ask him for money." I mouth the words barely loud enough for my own ears to pick them up and put them back inside me.

"Sorry?" the man asks, still in his quiet, humble voice.

"Ask him for money," I say again, but this time I speak it louder. I can't contain myself.

Out of habit, the old man says, "I'm sorry, sir." His expression sags. "I'm sorry to be asking you for change."

I've pulled a five-dollar note from my pocket, and I hand it to him.

He holds it like it's biblical. It must be rare for him to be given notes. "God bless you." He looks mesmerized with the money as I pick up my bags again.

"No," I answer. "God bless *you*." And I make my way home.

The bags slice through my hands, but I don't mind. No, I don't mind at all.

7 the secret marv

♥

He works. He drinks. He plays cards. He waits for the Sledge Game all year.

This.

Is Marv's life.

Well, that and forty grand.

On Tuesday I go over to Milla's place to see how she's going. I never get sick of being Jimmy, although *Wuthering Heights* is getting on my nerves a bit now. The trouble is, Heathcliff's a completely bitter arsehole and Catherine frustrates the hell out of me. My purest hatred, however, is reserved for Joseph, the miserable, complete bastard of a servant. On top of all his preaching and carrying on, it's hard to understand a word he says.

The best thing about the whole story is Milla. For me, it's her in the pages. When I think of that book, I think of her. I think of her old moist eyes watching me read as she listens. I love closing the book and seeing the old lady resting in her chair. I think she's my favorite message.

*　　*　　*

But then there's Sophie, Father O'Reilly, and the Tatupu family. Even the Rose boys.

Okay, okay.

The Rose boys is pushing it.

I'm walking the Doorman a lot lately, and as I do it, I remember all the messages so far. In one way, I feel like I'm cheating. This kind of reminiscing is supposed to be done at the end, and I haven't finished yet. I've got two messages to go. Two of my best friends.

Maybe that's why I'm letting the previous messages return to me.

I'm afraid for Marv and for Audrey.

I'm afraid for me.

You can't let them down, I lecture myself as each minute shoves past.

Afraid. Afraid.

I didn't come this far only to fail the ones I've known longest and care for most.

I run through them again, from Edgar Street to Ritchie.

Afraid. Afraid.

The messages give me courage.

"Any luck with the job search?" I ask Ritchie as we all get together at my place on Sunday night.

He shakes his head. "No, not yet."

"You?" exclaims Marv. "Get a job?" He falls into fits of hysterics.

"What's wrong with that?" Audrey interjects. Ritchie stays quiet, and we can see he's a little hurt. Even Marv. He tries to suck the laughter back and hold on to it.

He clears his throat.

"Sorry, Ritch."

Ritchie tucks the pain a touch deeper inside and gives us his usual, easygoing self. "No problems," he says, and secretly I'm glad Marv's stirred him up a bit. If anything, he'll keep trying now just to shut Marv up and see the look on his face when he gets hired by someone. There's a certain satisfaction in shutting up Marv.

"I'll deal," says Audrey.

When the game packs up it's close to eleven. Ritchie's already gone when Marv offers Audrey a lift home out on the front porch. For obvious reasons, she declines.

"Why not?" Marv objects.

"It'll be quicker to walk, Marv." Audrey tries reasoning with him. "And really, Marv, there are less mosquitoes out here than there are in *there*." She points at the prize vehicle on the road.

"Thanks a lot." He begins to sulk.

"Marv, do you remember what happened last time you gave me a lift? A few weeks ago?"

Grudgingly, Marv recalls it.

Audrey reminds him anyway.

"We ended up pushing it all the way to your place." She comes up with an idea. "You need a bike in the backseat."

"Why?"

This is getting interesting.

Almost entertaining.

"Oh, come on, Marv," she says. "I'll let you ponder that on your way home—especially if you break down."

She waves goodbye and walks onto the road.

"Bye, Audrey," I whisper. She's gone.

When Marv gets in his car, I hope for the inevitable, and it happens.

The engine fails seven or eight times, and I walk across the lawn, open the passenger door, and get in.

Marv looks at me.

"What are you doing, Ed?"

Quietly. Earnestly.

I speak.

I say, "I need your help, Marv."

He attempts to start the car again. No luck.

"With what?" he asks. He tries again. "You got something needs fixing?"

"No, Marv."

"You want me to clip the Doorman for you?"

"Clip?"

"Yeah, you know—whack him for you."

"What are you, Capone?"

Marv admires his own humor and still persists with the key, which irritates me no end.

"Marv," I say, "could you stop with the key and be serious for a minute or two? Would you do me that honor?"

He goes to try it again, but I reach over and grab the key from the ignition.

"Marv," I whisper. A whisper the size of a shout. "I need your help. I need money."

The moment slows, and I can hear us breathing.

A minute's silence passes.

This is the death of Marv's and my usual trivial relationship.

It truly feels like something has died.

*   *   *

314

It doesn't take much longer for Marv to get interested. The mention of money will do that to him. His eyebrows tense, and he looks over at me, trying to find a way in. He doesn't look too forthcoming.

He says, "How much, Ed?"

And I erupt.

I rip the car door open.

I slam it.

I lean back in and point my finger at the friend behind the wheel.

"Well, I should have known!" I get stuck into him. "You're the stingiest bastard, Marv. . . ." I point at him as ruthlessly as I can. "I can't believe this!"

Silence.

Street and silence.

I turn and rest back against the car as Marv gets out and walks around to me.

"Ed?"

"I'm sorry." *This is going well,* I think. I shake my head.

"No, you're not," he says.

"Marv, I just thought—"

He cuts me off.

"Ed, I haven't . . ." His words trail off.

"I just thought you could—"

"Ed, I don't have the money."

This is somewhat of a shock.

"Why not, Marv?" I step forward and face him. "Why the hell not?"

"I spent it."

His voice is somewhere else. It doesn't come from his mouth. It seems to show up from somewhere next to him. Vacant.

315

"On what, Marv?"

I'm getting agitated now.

"Well, not on anything." His voice is coming back to him. It's his again. "I put it in a fund and can't withdraw it for at least a few years. I put in, I earn interest." He's very serious now. Pensive. "I can't take it out."

"At all?"

"No."

"Not even in an emergency?"

"I don't think so."

I become loud again. My aggression seems to strip the street naked. "Why in the hell did you do that, Marv?"

Marv cracks.

He cracks by walking hurriedly around the car and getting back in, behind the wheel. Holding on.

Quietly, Marv cries.

His hands appear to be dripping on the wheel. The tears grip his face. They hold on and slide reluctantly for his throat.

I go around.

"Marv?"

I wait.

"What's happening, Marv?"

He turns his head, and his disheveled eyes angle for mine.

"Get in," he says. "I'll show you something."

On the fourth attempt, the Ford starts and Marv drives me through town. Tears stream his face. Less reluctant now. They veer down. They look drunk.

We pull up at a small weatherboard shack, and Marv gets out. I follow.

"Remember this?" he asks.

I remember.

"Suzanne Boyd," I say.

The words stagger slowly from Marv's mouth. Half his face is trodden with darkness, covered, but I can still make out the outlines, the forms.

"When her family left town," he says, "there was a reason they just disappeared. . . ."

"Oh God," I try to say, but the words are inhaled. They don't find their way out of me.

Marv speaks one last time.

When he moves, a streetlight stabs him, and the words flow out like blood.

He says, "The kid's about two and a half."

We get back in the car and sit in silence for a long time, and Marv begins to shiver uncontrollably. He has a tanned face, Marv, from working outside, but he's as white as paper as we sit in his car.

Now it all makes sense.

I see it.

Like words being typed across his face.

Punched in.

Black on white.

Yes, it all makes sense.

The pathetic car.

The obsessive watchfulness and abhorrent vigilance with money.

Even his argumentative disposition, to use an even more *Wuthering Heights* kind of phrase. Marv is suffering, completely alone, and he uses all of those things to sweep the guilt from his stomach every day.

*   *   *

317

"I want to give the kid something, you know? When it's older."

"You don't know if it's a he or a she?"

"No."

He pulls an old slice of notepad from his wallet. When he unfolds it, I can tell the address that's written there has been traced over several times to never fade.

17 Cabramatta Road, Auburn.

"Some of her friends," Marv speaks blankly. "When the family just disappeared, I went to her friends and begged them to tell me where she went. God, it was pitiful. I was crying on Sarah Bishop's front doorstep, for Christ's sake." The words seem to echo now, out of his mouth, which appears motionless. Almost numb. "Man, that girl Suzanne. That sweet Suzanne." He spits out a sarcastic laugh. "Cha—her old man was such a stern bastard—but she snuck out a few nights a week, an hour before dawn, and we'd go out to this old field where a man used to grow corn." He almost smiles now. "We had a blanket and we'd go there and have it a few nights a week. . . . She was so brilliant, Ed." He looks directly at me because if he's going to tell someone, he wants to do it right. "She tasted so good." The smile hangs on desperately. "Sometimes we'd push our luck and stay till the sun came up. . . ."

"It sounds beautiful, Marv."

I've spoken those words to the windscreen—I can't believe Marv and I are talking like this. Usually we argue to show our friendship.

"The orange sky," Marv continues, "the wet grass—and I always remember the warmth of her. Inside her and on her skin. . . ."

I imagine it well, but Marv murders it instantly with one savage breath.

"Then one day the house was emptied. I went to the field, but it was just me and the corn."

The girl got pregnant.

Not unusual in these parts, but obviously not condoned by the Boyds.

The family left town.

Nothing was ever said, and the Boyds were never really missed. People always come and go through here. If they make money, they move somewhere better. If they struggle, they move somewhere equally as shitty to try their luck somewhere else.

"I guess," Marv says later, "her old man was ashamed of having a sixteen-year-old girl of his getting stitched up, especially by someone like me. I guess he was right to be stern. . . ."

At this point, I have no idea what to say.

"They left town," he tells me. "Barely a word was spoken." Now he looks over. I feel his eyes on my face. "And I've been living with it for three years."

Not anymore, I think, but I can't be sure.

It feels more like wayward hope or desperation.

He's calmer now, but he sits stiffly in his seat. An hour goes past. I wait. I ask.

"Have you been to that address?"

He stiffens further. "No. I've tried, but I can't." He resumes telling the story. "About a week after that day at the Bishop place, Sarah came to where I was working. She hands me the note and says, 'I promised not to tell *anyone*—especially you— but I just don't think it's right.' Then she says, 'But you be careful, Marv. Suzie's old man says he'll kill you if you so much as set foot near her again.' And she left." A blankness blankets his face. "It was raining that day, I remember. Small sheets of rain."

"Sarah," I ask, "that's that tall, brown, pretty one?"

"That's her," Marv confirms. "After what she said, I drove into the city a few times. Once I even had ten grand in my pocket—to help out. That's all I want, Ed."

"I believe you."

Solemnly, he rubs his face and says, "I know. Thanks."

"So you've never even seen the kid?"

"No. I never have the neck to even turn onto the street—I'm pathetic." He begins to chant. "Pathetic, pathetic," and gently, fiercely, he beats his fist on the wheel. I expect him to explode, but Marv can't find the strength for any outflow of emotion. He's past that. For three years, since that girl left, his front has been impeccable. Now it peels from his skin, leaving the truth of him at the wheel of his car.

"This"—he shakes—"this is what I look like at three a.m., Ed. Every morning. I see that girl—that dirt-poor, spectacular girl. Sometimes I walk to that field and sink to my knees. I hear my heart beating, but I don't want to. I hate my heartbeat. It's too loud in that field. It falls down. Right out of me. But then it just gets back up again."

I hear it.

I imagine it.

His legs yield.

His trousers scratch the dirt.

Kneeling there with earth-bruised knees and a collapsing heart.

It hits the ground next to him, hard, and it . . .

Beats. Beats.

Beats.

It refuses to die or run cold, always finding its way back into Marv's body. But one night, surely, it has to succumb.

"Fifty grand," Marv tells me. "I'm stopping at fifty. At first it was ten, then twenty, but I just couldn't stop."

"Paying off the guilt."

"That's right." He tries to start the car a few times, and eventually we head off. "But it isn't money that'll fix me." He stops in the middle of the road. The brakes burn, and Marv's face ignites. "I want to touch that kid. . . ."

"You have to."

"There are plenty of ways to do it," he says.

"But only one," I reply.

Marv nods.

When he drops me back home, the night has turned cold.

"Hey, Marv," I say just before I get out.

He looks into me.

"I'll come with you."

His eyes close.

He goes to speak but can't. It's better unsaid.

8 ♥ each to each

Tomorrow is the day.

After I've walked in, I retire to the lounge room and sit there, completely exhausted, on the couch. Close to five minutes later, Marv calls and tells me. He doesn't say hello.

"We'll go tomorrow."

"About six?"

"I'll pick you up."

"No," I say. "I'll drive you in the cab."

"Good idea. If I get the crap beaten out of me, we might want a car that starts first go."

The time arrives and we leave my place at six, making it to Auburn by nearly seven. Traffic's heavy.

"I hope the bloody kid's still up," I wonder out loud.

Marv doesn't answer.

Pulling up at 17 Cabramatta Road, I can't help but notice it's exactly the same sort of fibro shithole the Boyds used to live in back home. We're on the other side of the road, in typical messenger style.

Marv looks at the clock.

"I'll go in at seven-oh-five."

7:05 comes and goes.

"Okay. Seven-ten."

"No worries, Marv."

At 7:46, Marv gets out of the car and stands there.

"Good luck," I say. God, I can hear his heart from inside the cab. It's a wonder it isn't bludgeoning the poor guy to death.

He stands there. Three minutes.

He crosses the road. Two attempts.

The yard is different. First go—a surprise.

Then, the big one.

Fourteen attempts at knocking on the door. When I finally hear his knuckles hit the wood, it sounds like bruises.

The door is answered, and Marv is there in jeans, nice shirt, boots. Words are spoken but I don't hear them, of course. I'm clogged with the memory of Marv's heartbeat and the knocking on the door.

He walks in, and now it's *my* heart I can hear. *This could be the longest wait of my life,* I think. I'm wrong.

About thirty seconds later, Marv comes rushing backward out the door. He hurtles. Through the doorway and onto the yard. Henry Boyd, Suzanne's father, is giving Marv a hiding he won't soon forget. A small trace of blood flows from Marv to the grass. I get out of the cab.

To give you an idea, Henry Boyd is not a big man, but he's powerful.

He's short but heavy.

And he has the will. He's a kind of pocket-size version of my Edgar Street message. Also, he's sober, and I don't have a gun.

As I cross the street, Marv is splayed on the front yard like a frozen starjump.

He gets kicked.

By words.

He gets shot.

By Henry Boyd's pointing finger.

"Now get the hell out of here!"

The small, steak-tough man is standing over Marv, beginning now to rub his hands together.

"Sir," I hear Marv plead. Only his lips move. Nothing else. He speaks to the sky. "I've got nearly fifty thousand—"

But Henry Boyd isn't interested. He moves closer to stand directly over him.

There's a kid crying. Neighbors are collecting on the street. They've come out to take in the show. Henry turns on them and tells them all to get their big Turkish arses back inside. His words, not mine.

"And you!" He punishes Marv with his voice again. "Never, *ever* come back here again, you hear?"

I arrive and crouch next to Marv. His top lip is extremely large and dipped with blood. He isn't particularly conscious.

"And who the hell are you?"

Shit, I think, very nervously indeed, *I think that's me.* I answer quickly. Respectfully. "I'm just picking up my friend here from your lawn."

"Good idea."

Now I see Suzanne. She holds a small kid's hand at the door. A girl. *You've got a little girl!* I want to shout to Marv, but I think very much the better of it.

I nod at her, at Suzanne.

"Get inside, Suzie!"

She nods back.

"Now!"

The kid cries again.

She's gone, and I help Marv to his feet. There's a stray drop of blood on his shirt.

Henry Boyd has tears of rage on him now. They puncture his eyes. "That bastard put shame on my family."

"So did your daughter." I can't believe the words I'm hearing from my own mouth.

"You better get moving, boy, or you two'll go home like twins."

Nice.

That's when I ask Marv if he can stand on his own. He can, and I walk closer to Henry Boyd. I'm not sure that's happened to him a lot. He's short but even more powerful the closer you get. At this point, he's stunned.

I look at him respectfully.

"That looks like a beautiful kid in there," I say. There are no shivers in my voice. This comes as a surprise, giving me the courage to continue. "Well, is she, sir?"

He struggles. I know what he's debating in his mind. He wants to strangle me but can smell the strange confidence that dresses everything I say. Eventually, he answers. He has sideburns. They move slightly before he speaks. "Damn right she's beautiful."

Now I point to Marv as I stand as straight as I can in front of Mr. Boyd. His arms hang. They're short and muscular. I say, "He may have brought you shame, and I know you left town for it." Again, I look at the slightly bloodied figure that is Marv. "But what he just did in facing you—that was respect. You don't get any more decent or proud than that." Marv shivers and takes a slight sip of his blood. "He knew this would happen, but here he is." Now I get my eyes to step into his. "If you were him, would you have been able to do the same? Would you have faced you?"

The man's voice is quiet now.

"Please," he pleads. I realize a giant sorrow has arrived in me for this man. He's suffered. "Go on. Leave."

I don't.

I remain in him a few moments longer, saying, *Think that over.*

At the car, I realize I'm alone.

I'm alone because there's a young man with blood across his mouth who has taken a few extra steps. He's walked forward, toward the house. The girl he used to meet in the field and make love to till dawn is on the porch.

They're staring, each to each.

9 ♥ the swings

A week treads past.

In the cab of that night, from Cabramatta Road, Auburn, Marv had just sat there, bleeding onto my passenger seat. He touched his mouth and his lip opened up, and the blood came sliding out, seeping. When it stained the seat, I told him off, of course.

He said one thing to that.

"Thanks, Ed."

I think he was glad to still be treated the same—even though he and I would never be friends like we once were. We had this in our memories now.

As I pull out of the Vacant Taxis lot one morning, I'm stopped by Marge. She comes hurrying out, waving me down. Once I've stopped and wound the window down, she hauls in her breath and says, "Glad I caught you—there's a job got called in for you last night, Ed. It sounded personal." I notice today that Marge has a lot of wrinkles. Somehow, they add to her friendliness. "I didn't want to broadcast it on the radio later on. . . ."

"Where is it?" I ask.

"It was a woman, Ed, or a girl, and she requested you specifically. Twelve o'clock today."

I feel and know it.

"Cabramatta Road?" I ask. "Auburn?"

Marge nods.

I thank her and Marge gives me a "No worries, love," and my first instinct is to call Marv straightaway and tell him. I don't. The customer has to come first. I *am* a professional, after all.

No, instead I drive past where he's been working lately, at a new subdivision out close to Glory Road. His father's truck's there, and that's all I need to know. I drive on.

At noon, I pull up outside Suzanne Boyd's abode in Auburn. She comes out promptly with her daughter and a special car seat.

We pause a moment.

Suzanne has long hair like honey and coffee eyes, though much darker than mine. No milk in them. She's skinny. Her daughter's got the same color hair but still fairly short. It curls around her ears, and she smiles at me.

"This is Ed Kennedy," her mother says to her. "Say hello, sweetheart."

"Hello, Ed Kennedy," the girl says.

I crouch down. "And what's your name?" It was Marv who got her in the eyes.

"Melinda Boyd." The kid has a prize smile.

"She's great," I tell Suzanne.

"Thanks."

She opens the back door and straps her in. It hits me hard that Suzanne really is a mother. I look on as her hands make sure Melinda's safely in the seat. She's as pretty as she always was.

Suzanne works part-time. She hates her father. She hates herself for never fighting. She regrets everything.

"But I love Melinda," she says. "She's the one piece of beauty among all this ugly." Suzanne sits next to her daughter and catches me in the mirror. "She makes me worth it, you know?"

I start the car and drive.

Only the engine sound fills the car while Melinda Boyd sleeps, but when she wakes up, she plays and talks and dances with her hands.

"Do you hate me, Ed?" Suzanne asks as we approach town. I recall Audrey asking me the same question.

I only look back in the mirror and say, "Why should I?"

"For what I've done to Marv."

The words that come to me are actually quite succinct. Maybe I'd rehearsed them subconsciously. I simply say, "You were a kid, Suzie. Marv was a kid. . . . And your father was your father. . . . In a way," I tell her, "I feel for him. He's pretty hurt."

"Yes, but what I did to Marv was unforgivable."

"You're in this cab, aren't you?" I look at her in back again.

After some thought, Suzanne Boyd gives me an acknowledging look and says, "You know, Ed?" Her head shakes. "No one's ever spoken to my father the way you did."

"Or faced him like Marv."

She nods her agreement.

I tell her I can take her to where Marv's working, but she asks me to stop at a nearby playground.

"Good thinking," I reply, and she waits.

There's a gap in Marv's hammering at the site. He's up high, with a few nails in his mouth. I take the chance, calling up. "I think you'd better come with me, Marv."

He sees the intent in my expression, pauses, spits the nails, drops his tool belt, and comes toward me. In the car, I think he's more nervous than the other night.

When we make it to the playground, we both get out.

328

"They're waiting," I tell him, but I don't think he hears. I sit on the hood of my cab, and Marv walks hesitantly on.

The grass is dry and yellow and not maintained. It's an old playground. A nice old one, with a big iron slippery dip, swings with chains, and a splinter-arse seesaw—just as it should be. No plastic vomit anywhere.

A slight wind taps the grass.

When Marv turns to look at me, I see the fear crouch down in his eyes. He walks slowly to the play equipment, where Suzanne Boyd waits. Melinda sits on one of the swings.

Marv looks so big.

His walk and hands and his worry.

I hear nothing, but I can see they're talking, and Marv's giant-looking hand shakes that of his daughter's. I can see he wants to hold her, hug her, squeeze her, but he doesn't.

Melinda jumps back on the swing, and after looking at Suzanne for permission, Marv gently, gently pushes his daughter into the air.

After a few minutes, Suzanne quietly escapes and comes back to stand with me.

"He's good with her," she softly says.

"He is." I smile for my friend.

We hear Melinda's shrill voice now. "Higher, Marvin Harris! Higher, please!"

He gradually pushes harder. He touches his daughter's back with both hands, and she laughs loud and pure into the sky.

When she's had enough, Marv stops the swing. The girl climbs off and grabs his hand and walks her father back toward us. Even from far away, I can see that Marv has tears on his face as clear as glass.

Marv's smile and the giant glass tears on his face are two of the most beautiful things I've ever seen.

10
audrey, part one: three nights to wait

I don't sleep that night—the day of the swings.

With each passing moment, I see Marv pushing that girl into the air, or I see him walking back with her, hand in hand. Close to midnight, I hear Marv's voice at the door. When I open it, he stands there, looking exactly how he feels.

"Come out," he says, and when I do, my friend Marvin Harris hugs me. He hugs me so hard that I can smell him and taste the joy that leaks from inside him.

So Ritchie and Marv are done. I've delivered those messages as best I can.

Now there's only one left.

Audrey.

I don't want to waste time. I've come so far since the holdup. I've plowed through eleven messages, and this is the last of them. The most important one.

The next night I go straight to Audrey's place and watch. For a while, I expect Daryl and Keith to show up again, but they don't. I know what I'm doing, and whenever that's the case, I seem to be left alone.

I don't sit exactly across from Audrey's place, but in a small park a bit further down her street. It's a new playground. All plastic and small. The grass is trimmed and neat.

Her town house is in one of those complexes with about eight or nine other places. They all seem stapled together. The cars are parked out front in rows.

I go there three nights. Each time, Simon shows up, but he never sees me camped out in the park. He has his mind firmly on Audrey and what they're going to do. Even from the distance of the park, I can see the desire on him as he drives in.

Once he's inside, I walk closer, to the letter boxes, and look.

They eat.
They have sex.
They drink.
They have more sex.

The sound of it slides under the door as I stand there, remembering the conversation I had with Simon at Christmas when he picked me up at Milla's.

I know what I have to give to Audrey.
Audrey doesn't love anyone.
She refuses.
But she loves me.
She loves me, and for one moment in time, she needs to allow it. She needs to hold it. Know it completely. Just once.

All three nights, I stay till morning. Simon leaves before the sun comes up. He must be rostered on for early morning in the city.

On the third night, I think it.

Tomorrow.

Yes.

I'll do it tomorrow.

J
♥ marv's afterthought

Just before I head over to Audrey's place the next night, Marv's at my front door again, this time with a question.

I walk out, and he refuses to follow me.

From the porch, he says, "Do you still need that money, Ed?" He looks at me, concerned. "I'm sorry—I forgot all about it."

"Don't worry," I tell him. "I don't think I'll be needing it after all."

I've got an old derelict cassette player under my arm with a tape inside it.

As I walk, Marv throws his voice out and ropes me back to face him.

He looks at me thoughtfully and says, "Did you ever need it?"

I walk closer.

"No." I shake my head. "No, Marv, I didn't."

"Then why"—he comes down the steps to face me properly—"then why did you say—"

"I kept that card I got in the mail, Marv." If Ritchie deserved the truth, so does Marv. I explain it to him. All of it. "Marv, I've

332

been through diamonds, clubs, spades, and I've got one more heart to go."

"Was that where I—"

"Yes, Marv," I answer. "You were in hearts."

Quiet.

Perplexed.

Marv stands on my front lawn and has no idea what to say— but he looks happy.

When I'm nearly gone, he calls out, "Is the last one Audrey?"

I turn and look at him, walking backward.

"Well, good luck!" he answers.

This time I smile and wave.

audrey, part two: three minutes to take

It all happens as usual, except tonight the radio I've brought sweats next to me as the moon rises, falls, and fades when morning finally approaches. I wonder for a moment why I didn't just set my alarm at home and come over at dawn, but I know I have to do this right. I had to suffer the night to do this properly.

My legs stretch out, but the night stretches further. First light frightens me.

I'm swaying toward sleep in the park when I hear a door slam and Simon's car start up. He exits the town house complex with a quiet, clumsy turn onto the street. A minute passes, but I realize that now is the time. It all feels right.

The radio. The light.

And now, my footsteps toward Audrey's front door.

I knock.

No answer.

Again, I clench my fist, but just as I'm about to hit the wood again, a crack appears in the doorway and Audrey's tired voice edges through it. "Did you forget some—" Her voice props.

"It's me," I say.

"Ed?"

"Yes."

"What are you—"

My shirt feels like cement. I wear wooden jeans, sandpaper socks, and anvil shoes.

"I'm here," I whisper, "for you."

Audrey, the girl, the woman, is in a pink nightie.

She opens the door and stands barefoot, removing some sleep from her eye with her fist. She reminds me of the little girl Angelina.

Slowly, I take her hand and bring her out onto the path. The heaviness has left me now, and it's just her and me. I place the radio in the bark-spattered garden, crouch down, and press play.

At first, a moderate static rustles through the air. Then the music begins and we can both hear the slow, quiet, sweet desperation of a song I won't mention. Imagine the softest, toughest, most beautiful song you know, and you've got it. We breathe it in and my eyes hook with Audrey's.

I walk closer and hold her hands.

"Ed, what—"

"Shh."

I hold her close now around her hips and she holds me back.

She places her hands around my neck and rests her head on my shoulder. I can smell the sex on her, and my only hope is that she can smell the love on me.

The music hits low.

The voice reaches high.

It's the music of hearts again—but much better this time—and we move and turn, and Audrey's breath places itself on my neck. "Mmm," she moans gently, and we dance on the path. We hold each other. At one point, I let go and twirl her slowly. She comes back and it's a small, small kiss she gives me on the neck when she returns.

I love you, I feel like saying, but there's no need for that.

The sky flows with fire, and I'm dancing with Audrey. Even when the song ends, we hold on a little longer, and I think it's about three minutes we danced for.

Three minutes to tell her I love her.

Three minutes for her to admit she loves me back.

She tells me when we let go, but no words of love exit her mouth. She just kind of closes one eye at me and says, "Well, Ed Kennedy, huh?"

I smile.

She points her finger. "But only you, though, right?"

"Right," I agree. I stare at Audrey's bare feet, her ankles, her shins, then make my way up to her face. I take a photo of her in my mind. Her tired eyes and morning mucked-up hair the color of straw. The smile gently scratching her lips. Her small ears and smooth nose. And the last remnants of love, holding strangely on. . . .

She let herself love me for three minutes.

Can three minutes last forever? I ask myself, but already I know the answer.

Probably not, I reply. *But maybe they last long enough.*

K♥ the end

I pick up the radio and we stand for a little while longer. She doesn't invite me in, and I don't ask.

What needed to be done was done, so I turn and say, "Well, I'll see you, Audrey. Maybe at the next card game. Maybe before."

"Soon," she assures me, and with the radio tucked back under my arm, I begin the walk home.

Twelve messages have been delivered.

Four aces have been completed.

This feels like the greatest day of my life.

I'm alive, I think. *I won.* I feel freedom for the first time in months, and an air of contentedness wanders next to me all the way home. It even remains as I walk through the front door, kiss the Doorman, and make us some coffee in the kitchen.

We're halfway through it when another feeling finds its way to my stomach, winds up, and spills.

I don't know why I feel it, but any contentment vanishes instantly as the Doorman looks up at me. We hear a latch open and shut from outside and a person rush off.

I walk slowly out the door, down the porch steps, and onto the front yard.

My letter box stands there. Slightly crooked. It looks guilty.

My heart shakes.

I walk on and shudder as I open the letter box.

Oh no, I think. *No, no. No!*

My hands reach in and my fingers take hold of one last envelope. My name's on it, and inside I can already see it.

There's one last card.

One last address.

I close my eyes and fall to my knees on my front lawn.

My thoughts stammer.

One last card.

Without thinking, I gradually open the envelope, and when my eyes find the address, all thoughts are cut down and left there to die.

It reads:

26 Shipping Street

The address is *my* address.

The last message is for me.

part five: **The Joker**

26 Shipping Street

J
the laughter

The street is empty and silent.

The Joker laughs at me.

Everything's quiet but for the silent laughter of the clown in my hands. He roars.

The grass is covered with sweat, and I stand alone with the wild card between my fingers. I've been watched all along, but never have I felt as vulnerable or scrutinized as right now.

Inside. I panic. *What's waiting inside?*

"Get in there," I say, and I walk across the sweat-soaked grass. Of course, I don't *want* to go inside, but what other choice do I have? If someone's in there, there's nothing I can do about it. My feet print the cement porch with wetness.

I walk through to the kitchen.

"Anyone there?" I call out.

But.

There's no one.

In.

My kitchen.

In fact, there's no one in my house at all except the Doorman, the Joker, and me. I all but check under the bed, even though I know it wouldn't be the style of what's been happening. They'd be drinking my coffee or taking a leak in my toilet or having a bath or something like that. There's nothing and no one in my house. Silence pervades everything until the Doorman yawns and licks his lips.

Hours pass until I have to go to work.
"Where to?"
"Martin Place, please."

With each pickup I grow more numb, and for the first time ever, I don't speak to a person all day. I don't discuss the weather. I don't talk about who won on the weekend, the state of the roads, or any disposable conversational crap that fills the void inside a taxicab.
That's the first day.
The second's the same.
On the third day, something happens.

I'm on my way back home when I nearly crash at a roundabout. A kombi in front of me attempts to go, but I look right instead of staying focused on the van. It stops abruptly, the brakes yell at my feet, and I manage to stop a few inches from the kombi's number plate.

I had the Joker on the passenger seat.

It springs forward.

It lands on the floor.

And laughs.

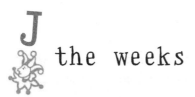 **the weeks**

Have you ever stretched your legs or touched your toes and tried for too much? That's how the days and weeks feel now as I work and wait for the Joker to unveil itself.

What will happen at my shack, at 26 Shipping Street?

Who will arrive?

On February 7 a hand reaches at my door, and I half rush, half stall on my way there. Is this it?

It's Audrey.

She walks in and says, "You've been quiet lately, Ed. Marv says he's been trying to call you, but you haven't been home."

"I've been working."

"And?"

"Waiting."

She sits down on the couch and asks, "For what?"

In no rush, I stand and walk to the drawer in the bedroom and pull out the four cards. When I return to her, I go through them one by one. "Diamonds," I say, "done." I let go and watch it flutter to the floor. "Clubs, done." Again, the card hits the carpet. "Spades and hearts—both done."

"So what now?" Audrey can see the paleness of my face and the jaded look of the rest of me.

From my pocket, I pull the Joker.

"This," I state. And I beg her. I nearly weep as I say, "Tell me, Audrey—please tell me it's you. Say you've been sending me these cards." I plead with her. "Tell me you just wanted me to help people and . . ."

"And what, Ed?"

I close my eyes. "Make *myself* better—make me worth something."

The words fall to the floor, to the cards, and Audrey smiles. She smiles and I wait for her to admit it.

"Tell me!" I demand. "Tell—"

She folds.

She tells the truth.

The words flow almost unconsciously from her mouth.

"No, Ed," she says slowly. "It wasn't me." She shakes her head and faces me. "I'm sorry, Ed. I'm so sorry. I wish it was, but . . ."

She doesn't finish her sentence.

J
the end is not the end

Finally, it comes.

Another knock rattles at my door, and I know this one feels right. It's late, the hand is harsh, and I place my shoes on my feet before I go to answer it.

Breathe deep, Ed.

I do.

"Stay here," I order the Doorman when he meets me in the hall, but he follows me back to the door.

When I open it, there's a man in a suit.

"Ed Kennedy?" He's bald and has a lengthy mustache.

"Yes," I say.

He comes closer to the doorway and says, "I have something for you—can I come in?"

He's friendly enough, and I decide that if he wants to come in, I should allow it. I step aside and let the man past. He's tall and middle-aged, and his voice is steeped with politeness and assertion.

"Coffee?" I ask, but he declines.

"No, thank you."

This is the first time I see the briefcase in his hand.

He sits and opens it, and inside he has a wrapped lunch, an apple, and an envelope.

"Sandwich?" he offers.

"No, thanks."

"Good decision. My wife makes an awful sandwich—I couldn't bear to eat it today."

Quickly he turns to business, handing me the envelope.

"Thanks." I speak with trepidation.

"You going to open it?"

"Who sent you?"

I shoot him through the eyes, and the man is taken aback for a moment.

"Open it."

"Who sent you?"

I can't hold myself any longer, though. My fingers work

their way inside the envelope, and the familiar handwriting greets me.

Dear Ed,
The end is near.
I think you'd best be getting down to the cemetery.

"The cemetery?" I ask, and I know that tomorrow is exactly a year to the day that my father died.

My father.

"My father," I say to the man. "Tell me—was it him?"

"I don't know what you're talking about."

"Why not?" I nearly take hold of him.

"I—" he begins.

"What?"

"I was sent here."

"By who?"

But the man can only bow his head. He speaks the words with purpose. "I don't know. I don't know who he is. . . ."

"Was my father behind it?" I talk at him. "Did he organize all of this before he died? Did he . . ."

I hear what my mother said to me last year.

You're just like him.

Did my father leave instructions for someone to organize this? I remember seeing him walk the streets at night when I was in my cab. He did it to sober up. I'd pick him up once in a while as he made his way home from the pub. . . .

"That's how he knew the addresses," I say aloud.

"Sorry?"

"Nothing," I answer, and no more words are spoken because I'm out the door. I'm running up the street and out to the ceme-

346

tery. The night is that blue black color. Clouds like cement are paved in sections to the sky.

The cemetery looms up, and I turn to the area where my father's grave is. Some security guards are standing close by.

Or are they?

No.

It's Daryl and Keith.

I slow to a standstill, and they watch me. Daryl speaks.

"Congratulations, Ed."

I catch up to my breath.

"My father?" I ask.

"You *are* like he was," Keith enlightens me, "and just like him, you were most likely to die the same way—a quarter of what you could have been. . . ."

"So he sent you to do this? He organized it before he died?"

Daryl answers the question, wandering closer. "You see, Ed, you were always an absolute no-hoper—just like your old man. No offense."

"None taken."

"And we've been employed to test you—to see if you can avoid *this* life." He points casually to the grave.

"The only problem is"—Keith steps in now—"it wasn't your father who sent us."

This takes a while to sink in.

It's not Audrey. It's not my father.

Crowds of questions stream through me like lines of people exiting a soccer ground or a concert. They push and shove and trip. Some make their way around. Some remain in their seats, waiting for their opportunity.

"What are you doing here, then?" I ask them. "How did you know I'd be right here at this exact moment in time?"

"Our employer sent us," Daryl replies.

"He told us you'd be here," Keith chimes in again. They're working well tonight. "So we came." He smiles at me, almost sympathetically. "He hasn't been wrong yet."

I try to think, to make some sense of all this.

"Well," I begin, but it appears that I have no more words to extend the sentence. I find them. "Who's your employer?"

Daryl shakes his head. "We don't know, Ed. We just do what we're told." He begins to wrap things up. "But, yes, Ed, you were sent here tonight to remind yourself that you don't want to die the same way your father did. Understand?"

I nod my agreement.

"And now we have one last thing to tell you, and then we'll disappear from your life forever."

I prepare to listen hard. "What is it?"

They already begin to walk away. "Just that you have a little longer to wait, okay?"

I stand there.

What else can I do but stand there?

I watch Daryl and Keith walk calmly into the night. They're gone and I'll never see them again.

"Thank you," I say, but they don't hear me. It seems a shame that they never will.

A few more days pass and I realize there's nothing else I can do now but wait. I've almost given up when I'm waved down by a young man in jeans, a jacket, and a cap on my way home from work one morning at dawn.

He gets in the backseat.

The usual.

I ask him where to.

The usual.

Then I get the answer.

"26 Shipping Street."

Not the usual.

The words paralyze me and I nearly pull the car to a stop.

"Just drive on," he says, but he doesn't look up. "Like I told you, Ed. 26 Shipping Street."

I drive.

We travel in silence until we make it to town. I'm driving cautiously, with nervous eyes and a badly beating heart.

I turn onto my street and pull up at my place.

Finally, the person in the backseat removes his cap and looks up so I can see him for the first time in the mirror.

"It's *you!*" I shout.

"Yes."

Something greater than shock or surprise has stolen every thought or reaction I might have had—because in the backseat of my cab is the failed bank robber from the start of this story. His ginger whiskers are still there, and he's as ugly as ever.

"The six months are up," he explains. He sounds friendly this time.

"But—"

"Don't ask questions," he interrupts. "Just drive on. Drive me to 45 Edgar Street."

I do it.

"Remember this place?" he says.

I do.

"Now 13 Harrison Avenue." And one by one, the failed bank robber takes me to each place. To Milla and Sophie, to the father and Angie Carusso, and to the Rose boys.

"Remember?" he questions me each time.

In the cab, I revisit each place, each message.

"Yes," I tell him. "I do."

"Good. Glory Road now.

"Clown Street and your ma's place.

"Bell Street.

"And you know the last three."

We drive the streets of town as the sun climbs higher in the sky. We go to Ritchie's, to the playground with the unkempt grass, and to Audrey's place. At each destination, remembering takes its turn in me as I drive. At times, it makes me want to stop and stay.

Stay forever.

With Ritchie in the river.

With Marv at the swings.

And dancing with Audrey in the silent fire of morning.

"Where now?" I ask when we return to my place.

"Get out," he tells me, and now I can't help it.

I say, "It was you, wasn't it? You robbed the bank knowing that—"

"Oh, could you just shut up, Ed?"

We stand by the cab in the morning sun.

Methodically, he pulls something from his jacket pocket. It's a small, flat mirror.

* * *

"Remember what I told you, Ed—at my trial?"

"I remember." And for some reason, I feel a warmness in my eyes.

"Tell me."

"You said that every time I look in the mirror, I should remember I'm looking at a dead man."

"That's right."

The failed thief steps away and stands in front of me. A small smile lands on his face, and he holds the mirror up to me. I stare right into myself.

He says, "Are you looking at a dead man now?"

In a flood inside me, I see all those places and people again. I hold the kid on her porch and go by the name of Jimmy to a marvelous old woman. I watch a girl run with the most glorious bloodied feet in the world.

I laugh with the thrill on a religious man's face. I see Angie Carusso's ice-creamed lips and feel the loyalty of the Rose boys. I watch the darkness of a family lit up by the power and the glory, let my mother unleash the truth and love and disappointment of her life, and sit in a lonely man's cinema.

Looking into the mirrored glass, I stand with my friend in a river. I watch Marvin Harris push his daughter on a swing, high into the sky, and I dance with love and Audrey for three minutes straight. . . .

"Well?" he asks again. "Are you still looking at a dead man?"

This time, I answer.

I say, "No," and the criminal speaks.

"Well, it was worth it, then. . . ."

He went to jail for those people.

He went to jail for me, and now he walks away with a few last words.

"Goodbye, Ed—I think you'd better get inside."

And he's gone.

Just like Daryl and Keith, I will never see him again.

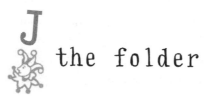 J the folder

As calmly as I can, I walk inside. My front door was open.

On my couch there sits a young man who pats the Doorman very quietly and happily.

"Who are—"

"Hi, Ed," he says. "I'm glad to finally meet you."

"Are you—"

He nods.

"You sent—"

He nods again.

When he stands up, he says, "I came to this town a year ago, Ed." He has fairly short brown hair, stands a bit smaller than medium height, and wears a shirt, black jeans, and blue athletic shoes. As each minute passes he looks more like a boy than a man, although when he speaks, his voice is not a boy's at all.

"Yeah, it was about a year ago, and I saw your father buried. I saw you and your card games and your dog and your ma. I just kept coming back, watching, the same way you did at all those addresses. . . ." He turns away for a moment, almost ashamed. "I killed your father, Ed. I organized the bungled bank robbery for a time when you were there. I instructed that man to brutalize his wife. I made Daryl and Keith do all those things to you, and your mate who took you to the stones. . . ." He looks down, then up. "I did it all to you. I *made* you a less-than-competent taxi driver and got you to do all those things you thought you couldn't." We stand now, staring. Waiting for more words. "And why?" He pauses, but he doesn't move back. "I did it because *you* are the epitome of ordinariness, Ed." He looks at me seriously. "And if a guy like you can stand up and do what you did for all those people, well, maybe everyone can. Maybe everyone can live beyond what they're capable of." He becomes intense now. Emotional. This is everything. "Maybe even *I* can. . . ."

He sits back down on the couch.

I recall the sensation of the town feeling painted around me and of feeling invented. Is this happening?

It is, and the young man sits there rinsing his hand through his hair.

Quietly, he stands up and looks back at the couch. There's a faded yellow folder sitting on a cushion. "It's all in there," he says. "Everything. Everything I wrote for you. Every idea I scratched around with. Every person you helped, hurt, or ran into."

"But"—my words feel smeared—"how?"

"Even *this*," he answers, "is in there—this discussion."

Shocked, amazed, dumbfounded, I stand.

Eventually, I manage to speak again. "Am I real?"

He barely even thinks about it. He doesn't need to. "Look in the folder," he says. "At the end. See it?"

In large scrawled letters on the blank side of a cardboard beer

353

coaster, it's written. His answer is written there in black ink. It says, *Of course you're real—like any thought or any story. It's real when you're in it.*

He says, "I'd better go now. You probably want to go through that folder and check for consistency. It's all there."

For a moment, I panic. It's that feeling of falling when you know without question that you've lost control of your car or made a mistake that's beyond repair.

"What do I do now?" I ask desperately. "Tell me! What do I do now?"

He remains calm.

He looks at me closely and says, "Keep living, Ed. . . . It's only the pages that stop here."

He stays for perhaps another ten minutes, probably due to the trauma that has strapped itself to me. I remain standing, trying to contemplate and recover from what's just transpired.

"I really think I'd better go," he says again, this time with more finality.

With difficulty, I walk him to the door.

We say goodbye on the front porch, and he walks back up the street.

I wonder about his name, but I'm sure I'll learn it soon enough.

He's written about this, I'm sure, the bastard. All of it.

As he walks up the street he pulls a small notebook from his pocket and writes a few things down.

It makes me think that maybe I should write about all this myself. After all, I'm the one who did all the work.

I'd start with the bank robbery.

Something like, "The gunman is useless."

The odds are, however, that he's beaten me to it already.
It'll be his name on the cover of all these words, not mine.
He'll get all the credit.
Or the crap, if he does a shit job.
But just remember that I was the one—not him—who gave life to these pages. I was the one who—
I tell me to stop.
It's an inner voice and it's loud.

All day, I think about many things, though I try not to. I look through the folder and find everything as he said. All the ideas are written in and people are sketched. Scratchy excerpts are stapled together. Beginnings and endings merge and bend.
Hours wander past.
Days follow them.

I don't leave the shack, and I don't answer the phone. I barely even eat. The Doorman sits with me as the minutes pass by.
For a long time, I wonder what I'm waiting for, but I understand it's just like he said.
I guess it's for life beyond these pages.

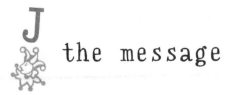

J
the message

One afternoon, I hear what feels like the last knock at my door, and standing there, on my cracked front porch, is Audrey.
Her eyes dangle for a moment, and she asks to come in.

In the hallway, she falls back against the door and says, "Can I stay, Ed?"

I go to her. "Of course you can stay the night." But she shakes her head and her dangling eyes finally fall. Audrey walks forward and reaches into me.

"Not for tonight," she says. "For good."

We sink to the floor of my hallway and Audrey kisses me. Her lips join up with mine, and I taste her breath and swallow and feel and lunge for it. It streaks me inside with streams of her beauty. I hold her yellow hair. I touch the smooth skin of her neck, and she keeps kissing me. She wants to.

When we finish, the Doorman walks to us and settles down at my side.

"Hey, Doorman," Audrey says, and again her eyes stream. She looks happy.

The Doorman looks at both of us. He is the sage. He is the wisdom. He says, *About bloody time, you two.*

We stay in the hall for close to an hour and I tell Audrey everything. She listens intently as she pats the Doorman, and she believes me. I realize that Audrey has always believed me.

I'm about to relax completely when a final question slips inside me. It tries to get up but slips over again.

"The folder," I say.

I get up and walk hurriedly to the lounge room. On my knees, I go through the folder incessantly. I sit there and comb through it. I rummage and plow among the loose papers.

"What are you doing?" Audrey asks. She's come in and stands behind me.

I turn and look up at her.

"I'm looking for *this*," I tell her. I wave my hand at both of us. "I'm looking for you and me, together."

And Audrey only crouches down. She kneels with me and places her hand on mine to make me drop the papers.

"I don't think it's in there." She says it softly. "I think, Ed . . ." Her hands hold me now gently on my face. The orange light of late afternoon is attached to her. "I think this belongs to us."

It's evening now, and Audrey and I share a coffee with the Doorman on the front porch. He smiles at me when he's finished and falls into his normal gentle sleep by the door. Caffeine doesn't affect him anymore.

Audrey's fingers hold on to mine, the light remains a few moments longer, and I hear the words again from this morning.

If a guy like you can stand up and do what you did, then maybe everyone can. Maybe everyone can live beyond what they're capable of.

And that's when I realize.

In a sweet, cruel, beautiful moment of clarity, I smile, watch a crack in the cement, and speak to Audrey and the sleeping Doorman. I tell them what I'm telling you:

I'm not the messenger at all.

I'm the message.

MARKUS ZUSAK received the Children's Book Council of Australia's Book of the Year Award for *I Am the Messenger* (published in Australia as *The Messenger*). His previous books for young adults include *Fighting Ruben Wolfe*, an American Library Association Best Book for Young Adults, and *Getting the Girl*.

Markus Zusak began to write during high school, where he led a "pretty internal existence. . . . I always had stories in my head. So I started writing them." He lives in Sydney, where he writes, occasionally works a real job, and plays on a soccer team that never wins.